American Pimps
The Vinnie Mac Story

VINCENT E. JORDAN

NEWMAN SPRINGS PUBLISHING
320 Broad Street
Red Bank, NJ 07701

First originally published by Newman Springs Publishing 2021

This is a work of fiction; any reference or similarities to actual events, real people, living or dead, or the locations are intended to give the novel a sense of reality; any similarity in other names, characters, places, and incidents is entirely coincidental.

ISBN 978-1-63692-934-7 (Paperback)
ISBN 978-1-63692-935-4 (Digital)

Printed in the United States of America

I dedicate this book to my sons Vincent E. Jordan Jr., Jerron Jordan, Vinnie Mac M. Jordan, Cordon Jordan, and Ronzay Jordan. They inspire me to keep my dreams alive and to not give up.

Thanks, Nina Jordan; to my grandmother Lenora "Nanny" Taylor; Grandmother Mary Broomfield; and to my mother, Lula "Braden" Davis; Aunt Helen. May you rest in peace.

To Aunt Marie and Aunt Leretta, love y'all. Aunt Thelma in Oakland, love ya. To cousin Ronnie, cousin Kenneth, thanks for never turning me down. To Jimmy, Shawn, Cookie, Linda, Brent, and all my other cousins. Oh yeah, to cousin Jeffery in New York.

To my dad, my hero, thanks for the talks you had with me, it helped me stay focused.

I would like to thank God for giving me the grit to put my words and thoughts into picture that I paint and for giving me the talent to achieve my goals in life and for giving me a good life and for keeping me alive to talk about life. I appreciate you for giving me the inspiration to compose this book and for all the blessings.

Most of all, thanks to everyone that purchased this book.

And to all the true players in the game, remember, life is what you make it.

Preface

God has uplifted me and my best friend, Speedy Mac. Me and Speedy Mac pimped together, sold dope, banged, and did all kinds of other things. When Speedy was in his dark place in life, God called him to become a preacher. Not just a preacher, but a great teacher of the Word of God. He's now called pastor Lynwood Young.

I'm in a dark place in my life right now. I have learned not to let my past paralyze my future. Speedy's been there for me as I purged myself of the things from my past. I'm sharing them with you in this book that I now write in hopes that it will enlighten you. To let you know that the game is real. If you cross that path, you can end up in a dark place in your life. Watch your back at all times, and keep God in your life because you will always need him. Without Jesus, we're lost. Words from a blessed soul.

1

It was Sunday morning, the day before I was going to catch my flight to Utah. I'll be leaving Long Beach and its great weather, beautiful sand, blue seas, and palm trees for the smell of horse and cow shit, white folks, mountains, and snow.

I always wanted to be a chef. This was my first step. I'm getting a chance to graduate from high school and cooking school at the same time.

When I get back in a year or so, my friends will just be getting out of high school. After attending their prom, I will already be working for more than that minimum wage most of them will be getting because they won't have experience. I will be working by the time I'm eighteen.

The employment office said they would help me when I got back home. The recruiter said they put money aside so I will have a nice check after coming home. It was a great opportunity.

My baby momma and my first love was still asleep after a long night of lovemaking. I kissed her all over for the first time. She had beautiful big breasts, and I was sucking and licking them like there was no time and no tomorrow. We had sex four or five times. She was out of it. She was three months pregnant.

I decided to go to Job Corps after I found out she was expecting a baby. I wanted to be a good father to my child. I wasn't raised by my father, but he was there when I needed him the most.

He paid child support for me and my brother. Once I turned sixteen and my brother was seventeen, so we could take care of ourselves, he took us shopping for winter clothes. He also got me boots, gloves, coats, and a scarf. He paid for everything.

I was a young hustler. Everyone knew me on the block. I sold drugs, weed, and Lovely (PCP, phencyclidine). On Twenty-First and Lemon, me and the boys, we had a shack there—behind my friend Charles's house.

The shack was his garage. That's where we hung out at. We smoked weed, shot dice, and had our club meetings. We were Twenty-First gangsters—some of the baddest niggas on the east side of LBC (Long Beach, California).

My mother, bless her heart, was a real gambler; she shot dice, played the horses, and played cards for money.

She was gone most of the time; we raised ourselves.

My mom got on a losing streak, and we got evicted out of our apartment. That's how we met our foster mother. Her name was Ms. Williams. She was our friend's mother. His name was Bruce; we were from the same gang.

Bruce told his mother what had happened to me and my brother—that we had got put out.

He told his mother that we would give her $50 a month; she let us move in. We moved on Twenty-First and Lemon in the county apartment building #3.

Ms. Williams was a thickset woman. She was of brown skin with salt-and-pepper hair. She had a nice smile, and she stood about 5'2". She was very nice to us. She loved money. On top of the $50 we gave her every month, we gave her extra money. She had three kids of her own. Bruce was seventeen, and she had two kids under him. The money came in handy. She cooked every day—breakfast, lunch, dinner. She made sure that we had everything that we needed.

I made $100 a day. That was good enough for Debbie, my girl-friend, who was 5'2", with long black hair, big titties, a small waist, and with caramel-colored complexion. She was fine as hell. She didn't want me to go to Job Corps. She liked the way I was getting money, plus I was gangster. She didn't want me to leave her alone. Debbie didn't want to wait a year or longer until I got back. We went back and forth about the matter. I told her it would be best for the both of us. I could give her money before I leave so she could move and find an apartment and fix it up the way she wanted it. Debbie still didn't like the idea.

My brother didn't want me to leave either. He was a good hustler. I worked side jobs with him. He was a pro at burglarizing homes. Eddie was about 5'9", with sandy-colored hair and eyes. He had long hair in cornrows. He had a nice build and was strong as hell. He had been to camps for boys a couple of times. The girls loved him. Plus we dressed sharper than a mothafucka suited and booted with jewels to match. Eddie has been out of jail for only six months, and he was getting a lot of money, him and his crew. Bruce was on the crew too.

Bruce wanted me to stay also. We talked about it all the time. We were stacking a lot of money, and we were known gangsters, and nobody fucked with us.

It was getting hot. The cops were asking a lot of questions. I didn't want to end up going to jail. We were having our first child, and I wanted to be able to provide for him. Going to jail wasn't going to help me do that.

I told Bruce, "That's it, that's all. I don't want to talk about it anymore."

I woke up early, thinking, *This is it. I will be out of here tomorrow and on to a different environment.* I'm taking an ounce of weed and a half ounce of PCP to make Lovely out of and my dice—I'm going to hustle wherever I'm at.

I went to sleep thinking about things. I woke up and went to the bathroom, turned on the shower, brushed my teeth, and then got into the shower.

I took my time, soaped up my face, toweled real good, and washed myself up—seemed like I was in there an hour. I was just about to get out when Debbie got in with me, taking off all her clothes.

"I see you're taking a shower without me," she said at the same time. She got down on her knees and started licking the head of my penis.

"Damn, that feels good as a mothafucka. You gonna make me cum." She had both hands on my balls and kept sucking. My manhood got harder and harder, and I said, "Whoo, shit, don't stop please. I'm about to cummm!" I came in her mouth, and she spat it into the toilet. We wrapped a towel around ourselves and went into the room.

*****

"I see you got up. I thought you would sleep a couple more hours after I put that dick on you."

"Shit, I thought you would sleep longer after all that pussy I put on you." We both started laughing our ass off. We lay back down for an hour.

I woke and rubbed her body and touched her face and said, "I love you."

She looked into my eyes and said, "I love you too." Her eyes were beautiful.

She started rubbing my thing again, and it started growing. Debbie took her time and started rubbing my nuts. I started rubbing her pussy and put my fingers inside. She was very wet.

She said, "Let me suck it again, my pussy is worn-out."

I said, "Damn, baby, you trying to make a nigga stay home and miss my plane tomorrow."

She smiled, and this time she sucked even better. I got on top of her and stroked my penis between her tits until I came again. She said, "If I can't talk you into staying, I'll suck and fuck you into staying." We both were laughing once again.

After that, she went right to sleep. I kissed her and said, "I love you with yo fine ass."

I started to get dressed. All my clothes were packed. I left out a pair of Stacy Adams, slacks, a button-down shirt, vest, and a hat.

I was dressed to impress. I put on some perfume. I went into my stash and pulled out fifteen bags of weed and headed to the spot on Twenty-First and Lemon. As soon as I walked out to the front apartment, my homie was headed to my house; he wanted three bags of weed. He asked me if I was leaving town. I told him yeah and that

I would be gone for over a year. I gave him a bag on the house. He said, "I'm going to miss you, dog."

I gave him daps and said, "I'll miss you too, homie."

*****

It was a nice day in Long Beach. The sun was shining, and there were no clouds in the sky. Everything was all right. I decided to put up the weed and go to church. I hadn't been in a while. I wanted to go and pray for a safe trip. This would be my first trip on an airplane.

Church was great. The preacher had a great sermon. The message was about a man's safe travel and his faith in God. I saw Ms. Price, Debbie's mom; she also prayed for me to have a safe trip, and I thanked her.

After the church service, I went back home to pick up my weed and some money. To my surprise, when I walked into the house, Debbie and Ms. Williams were cooking.

Damn, it was smelling good, and I was hungrier than a motha——.

"You ready to eat?" Ms. Williams asked. "I cooked. We cooked some bacon, eggs, potatoes, and toast."

"That sounds great," I said.

Debbie said, "We're also cooking fried chicken, collard greens, yam, and potato salad for dinner."

"Have you seen your brothers this morning?"

"No, Ma."

"Okay, I'll put their food in the oven."

After we were done eating, I told Debbie, "I saw your mother at church. She said to tell you to come home after I leave tomorrow. She needs you to watch your brothers and sister. She has a doctor's appointment."

"Damn, that's all she wants me to do—watch them damn kids. I'll be glad to get my own apartment," Debbie said.

I said, "She will still want you to watch them." I laughed.

She said, "That's not funny."

"I got the money saved up for you. All you have to do is find an apartment. It's all on you."

Ms. Williams smiled and said, "How was church?"

I said, "Great."

We put up the dishes that Debbie had washed. Ms. Williams said, "I'm going to miss you."

"I'll miss you too." Me and Debbie went back upstairs to the room.

Debbie went back to sleep. I rolled up and smoked some weed and got high. I went back into my stack and got out ten bags of weed and some change—twenty $1, five $5, and four $10 bills. I grabbed my dice and headed back out the door on my way to the shack to check what's up with the homies—what they hit for. The dice game was cracking. Hump was shooting the dice. He was wearing a white T-shirt, tan khakis, and blue and tan croker sack shoes.

"Shoot two," he said.

I said, "Come on, two. Who else thinks he will hit?"

His brother Peter said, "He hits for two." Peter was wearing a white T-shirt, black corduroys, and black Wallabee shoes.

I said, "Come on, two." *Does anybody else think the dice will hit?* Nobody else wanted to bet.

Hump picked up the dice and rolled an eight.

Babs said, "I'll make eight for three." Babs was dressed in a button-down blue shirt and tan slacks and a pair of blue Stacy Adams shoes.

Pee Wee said, "He makes it for $5." Pee Wee was dressed in a black button-down shirt, black slacks, gray Stacy Adams, and a gray godfather hat.

I said, "Come on, $5."

Babs said, "Let me get two of that $5."

I said, "Okay." Hump picked up the dice and rolled six. I asked if anybody had seen my brothers.

Pee Wee said, "Him and Bruce came by my house this morning and asked me if I wanted to go hustle with them. I said I was cool."

Humped picked up the dice and rolled a seven. It was a good dice game. I made $120. Me and my boys walked to the liquor store and got TJ Swann Mellow Movements wine.

We rolled up some weed. We drank and smoked. We started talking, and Babs said, "You really gonna leave tomorrow?"

I said yes. "You going to leave that fine-ass bitch by herself?"

"I got to handle my business. She knows what's up."

"Good luck, homie."

Pee Wee said, "Vinnie, I know you have some Lovely. Let's get fucked up this one last time."

I said, "Okay, I'll be right back, it's at home. I'll dip one, and I'll be back."

We got fucked up in the summer sun and had fun in the streets of Long Beach.

*****

A green Impala glasshouse on rims and five twenties size tires came down the street, hitting witches. Babs and Pee Wee said, "Who the fuck is that in that clean-ass mothafucka?"

I said, "I don't know, but it's clean."

It was a 1970 green Impala with white interior; the beat was kicking. The closer it came, the music got louder, and then it got lower. Somebody hollered, "Two one, two one, two one." That's our call for the Twenty-First gangsters.

When the car came to a stop, my brother Eddie jumped out. Eddie was dressed in green. He had on a green godfather hat, a white button-down shirt, green slacks with white stitches going down the sides, and a green and white pair of Stacy Adams shoes.

That nigga was razor-sharp, cleaner than a mothafucka. Eddie said, "What's up with it?" I was just coming down off my high.

Pee Wee said, "Is that your car?"

Eddie said, "It sure the fuck is. I told you to come with me. You could have got paid too. I hit $5,000. You woulda been fat like me."

Pee Wee said, "Damn, I should have gone with you."

I couldn't believe my eyes. I said, "Nigga, is that really your car?"

"Yeah, look, I'm dressed just like my car."

Hump said, "That shit is clean. Turn the music back on." We started dancing in the streets.

Eddie called me over to the side and showed me his bankroll and said, "You still want to leave?"

I said, "Momma already signed the papers. She will kill me if I don't leave tomorrow."

He said, "Yeah, I know. Let's go out and have some fun with our girls then."

We had a great time. I was proud of my big brother.

*****

The next morning, Eddie, Debbie, and Bruce drove me to the airport. I gave my brothers daps and kissed Debbie and then walked into the airport. I watched as they drove out of sight.

2

As I entered the plane, the stewardess asked for my ticket and said, "Your seat number is twenty-seven, that's a window seat." After everyone was seated, they went over the safety measures.

Then the pilot said, "Good afternoon, folks, this is flight 324 to Salt Lake, Utah. We will be arriving in approximately one and a half hours. At this time, I'm asking everyone to fasten your seatbelts and enjoy your flight."

We were in the air in no time. It was a smooth takeoff. After I was able to take off my seatbelt, I went to the restroom. I noticed five other young black guys on the plane. On my way back from the restroom, I asked if they were headed to Job Corps. They said yes. It was a brother that dressed kind of like me. He had a perm in his hair and Stacy Adams on, brim slacks, multicolored shirt, and he was looking player. I had asked him where he was from. He said LA. I asked if anyone was sitting in the seat next to him. He said no. I sat down and asked his name.

He said, "AD. And what's yours, brother?"

"Vinnie," I said.

"Would you like a drink? I got some in this flask."

"I like those Adams you got on."

"I like yours too."

"How much did you pay for yours?"

"Seventy-five dollars, and you?"

"The same."

AD said, "I'm pimpin'."

"I ain't no pimp. I'm a hustler."

AD said, "Pimpin' and hoein' is the best thing going. If it ain't white, it ain't right."

"Maybe you can teach me some of that pimpin' you got," I said.

"It's got to be in you, not on you."

"It will be in me as I learn it from you," I said.

"It's called game. I'll see. Can I fill up your game tank?"

"Thanks, AD."

*****

A voice came over the speaker and said, "Buckle your seat belts, we'll be landing shortly, and thanks for flying with Hughs Airlines."

"Damn, we got here quick," I said.

AD said, "That's what happens when you chop up game."

"Yeah, I see, I like the game already," I said.

"I got some pimp books I will let you read, ya dig?"

"I dig."

*****

We entered the airport, picked up our suitcases, then we spotted a man holding a sign. It said, "Welcome to Job Corps." All of us met him across the street, and he escorted us to the bus that would take us to Clearfield, Utah. He informed us that it would take about thirty minutes to get to the campus.

We arrived at the campus; it was very nice. We all started commenting on the place. We went to orientation. We found out which dorms we were assigned to. I was in dorm C, and AD was in dorm G. They told us that this campus was coed. Girls were in dorms M through Z.

As the bus drove in the rest of the way, we got a chance to look around. We saw two huge parks; students were sitting in the grass playing music, cars, and other games. I saw cute girls all over the place.

Some students were studying. They had a movie theater, gym, swimming pool, recreation center, cafeteria, and a lot more. The bus pulled over and let us out by our dorms. Dorm C was right up the ramp. I told AD I would meet him by the park closest to the dorms. I walked into my dorm and met my counselor. His name was Dan. He explained rules and regulations. He also told me where my room was. They called them cubes. I was in cube 47, and I had three other roommates. I unpacked and checked out the rest of the dorm. It had pool tables, a nice fireplace in the group meeting room, and plenty of showers. It was like a college.

I met the other guys that I was sharing the cube with. Their names were Richard, Mark, and James. We talked for a minute. I headed outside after that.

AD was standing out in the front. I ran into him. We walked to the park. We saw some of the students smoking weed.

I found out that a joint of weed cost $2 a piece. I had a whole ounce. *Cool,* I thought. Then I told AD, and he asked if he could be down with me.

I said, "You teach me how the pimp game goes, and I'll teach you how to hustle."

"Cool," he said. I told him to wait till payday. All 1,800 of us students get paid on the same day. I told him that. I had some PCP, and it cost $7 for a pinhead. My roommate told me that whatever I had would be sold in an hour. Nobody had any in five months. AD said, "We gonna get paid, ya dig?"

"I dig."

"We'll get all the girls too."

I said, "Cool, but let's take our time."

I pulled out two joints; it was some of that good Cali weed. When the students smelled it, they wanted to buy some right then.

As the weeks went by, we met T. Money; he had a perm, and it was down past his shoulders. He was kicking pimping too. AD had two brothers already here. One of them was named King; Danny was the other. Both of them were in the pimp game too. We were labeled the West Coast pimp crew.

King was nineteen years old. He got us a motel room when we went into the city so we could roll up the weed and the Lovely (PCP).

The Job Corps bus took us to Ogden; it was a better spot for us to handle our business. We could go there or to Salt Lake City.

Out of the ounce of weed I brought, we rolled 175 joints. Out of the weed-mixed PCP, we rolled 150 pinhead joints. I made over a thousand dollars of the PCP and over $400 off the weed. I kept $900 and split the rest.

AD and the rest of them had over $150 apiece. I told AD I was going to call my sister and have her send me two ounces of weed and one ounce of PCP in about six weeks.

He said, "Cool."

*****

Three of us had girls. I had met a girl named Diane from the Bronx. King had a girl from Los Angeles named Kathy, and Danny was fucking her sister Pam.

AD and T. Money were kicking pimping every day; they didn't want anything but a white girl so they could teach her how to be a ho. I started learning more about the game.

AD blessed me with those pimp books. One was *Iceberg Slim*, and the other was by Donald Goines.

*****

Another three months had passed. King and Danny graduated and went home back to Los Angeles.

T. Money had been sent home for taking money out of the counselor's pure. He said he was going pimping, that Job Corps was too slow for his fast pimping ass.

It was just AD and me; the rest of the West Coast pimping gang were gone.

It took two more months for the package to arrive from my sister. She sent one ounce of PCP and two ounces of weed. I was on, once again.

I called her to thank her and to ask her if she had heard from Debbie. My sister told me that she had the baby, and it was a boy. She named the baby after me, and he looked just like me.

Then she told me something that I would never forget. She said, "Debbie got back with her first baby daddy. Her ex-boyfriend." I couldn't believe it. I was hurt. I was pissed the fuck off. *That punk-ass bitch. I gave her all that money to find an apartment*, I thought. No wonder that bitch didn't write me about my son. Her mother said she moved out and got an apartment on Myrtle and New York in Long Beach. She hadn't heard from her.

I told AD, and he said, "That's why I want my hoes to sell pussy instead of giving it away, ya dig?"

"I dig."

"A chicken ain't nothing but a bird, an' a ho won't keep her word."

*****

I had my eighteenth birthday in Job Corps. Diane was my new woman now. We went to Ogden and rented a motel room. It was to be the first time we made love.

She got me some gifts and a small cake for my birthday. I was surprised, and I had something for her too—a diamond ring. And I got her flowers; she was graduating next week also. We went to Sizzler steak house. For dinner, we ordered shrimp, lobster, steak, and salad from the bar; it was a great meal.

Once we were back at the motel, we took a shower, and we had a couple of drinks. She lit some candles, turned down the lights. We started kissing first, then we started sticking our tongues down each other's throats.

I rubbed on her beautiful big tits and down to that hairy pussy. She rubbed my chest. I started licking her all over. Diane started to moan. Her body was rocking back and forth. I licked her nipples, and they were rock-hard. She moaned louder and louder. She rubbed my dick; it became hard as hell. All ten inches was right in front of her.

She said, "Damn, I never seen anything this big, please take it easy."

I said, "Okay, I will." I moved my fingers inside her. With my other hand, I played with her pearl tongue. She humped and moved her body up and down until she had an orgasm.

Diane sucked my cock; it was the best I've ever had.

I laid her on her back and slid my big hard dick into her pussy. She gasped. I pushed deeper into her. She said, "It's so large." I told her to get on top and ride it. She had two more orgasms. I nutted inside her. We fell asleep just like that.

*****

Diane had gone back to New York. My best friend AD went back to Los Angeles. He said he was gonna go pimping in Hollywood. I told him that once I get back, I'd call, I would look him up. I had six more weeks until I graduated. I met Beverly; she was from Cali. I was feeling, "Baby, she's superfine—five foot two, 38 Ds, small waist and cute in the face, thick thighs and pigeon-toed, long black hair, brown eyes." She had a dark-brown complexion, a gorgeous smile, and a sexy walk.

We spent every day together. She never had sex. I wanted to be the first to tap that pussy. She was nineteen years old. She was a year older than me, and that was no problem. My game was up a couple steps ahead of her. All I thought of was hitting that pussy, but I had to take my time with her. All we did was kiss and grind a few times.

I told her I would call her once I got home; she gave me her mom's phone number, and I gave her my sister's phone number.

*****

I had graduated. I spent my last days with Beverly. I had to get up early the next morning to catch my flight back to Cali. Beverly got up early to walk me to the van that would take me to the airport. I kissed her goodbye, and I was gone.

*****

I was waiting out in front of LAX for the cab to Long Beach. I had been gone for over a year. I was excited to be back home.

It was Friday. I didn't have to be at the employment office until Monday. I wanted to see my baby boy as soon as I could.

I had a taxi take me to Debbie's mom's house so I could get the address of Debbie's apartment.

"Hi, Ms. Price, how have you been?" I asked.

"We're blessed," she said.

I got the address and was off to see my baby momma and Lil Vinnie. I had the cab wait in front in case nobody was there. I knocked on the front door; nobody answered. I looked in the window and spotted my son. I went to the side window and saw Debbie and some nigga slow-dancing and kissing.

I went back to the front door and checked it, and it was open. I went inside. I started to go in there and fucked both of them up, but I was a different person now. I wasn't the gangster nigga I was before. I was a smooth player, a pimp mothafucka now. I picked up my baby boy and kissed him; that nigga looked just like me. I looked into his eyes and said, "Don't worry, Daddy's got you, baby boy, but me and your momma are done." I put a hundred-dollar bill in each of his hands and left. I jumped back into the cab and headed to my sister's house.

I told her what had happened. She said, "I told you what I had heard, so it is true. That's why we haven't seen the baby. So what's next, brother?"

"Well, I'm going to get a job. The recruiter said the employment office helps everyone that graduated from Job Corps get a job," I said. "I'm going to be a pimp as soon as I learn more about it. I'm not the same nigga I used to be. A bitch can pay me or pay me no attention."

"Say, *boy*—or shall I say, *young man*, watch yo mouth," my sister said.

"I mean what I said, but I will respect yo house."

"Is that what you learned in Job Corps?"

"Yeah, I sure did, and I'm going to be the biggest pimp in Long Beach or the West Coast. You just watch me."

"I hear you, brother, as long as you respect me. I'm not yo bitch."

"I'm sorry, sis, I'm just mad right now, but it's all good." I reached into my suitcase and pulled out a Crown Royal bag. It had $5,000 in it. I pulled off $1,500 off my bankroll and gave it to my sister Peaches.

"Thank you," she said. My sister then started laughing and said, "I almost pissed my pants when you said you wanted to be a pimp."

"I meant what I said. I'm going to be a pimp. I've been reading some pimp books. I've been around pimps too."

"So you went to Utah to learn how to be a pimp? You could have stayed home and read books about that Mom gambles with hustlers and pimps all the time. You didn't even notice them hoes at the gambling house? They're in and out of there all the time."

"Well, I didn't notice back then."

"Peaches, you want to have a drink with me?"

"Yeah, brother, we can have a drink. So tell me all about your time at Job Corps." I told her all about my time at the Corps.

We had fun drinking and laughing. I was glad to be home with my family and friends. I went and saw my mother. I gave her $1,000. She hugged and kissed me. It was one of the best days of my life, even though my baby momma had left me and got back with her ex-boyfriend; she might have been fucking with him the whole time, who knows.

I know one thing's for sure: the next bitch, yeah, that's right, *bitch*, will pay what she weighs and make my troubles go away. Mr. Pimp Vinnie is back in town, so all you hoes better look around.

After that, I took my drunk black ass home to sleep.

3

Monday morning, I headed to the employment office. I stopped at the doughnut shop and picked up some coffee and two doughnuts. I sat down inside and started looking at the Long Beach *Press-Telegram* newspaper, the classifieds section. I was excited because I would be looking for my first job.

The bitch Debbie had come by my sister's house, trying to run game on me. I had gone to church and talked to Debbie's mom and gave her $1,000 for Lil Vinnie and a few hundred for herself. Ms. Price was always nice to me. I told her what had happened when I had gone to Debbie's. Her mom told her that I had seen her and that nigga through the fucking window.

I told that punk-ass ho I was pimping and that I would see my son at her mother's house. The fag was going to school to be a nurse, and her mother watches my baby on Mondays, Wednesdays, and Fridays. I told Ms. Price that I would pay her to keep him. I gave her the thousand to get my baby whatever he needed. I was done with Debbie, and she was done fucking over me with her slick ass.

Once I got to the employment office, I was informed that I would receive my check from Job Corps; the program saves $50 a month for me, and that was great because I had spent a lot of money.

The employment office set up a job interview for me. It was at the Belmont Pier. I used to fish there all the time. My mom would drop us off there in the summertime. I loved going there. We would fish while my mom went to work; it saved her money, and we didn't need the babysitter while we were there. By noon, I had my first job cooking at the snack bar and grill restaurant.

I had a good shift—noon till 8:00 p.m. The chef's name was Emual. He was Jewish, with short curly hair and glasses. He seemed to be in his fifties. The pier was cool.

*****

There were a lot of people fishing, kids running and playing, people skating back and forth. There were tourists sightseeing. The place I worked at was on the backside of the bait-and-tackle shop. It was a large building. The snack shop and grill were at the bottom floor, and the restaurant was upstairs. We did all the cooking down-stairs in the snack and grill and sent the order from the restaurant up in the dumbwaiter; it was a small elevator.

The snack shop served hamburgers, french fries, onion rings, fried clams, popcorn, soda, candy, cigarettes, wine, and beer. The restaurant was very romantic with all the tables and candles on them.

It served beer, wine, with a great menu of prime ribs, steak, lobster, king crab, jumbo shrimp, oysters, clams, and all kinds of seafood salads.

It had a fantastic, breathtaking view of the ocean.

*****

It was summertime. I had been working there for about six months. I went upstairs to help the waitress out. Her name was Heather. She was a perfect ten. Heather was 5'9", with 38-D breasts, a twenty-four-inch waist, and had long blond hair down her back to her perfectly shaped ass.

Her eyes were ocean blue, and she had a deep dark tan. We used to talk all the time. I was really digging that snow bunny, as AD used to say. I decided to ask her out on a date, just to see what she would say.

I said, "I don't care."

"But I do. Why don't we just fuck? I know that's all you want, that's all the others want. I've never been with a black guy before. I've always wanted a big black cock inside me. This is your lucky day, and this will be your first and last time if your cock is small."

I said, "When?"

She said, "Now. The place doesn't open until another half hour. That's plenty of time. You're not going to last that long anyways."

We went into the storage room. I went right to work on those big-ass breasts, licking and sucking them. She stepped out of her stockings. Her uniform was short. I played with her pussy.

She said, "I want you to eat this pussy," and then pushed my head down there. Her pussy tasted sweet. I could have sucked it all night. She got up and bent over and said, "Ram that big black cock in me." I did just that. She screamed, "Yes, yes, damn it, fuck me, pull my hair, that's it." She moaned. "Oh yeah, pull my hair, slap my ass, harder, oh harder, oh yeah, fuck, you're huge, make me cum, oh, I'm, I'm, oh shit, I'm cummmmmmmmming." She screamed with pleasure. Her legs started to shake; she was limp. "Cum in my face, cum in my face." I nutted all over her face, and she sucked the rest of it out. It seemed like an hour, but it was only ten minutes. She lay there. "That's the best cock I've ever had." She still couldn't talk right. "You can have this pussy anytime you want. Damn, Vinnie, I can hardly get up." I helped her wash up and washed myself up too. She reapplied her makeup, kissed me, and said, "Thanks."

*****

I got a better job after the first year. I got a job at the Copper Penny. It had better benefits, and it was a bigger company—seven hundred stores; they gave me an extra dollar per hour. I had a chance to go into management. After six months, I became the crew chief. I got to wear my own clothes. I stayed suited and booted, with a tie on.

I waited tables, worked the cash register, and helped out in the kitchen.

One day I was seating people while my hostess was on break, and in walked AD and T. Money. I couldn't believe my eyes.

"Vinnie," AD said. I was so happy to see them. It had almost been two years.

"Come on, have a seat over here in the closed section. Order whatever you want, I got y'all. We will talk after my hostess comes off her break. I'm the manager."

We talked and caught up on things. I said, "You niggas ain't pimpin'?"

AD said, "I've had a few hoes, and T. Money has too."

T. Money said, "We're in hot pursuit of a new prostitute."

AD said, "My bitch just got busted."

I said, "Where at?"

He said, "On PCH, here in Long Beach."

"No shit," I said.

AD said, "That's why we're here on Ocean Boulevard. The court is down the street."

T. Money said, "The bitch goes to court at one thirty."

AD said, "The bitch should get time served." I asked where they were staying at. AD said, "We have a room on PCH and Cherry."

"When I get off at 5:00 p.m., we will hook up."

T. Money said, "Our room number is 35, come on over." They had finished their food and headed to the court building. I had to work overtime and never got the chance to hook up with them that day. I went there the next day; they had checked out.

*****

I wanted to buy a car, but I was too young, and I hadn't been working at my job long enough to get this Cadillac I wanted, so I tracked my mom down at the gambling shack. I told her I wanted to buy a car and that I needed her to cosign for me. I told her I would give her a thousand dollars if she did. She had tried to talk me out of buying a Cadillac. She said, "It burns too much gas." I told her I needed it. "For what?" she asked. I told her I was going to be a pimp. "A pimp!" She started laughing. She shook her head and said, "You better keep that job and pay for this damn car."

I said, "I will."

The Cadillac was a rust color and had a tan top, with tan interior. It was the happiest day of my life. I gave my mom her money

26

and took her back to the gambling shack. She told her friends to look at my car; they said it was a nice car. She said to her friends, "Remember that car there will be a pimp driving it."

"What pimp?" they asked.

"Vinnie," my mom said, and all her friends started laughing. "My baby is becoming a man." She pulled me to the side and said, "Go to the barbershop and see Mac. He will pull your coattails. He's one of the biggest pimps in Long Beach. Tell him you're my son." She gave me the address, and I was off to see him.

*****

"Hi, Mr. Mac. I'm Lula's son. She told me to come and see you. I need my perm redone, and I'm trying to be a pimp, and she said you could help."

"Man, I haven't seen your mother in years. How is she?"

"Fine," I said.

"What's your name, son?"

"Vinnie."

"Yeah, I can help." He did my hair, and it was the flyest perm I've ever had. I would go there every week; he started calling me *Vinnie Mac*. I liked that name, and every time I got my hair done, he would kick game at me.

One day I went to see him, he gave me a tailor-made suit. He said, "Vinnie Mac, this is for you. It was one of mine. I used to be the same size as you. I had your name put in it." I was very thankful.

I went there one day. I was off work. I said, "This is the day. I feel real good. I'm going to knock my first ho."

Mac said, "Oh, you're feeling it today."

I said, "Yeah, I'm feeling it, and I'm down for my crown."

Mac said, "Give me a report next time you come get your hair done."

I said, "Okay, I will."

I went home, smoked me a joint, and took a shower and put my tailor-made suit on. I was looking fly as hell. I took a couple of joints with me. I jumped into my Cadillac and hit the ho stroll. On

Pacific Coast Highway, there were a lot of hoes out there. I had been seeing three young hoes out there. I knew one of them; her name was Cherri. I hadn't seen her in years; she used to come into my sister's store.

I said, "Cherri, get in and let me holler at you."

She said, "Drive around the corner, and I will meet you there."

She came around the corner and jumped right in. "Look at you looking all fine and shit."

"What are you doing out here looking like a pimp? You got some girls out here?"

"Yea, I'm talking to her." She smiled.

"It's slow out here. Would you take me and my friends to Inglewood, by the Hollywood Racetrack?" she said. "It's a ho stroll out there, and we will pay you $40 each if you give us a ride and wait for us to get done working."

"I'll pick you guys up in five minutes."

"Okay." She got out, and I drove up the street to the store and got some yak. I needed a drink to compose myself. I got some Zig-Zags and some yak. I headed back to pick them up. I was so happy. I didn't want them to know. I was pimping, and it seemed so easy. I lit my joint on the way back, and they were there waiting just like she said. "This is Rohda, and this is Pam, and this is Bam."

"Wait, they call me Vinnie Mac."

Cherri said, "You changed your name."

I said, "Yeah." Rohda asked if I had another joint. I pulled out two more joints.

Cherri asked if they could have one so they could get it dipped in PCP; they said, "It would make them work better."

I took them to get it dipped and drove to Kings Park. We got out. I left the music on. They smoked their dipped joint, and I smoked my weed. After they were done, we headed to Inglewood. Once we got to the ho stroll, I dropped them off. I told them I would be back in a couple of hours. I went to the racetrack. I played a couple of horses, and I won $300.

When I got back to the stroll, they were ready to go. I picked them up on the side of the street. They jumped in. I drove away.

Cherri handed me her money; Pam and Rohda did the same thing. I was thinking, *I'm pimpin' now*, with a smile on my face. I dropped Pam and Rohda off at Pam's house. I took Cherri home, and she asked me to come in. Once we got in, Cherri went to take a shower.

She said, "Make yourself at home. I'll be out in a minute." Once she was done, we went and got another dipped joint and something to drink from the liquor store, and I bought some Newports. Once we got to her house, we started talking. She asked me to be her pimp.

I said, "I already am. You gave me your money."

She said, "That was for giving me a ride, me and them.

"You've never had a ho before?"

"You will be my first ho. I'm just getting started."

"I could tell," she said.

"Here." I counted the money, and it was $240.

"Yeah, I make more than that if I'm happy," she said.

I asked, "Are you happy now?" She smiled.

I drove to my sister's and picked up some more weed. She said hi to my sister. My sister knew her. Her mom lived around the corner.

After we got back into the car and drove off, she told me, "Rohda and Pam made over $700, and they were calling you a cabdriver and said you wasn't a pimp."

Cherri said, "The next time they get in your car, you tell them to break themselves, tell them you're pimpin', no bitch rides for free." Cherri added, "I'm gonna call you *Daddy*—that's a form of respect. All the hoes should call you *Daddy*." She told me that pimps didn't give hoes rides unless they were trying to choose up. Cherri was my first real ho.

Cherri taught me a lot about the game. Cherri told me that she had an old record for robbery and that she would have to go to jail for sixteen months. Her mother had put up her house to get her out of jail. She told me that she loved me and wished she had met me first. All I could do was look into her eyes and tell her that I had love for her too.

Cherri and I were together for three months before she had to turn herself in.

I drove her to the court and dropped her off. I didn't want to go in and see her cuffed. I kissed her, and she walked in the court building with her head held high. She was a real ho; now she was gone. I knew there would be no other like her; she had given me game from a ho's standpoint.

I drove to Mac's barbershop to get my hair done and told him I had dropped the ho off at the courthouse.

*****

I had run into Pam and Rohda; they had asked me for a ride, and when they got into my Cadillac, I told them to break themselves. When they didn't want to choose up, I took their money and their clothes and put them out in their panties and bra. The bitches started cussing and hollered, "You ain't no pimp. My pimp is going to fuck you up, mothafucka."

I yelled, "Tell him Vinnie the Pimp broke you for being out of pocket, bitch." I burned rubber. "I'm pimpin', bitch!"

4

I had just got off work and had to go right back. I was assistant manager now. I was working twelve-hour days.

One of the cooks didn't show up for work last night. So I had to work a double shift.

I only had time to take a shower and change clothes and went back to work.

I was in my office, working on the time cards, when a waitress walked into my office and said, "Your brother's here to see you."

"Thank you, tell him I'll be out there in about ten minutes. Give him a menu. Sit him on the side where I sit and do my paperwork."

When I walked out, it was AD; he was dressed in a multicolor shirt, brown cowboy hat, and snakeskin boots. I was impressed. I asked him where he had been, and he told me that on the way from the courthouse, the police pulled him, T. Money, and the white bitch over on PCH and took him to jail for a warrant. He said he had stayed in jail for eight months.

We ate dinner and then went outside to smoke a Newport. I had shown him my new Caddy; he couldn't believe it was mine. He asked me if I got off at 5:00 p.m. I told him I got off at 10:00 p.m.

He said, "Hollywood is full with over five hundred hoes on the ho stroll. They work all day and all night."

I said, "Damn, we will go there after I get off work." I let him drive my Caddy and told him to pick me up at 10:00 p.m.

*****

He pulled up, and I was standing outside smoking a Newport. I let him drive.

We jumped on the freeway and headed to Hollywood.

I told him about Cherri. I told him that she was an ugly bitch but a pretty ho. I told him what I had done to the other hoes, Pam and Rohda, for playing with my pimping and calling me a cabdriver.

He laughed and said, "You've been doing your thang pimpin'."

I said, "That's for sure."

I told him all about Mac, the barber, and told him that we would go there tomorrow and get our hair done and kick game.

*****

There were very many hoes in Hollywood; it looked like there was a parade going on. The ho stroll was packed with cars; tricks were pickin' up hoes on every corner. There were twenty hoes on every block for miles and miles. It was the first time I'd seen the true meaning of the ho stroll. It was going on for real. I had never seen so many pimps and hoes.

There were some of the flyest cars I've ever seen. Caddys, Benzes, Double Rs, Excaliburs, and Zimmermans.

The pimps were in tailor-made suits, had big jewels on, snake-skin shoes, and fly hats.

AD said, "We're not here to make friends, we're trying to knock them niggas' hoes and give them some news they can use." He knew a lot of pimps already; he kept blowing the horn at the hoes. AD said to one of the bitches, "Let your next move be your best move." We campaigned all night. I had made up my mind right then that I was going to be one of the biggest and flyest pimps in the game. I had to step my game up. We pulled over to a Copper Penny in Hollywood and had breakfast. We kicked it with some of the pimps inside the restaurant; after we were done, we headed back to Long Beach.

*****

We went to see Mac the next day. I told him all about the night before in Hollywood. He said, "Your game better be tight, or them pimps will service you for your hoes." He added, "It's pimps from all around the globe there. That's the biggest ho stroll in America." AD told him about Joe Kadoe and that he had thirty hoes.

Mac knew him and all the major players in Hollywood; he said Joe and he go way back and that Joe had two double Rs and that he has ten other fly rides.

He finished our hair, and we went to lunch. AD said he heard of Mac before and said that he had nine hoes and that he had dope in his game, and he had gone to jail for some cocaine, and that when he was at the top of his game, he had some racehorses and some homes.

"Yeah, that's him. He doesn't pimp anymore. He's on parole, and he's staying out of the way until he's off paper."

*****

We drove to the car wash on PCH. While the car was getting washed and detailed, we walked down the track. There were a few hoes down. I saw a snow bunny with hair down past her ass. She was walking with two other hoes. AD said, "Switch, you got a real pimp watching."

We followed the hoes; they ran across the street.

I said, "That's right, you hoes better stay in pocket."

AD said, "Let your eyes be your guide."

I said, "I think that's Hollywood snakeskin shoes."

AD said, "I'll service him too. Pimpin' is one thing, friendship is another. We got to do our jobs."

"Yeah, you're right."

"I heard that Smokie knocked Philmo Slim for two hoes."

I said, "I think that's them hoes. They look like veteran hoes right there. You see how fast they ran across the street?"

AD said, "How do you think he got them hoes off the track?"

I said, "You see those other hoes down by the A&W Root Beer. I think those are pimpin' Shawn hoes."

"Let's go check on the car."

It was ready. I gave the worker a tip, and we jumped in and got pimping.

*****

The next week, I took my Caddy and got some shoes put on it. I got true rims and Vogue tires. It really made my car stand out.

*****

We went to Hollywood for the next three months. AD was driving the car while I went to work at the Copper Penny. He called the job and told me he had knocked a snow bunny. He said he's got her down on PCH, and he rented a room on the track.

He said he moved from the track in Hollywood; she gave $250, and he filled up the gas tank.

I told him when he got finished working to bring her in to get something to eat. He said, "I'm calling to let you know we were coming there."

I said, "Cool, I'll see you when you get here."

They showed up two hours later. She was a bad bitch. I had to give it to him, I was proud of him. They had dinner; he told me he would pick me up after I got off work.

I was standing outside smoking when he showed up. He was by himself. I asked, "Where your folks at?"

He answered, "She's at the room."

"You letting her rest up?"

"Yeah, she gave me $360." He said, "Now it's time to service the pimpin' for the bitch." It was the first time I would hear some pimp get news for his ho.

He called the motel that the ho gave him to service pimping for the bitch. He said, "It's ringing."

Someone answered and said, "Baby, you all right? I thought you were in jail. What happened? I've been looking for you all day."

AD said, "What's up, pimpin', this is AD the P. For the record, man, I got you for the bitch. She chose up."

The voice on the other end of the phone said, "Let me talk to the bitch."

AD said, "Is this Mac D the P?"

He said, "Yeah."

AD said, "How do you think I got your phone number? Anything you gotta say to the bitch, you can say it to me."

He said, "Put the bitch back down and give me action at the ho."

AD said, "The bitch gave me $500. She's been down all day and half of the night."

He said, "Where you at?"

AD said, "I'm like the air, I'm everywhere." And then he hung up the phone.

I said, "Pimp, son," and we laughed.

AD said, "He can keep them clothes and save them for the next ho. I'll buy the bitch something new every day. It will give her something to look forward to."

*****

AD pimped on the bitch for a month. The nigga found out where she was working at. He ran the ho all over the track—up and down the ho stroll, from one side of the street to the other. She stayed in pocket; she acted like she didn't even know him.

The police came and took them both to jail; it turned out that they had warrants all over the state. She was gone, and AD couldn't do anything about it. AD said, "The buster-ass nigga got my ho knocked by the police. It's cool, that's part of the game. I stacked a bank on the bitch. Now on to the next bitch."

I said, "That short-haired, blue-eyed blond ho got you paid in full."

He smiled and said, "If it ain't snowing, I ain't going. I only fuck with white hoes. If you see me with a black bitch, I'm holding her for the police. I don't want nothing black but a Cadillac, ya dig?"

I said, "I'm like Peter, and, Paul, I'm trying to get them all." We jumped into the Caddy and drove down the track looking at and sweating the hoes out there.

AD said, "Let's go to Norms and grab a bite to eat. A pimp is starving." I drove to the restaurant and parked. We got out and headed in to Norms.

*****

"Hey, what's up, Diane, how have you been?" I said.

She said, "Missing you. When are you gonna come and see me?"

Me and Diane had been talking off and on; she stayed on my mind all the time. I told her I would fly out for one day so we could see each other. She said, "You got it like that?"

I said, "Yeah, for you and only you." I could sense her smiling through the phone.

"When I come, we're gonna kick back and make love like we used to."

She said, "I can't wait to see you."

I said, "I'll call you next week and let you know what time and day I will be there." I got back to work. I had a lot to do; it was the day before payday. I had to go to the bank and deposit money, and I had to help cook; it was going to be a busy night.

The next day I called her and told her I would be there that following week so she could get things together on her end.

That week went fast. I was going to be off on Wednesday; we talked a couple more times. I told her I would call her tomorrow and tell her what time I would be there.

"Hey, sweetheart, my flight lands at 2:30 p.m."

She said, "I'll be there. I'm going to be in front waiting for you."

5

Diane had rented a car to pick me up from the airport. We drove to Atlantic City. I got a suite for us. I had $3,000 with me, so we could do anything we wanted. Diane asked me if I was pimping. I told her I tried it for a couple of months. I told her the money was great and that the West Coast was full of hookers just like New York. She said, "I'm not a ho." I thought, *You will be when I'm done with you.*

The room was very nice; it came with room service and a mini-bar. We had a couple of drinks, then we got into the bathtub; it was full of bubbles, and it smelled wonderful. We stayed in there for an hour. We talked and laughed; it was as if we hadn't been apart for over a year. We got out and dried each other off, kissing and touching each other. We walked over to the bed. I took the towel off her. She was super fine—5'8", 36-D breasts, twenty-four-inch waist. She was a redbone with green eyes. She had a short-styled haircut; it looked great on her. I laid her down and licked her tummy, down her legs, to her inner thighs; she started moaning.

I licked all the way back up to those beautiful breasts. They were huge. I licked around the nipples. I put two fingers insider her vagina, and she started grinding on my fingers. I could feel her getting very wet; she started moving faster and faster. "I'm cumming!" she shouted.

I made her cum again and again.

She kissed me with passion and love, but it was the first time I really knew that she did love me. After a few minutes went by, and her legs stopped shaking, she dropped to the floor and licked my balls, down my legs, and between my thighs. It felt so good. She sucked my rod so good she made me cum, and she swallowed every bit of it. "Vinnie, I love you." Then she licked my thighs and sucked my dick until it became hard; we made love all night until the sun came up.

That morning we called for room service. We ordered some breakfast—steaks and eggs, hash browns and toast. We had some fruits also.

We got a couple of hours of sleep. We got up and got dressed and went to gamble; we had a couple of drinks, and I took her shopping. We had a great time. She only spent a few hundred dollars. I gave her $500 to pay off the rental car. I knew that was more than enough. We stopped and had lunch. I had to get back to the room so I could pack my things. We had a couple of hours before I had to leave. We made love for an hour, and she drove me to the airport.

She said, "I had a great time. I hate that you have to go. I've been thinking about being your ho. I love you, and I'll do anything for you, Daddy." I couldn't believe it; she was thinking about it.

I said, "Take your time and think about it, and when you're ready, I'll fly you out to the West Coast."

She said, "I've got a brother out there in Compton. I would like to see him. It's been eight years."

"Cool, you could do that for sure, just let me know. I love you." I kissed her and grabbed my suitcase and headed into the airport.

She said, "Daddy, let me walk you into the airport." We walked, she hugged and kissed me, and I was off to get on the airplane.

*****

I had a wonderful time with Diane in Atlantic City. I stayed in her ear while we were making love, asking her to work for me. I was glad that she was in love with me, and she said she would think about it. That's all I can ask of her, and she didn't let me down; that was good enough.

I told AD all about it. On the drive back from the airport, I was tired as hell; it was from jet lag and all that sex. I had to be at work in a couple of hours. I told AD to drop me off and come back and take me to work.

*****

When I got to work, the place was packed. There was a convention in town at the Long Beach area; the Copper Penny was right down the street from there.

I had to get right to work. I was maneuvering my way around, in, an out of the kitchen, helping the cooks, working the cash register, seating people, and carrying trays of water to give to the customers at the tables. I worked twelve hours. I fell asleep in the car after AD picked me up. When I woke up, we were in Hollywood. I was so tired that I had slept all night. It was morning when AD said, "You wanna get some breakfast?"

I wiped the sleep out of my eyes and said, "Yeah, how long was I sleep?"

AD said, "About six hours."

"I'm feeling better. What day is it?" I asked.

He said, "It's Friday."

"Good, I'm off today." We finished eating and headed back to Long Beach. We drove down the streets on the way back. We hit Western then Figueroa in Los Angeles, then we drove to Long Beach Boulevard in Lynwood, the Compton, and we hit the city of Long Beach. It was a long drive. We worked the ho stroll on Long Beach. PCH had about twenty hoes out there. I think I saw that bitch Rohda; she jumped in that truck with that trick. I asked AD if he saw that ho get into the truck.

AD said, "I see that black girl?"

I said, "That was that ho I was telling you about, the one I broke."

AD said, "I see that bitch all the time when you're at work. Every time she sees the car, she puts her head down and keeps pushing."

*****

I was awakened by the sound of the phone ringing. It was my mother; she said, "Your car note is due today."

I said, "Okay, I'll take care of it."

Mom said, "I need you to bring me some money. These niggas are kicking my ass on the card table."

I asked her, "How much do you need?"

Mom said, "Bring enough for me and you. I want you to help me kick these niggas' ass on the table."

"I'll be there in an hour. As soon as I come from the car lot."

My mother said, "Stop and get me a pack of cigarettes and a beer and a shot of liquor."

"Okay, give me a minute, and I'll be there. AD, wake up, I need to go and pay my car note then go and holler at Mom's."

He said, "Go ahead, I'll holler at you when you get back."

I said, "Okay, I'm off today, you know how Mom is."

"Yeah, that's why I'm staying here till you get back."

*****

The game was in full swing. When I walked in, my mom said, "Here's my baby. Now we gonna kick y'all asses."

The lady dealing said, "How much you want?" They were playing blackjack. My mother was the third person to the left of the dealer. There were only seven seats.

The dealer's bank was $360. The first person asked for $60, the next person asked for $40, and my mother said, "Bring me the rest, $240."

The dealer said, "There's $240."

My mother looked at me. I gave her $1,000 in all twenties, and she said, "Bring it on."

The remaining people at the table didn't get a hand.

The dealer was Ms. Pat; she said to the first person, "You stay or hit?"

"Stay," the first said.

The next person, which was Ms. Eleine, said, "Hit me," and she busted out the third person, which was my mother.

She said, "Stay."

The dealer turned over her hand and said, "I've got nineteen. I'm paying twenty. The first person had eighteen and lost." Ms. Pat said, "Lula, what you got?"

My mother said, "Pay me, bitch. I got twenty."

Ms. Pat said, "Damn, bitch, with your lucky ass." My mom ended up winning $1,300. We split it. I kissed my mom and left.

"Nigga, wake up. Look what I won. Mom's won all the money. We split it. $1,300."

"What's up for the day?" AD asked.

"Let's get pimpin'."

*****

We went to the ho stroll and sweated some hoes and got the Caddy washed. Then we went to get some weed and stopped at the liquor store and picked up something to drink. We ate at the pad and just kicked back. I split my money with AD, and I went to sleep; it was a good day.

*****

I was at work taking a break before the dinner rush. The Copper Penny was a very nice restaurant. The booths were brown, and it had a multicolored carpet. It was open twenty-four hours a day, seven days a week, and in a busy part of downtown. Ocean Boulevard was lined with beaches, luxurious apartments, large homes, banks, hotels, the Long Beach arena, and the convention center. People came from all over the world to see the *Queen Mary*, one of the largest ships in the world, with its three smokestacks.

The Copper Penny stayed busy. I had a good job. I was the youngest black manager in the company. I had proven myself in the area.

While I was eating, I thought about Job Corps and the first time it snowed. It was colder than a mothafucka. The snow was knee-deep, and the wind was blowing, pushing the snow back and forth.

It took a month of slipping in that snow, and my face being frozen, me and Diane played in that snow. They were fun times, but I didn't want to live there.

I did have a great time while I was there. It paid off. Now look at me, driving America's finest car, working for a huge company, but I can't get pimping out of my mind—the girls, the money, the cars, the jewelry, the street fame. I made $700 every two weeks, and a ho makes it in a day or two.

I was the boss at the Copper Penny, but I wanted to be a boss in the streets. It seemed like the game was calling me. I had dreams of being the best pimp in the world.

The world anyway. Beautiful prostitutes was a nightly vision. The tailor-made suits, fly brims, reptile shoes, money stacking high, enjoying being called Daddy, and having fine hoes on my arm.

*****

"Good evening, sir. How many in your party, smoking or non-smoking?" I asked as the dinner rush had started. The customers began to pour in. A nice-looking girl asked if we were hiring. I told her, "Come back around 2:30 p.m. tomorrow."

She said, "Okay," with a bright smile. I was working from 11:00 a.m. till 11:00 p.m. I liked that shift. I didn't have to get up too early, and I could go to bed late. I still could get enough rest before my next shift. The only thing was I worked twelve hours a day, six days a week. It was cool. I stayed dressed fly every day at work. People complimented me on my attire all the time.

A lot of good-looking women came into the restaurant on a daily basis. I got a lot of action all the time. I knew one day I would meet someone I could have working the ho stroll for me, and being the street boss I wanted to be. A pimp, ya know!

6

The girl came back the next afternoon and filled out an application. Her name was Crissy. She had red hair, green eyes, and freckles. She was about 5'5", and she had a sexy shape. I gave her the job. She would be working the night shift. We became real, real good friends.

I was telling AD about her. I had fucked her three or four times. I had stopped having sex with her after that. She wanted to become my girlfriend.

I wanted a ho—that's all I could think about. I didn't want to mix that shit up with work. And I didn't want everybody at work to know anything about my desire to become a pimp. I never told Crissy about the life of being a hooker. She said I was a womanizer and a flirt. Me and Crissy, we're cool the way things were. If I ever needed some pussy, she would be there with her legs open quickly. I was always good to her.

*****

It was a sunny day in Long Beach. I could smell the ocean breeze. Not a cloud in the sky—I noticed as AD drove me to work. I told him, "One of these days, we should go to the beach. We might meet a cool bitch there."

AD said, "If I did, I would have to turn her out to the game, if she was going to be your ho." He said, "I like to get mine off the track because they're already in the life. The only thing I would get from the beach is a girlfriend or some pussy. I want the money and the honey, ya dig?"

I said, "I dig ya."

He was younger than me but had more game than me. That was cool; he was teaching me the game. I wanted to learn how to be the best pimp there was.

*****

"Good morning," my sister said.

"The same to you." I loved my sister. I stayed with her and her husband. I moved in with them after me and Debbie broke up.

My sister was very good-looking. She had pretty eyes and a nice shape, with a wonderful smile.

The nickname *Peaches* fit her. My grandmother named her that as soon as she was born. Her skin looked like a peach. She asked me if I would cook breakfast. I cooked bacon, eggs, potatoes, and toast. We had coffee and orange juice.

As we were eating, she said, "A girl named Beverly has been calling for you. She left her phone number."

*****

"Hello, is Beverly there?"

"May I ask who's calling?"

"Ms. Smith," I said, "it's Vinnie. I met her in Job Corps."

"Okay. Bev!" she shouted on the other end of the phone.

"Yeah, Mom," I could hear Beverly saying from somewhere in the house.

"Telephone," her mom said.

"I got it." I could hear her picking up on the other line. "Hello."

"Hi, what's up with you?"

"Oh, it's you, how have you been?"

"Fine, just working hard and thinking about you," I said.

"I called your sister a couple of times, but you were never there."

"How long have you been home from Job Corps?"

"Two weeks. I'm glad to be out of that snow. It was hard going to school in all that cold-ass weather," she said.

44

"I know the feeling. I was glad to come back to Cali. I have a car. When can I come and scoop you up?"

"I want you to meet my family. I've been telling them about you," she said.

"Well, I'm off on Wednesday. I work six days a week," I said.

"Okay, come next week on your next day off."

"What do you want to do?" I asked.

"Have dinner with my family, and we will see what's up after that."

I asked, "Do you want me to bring something?"

"Yeah, bring something, my mom likes beer."

"What kind?" I asked.

"Schlitz Malt Liquor."

"Oh, the bull, yeah," I said, "my mother drinks the same thing."

She said, "Well, I guess I'll see you next week."

I said, "Yeah."

And we ended the call.

*****

I took my car and got it detailed. It was looking new. I had my hat in the back window; it was the same color as my car. The hat in the window was a sign of a player. I was nervous meeting her family. I stopped at the liquor store and picked up two six-packs of beer, and I got a case of soda. I walked out of the store then turned around and went back in and got two packs of Newports for Beverly.

I lived in Long Beach, and she lived in Watts. It was a cool little drive. All I could think about was all the fun me and Beverly had in Job Corps. I really liked her. I pulled up to their house, and Beverly was standing on the front porch smoking a cigarette. There were two guys out there with her. I blew the horn in my car. She was smiling from ear to ear. I got out and walked to the gate and asked if there was a dog.

She said, "Yeah, but we have him tied in the backyard. You can come in."

"Oh, let me get the bags out of the car," I said. "I bought you some Newports."

"Thanks," she said. We walked inside the house; they had a very nice home. It had a huge living room, dining room, and den. It was a five-bedroom house.

Beverly said, "These are my brothers Flipper and Eddie. My mom is in the kitchen." She walked me into the kitchen to meet her mother.

I said, "Hi, it's nice to meet you, my name is Vinnie."

"I know who you are, it's nice to meet you too," she said.

"I brought you some beer. Two six-packs."

"Thank you." I set the bags on the table, and me and Beverly walked back outside.

Beverly said, "My dad will be home at 4:00 p.m. My mom likes you, I can tell."

"She's very nice."

"Most of the time."

"Yeah, I know how moms can be. My mom is a trip sometimes too," I said. "Man, that food smells good."

"Do you eat pork?" Beverly asked.

"Hell yeah."

"Mom is frying pork chops with mashed potatoes, gravy, green beans with bacon in them, yams, salad, and cornbread," she said.

*****

"Hi, sir, my name is Vinnie, it's nice to meet you."

"My name is Paul, Paul Smith. Is that your car out there with that hat in the back?" he asked. "What kind of work do you do?" He gave me a strange look.

"I work at the Copper Penny restaurant, I'm the manager."

"Oh, you must make good money, driving a car like that," he stated.

Beverly said, "Daddy."

"Well, anyway, it's nice to meet you," he said.

"Daddy, Vinnie brought you some beer, would you like one?"

"Yeah, thanks, son, that was nice of you."

Beverly walked into the kitchen and got a can of beer and gave it to her father. Beverly and I went outside to smoke a Newport.

"Your dad doesn't trust me."

"Don't mind him, he's like that. But he's cool." Her sisters came over; one's name was *Summer*, and the other was *Nunu*.

We all sat down and ate dinner. Mr. Smith was cool. He told jokes. We laughed and talked. I told them about my job. I joked about some of the people that came inside the restaurant. The dinner was great. I had to admit, her family was all right.

I felt right at home. After the dinner, we walked outside and smoked a Newport. Her brother Eddie asked if I had any weed. I told him I had some in the car.

He said, "Let's smoke."

"Jump in, we'll ride and get high."

Beverly said, "My dad knows we smoke weed. We smoke out in the back. Anyways, the police is hot around here. You don't want to smoke in that Cadillac." I grabbed a bag of weed out of the car. We rolled out and headed to the backyard. They had a huge yard. They had a table and chairs. We played cards and had a couple of beers. I had a cool time. When we were finished, Beverly walked me to my car and gave me a hug and a kiss.

I told her, "Next time, we will go to my house." I looked at her and smiled.

7

"My main man," Mac said as I walked into the barbershop.

I said, "What's up with you?"

He said, "It's always good to see you, playa. There are three people ahead of you."

I said, "It's cool. I got time, playa." I picked up the newspaper and glanced through it. I found the sports section and looked at the horses. I planned on going to Hollywood Park Racetrack to try and win some money. I've been playing the horses. I asked Mac, "What do you like in the third race?"

Mac said, "I played the three over the four in exacta box."

I said, "It looks good. I'm going to play the same thing." It was my turn in the barber chair. I got a wash and set.

Mac asked, "How do you want your hair set?" after he was done rolling it up.

I said, "Just make it fly like always."

"So tell me about it, playa."

"I'm staying down for my crown. When I leave here, I'm going right to work on a bitch's ass."

He said, "That's right, pimpin'."

I said, "It might be my time to shine, ya dig?"

"I'm near ya not to hear ya," he stated.

"I just bought some snakeskin boots to match that tailor-made suit you laid on me. I'm going to work that outfit you gave me today. You gotta stay fly if you gonna be a pimp, ya dig?" My hair was laid once he was done. "Mac, I'll see ya next week."

I was going down PCH, and I spotted two ducks walking on the ho stroll. They were watching the cars as they drove by. I thought to myself they must be turnouts; as I drove past, they waved at me. I blew my horn and told them to meet me around the corner. One of them was redbone with big tits. She was about 5'7", with brown eyes and brown hair. The other one was 5'9" with big tits, dark-skinned, dark eyes, curly long black hair. I turned the corner and pulled over. They slowly walked around the corner and walked to my Cadillac. I asked them their names; the redbone said, "Stacy," and the other one said, "Michelle."

I said, "What's up with y'all?"

Stacy said, "Just trying to find something to get into." I told them to get in, and they did.

I drove the backstreets. I asked them if they smoked weed and if they wanted something to drink. They said yes. I pulled over to the liquor store and sent Michelle into the store. I asked Stacy if she had a man. She said no.

I asked her, "What about Michelle?"

She said, "Her and her nigga she was fucking with had a fight, and she's mad at him."

I asked, "Were you guys out there trying to make some money when I picked you guys up?"

She said, "Yeah, I've been only been doing this for two weeks."

"And how about Michelle?" She told me that she had been working for over two months. "Does she give her money to the guy she's been fuckin' with?"

She said, "That's what they were fighting about. He spends up all the money, and she has to work all day to pay the room rent and to get something to eat."

Just then Michelle walked back to the car and said that the man in the store wouldn't let her buy the liquor because she didn't have her ID. I got out of the car and walked Michelle back into the store and got the drinks.

I asked her, "What's up with the nigga you fucking with?"

She said, "I'm tired of his shit. He goes and fucks off all the money and then wants me to work my ass off all day. I can't stand it anymore." I asked if he was a pimp. She said, "He's a wannabe pimp."

"Does he have a car?" She said no. I paid for the drinks, and we walked out of the store. We got into the car and drove off. I took them to the beach. It was a beautiful day; people were swimming, suntanning. There were other people playing in the sand, building sandcastles and flying kites.

I asked them where they stayed. Michelle said, "At a room on PCH called the Poolside."

"Do you guys pay the rent?"

Michelle said, "Hell no. I'm leaving his ass."

Stacy asked, "What's your name?"

"Vinnie Mac."

She asked, "Are you a pimp?"

Michelle said, "Girl, look at him—with his fine ass, his hair curled up, he has tailor-made clothes and snakeskin boots. He's a pimp for sure."

I said, "That's why I brought you all to the sand so you could choose a real man."

They laughed and said, "Sho, ya right." We finished our drinks and got into my Cadillac. I fired up the weed, and we smoked. I asked how much money they had.

Michelle said, "I've only got eighty."

Stacy said, "I only had two dates—one for forty and the other for thirty."

Michelle said, "We just got started when you picked us up.

"I'm giving him my money. I don't know about you." Michelle reached into her bra and pulled out her trap and handed it to me. She said, "I knew you were a pimp the whole time, I just wanted to see how you would act when we got into your car. You're the kind of nigga I want, and I mean that in a good way."

"He's a cool-ass pimp, and he's good-looking," Stacy said.

Stacy reached me them ends she had stashed in her front pocket. I said, "You doing the right thing. You taking a chance to advance. You will advance fuck with me." I turned up the music, and we smashed off.

Stacy said, "You sure do have a nice car."

"Thanks. Do you guys have clothes?"

"Yeah, they're in the room."

I said, "Y'all are with me now. I want you hoes to call me Daddy."

"Yes, Daddy," they said.

I said, "Pimpin' an' hoein' is the best thin' goin', ya dig?"

"We dig."

"I'm going to give you guys nicknames," I said. "Stacy, I'm going to call you Red Bone, and, Michelle, I'm going to call you Sexy because you have a sexy-ass walk." Michelle smiled. "Stacy, I'm calling you Red Bone 'cause you're light, bright, and damn near white, ya dig?"

She smiled and said, "Daddy, we need to get our shit out of the room."

"Our purses are in there," Michelle said.

We pulled up to the motel, and I said, "You bitches hurry up and get your shit." They jumped out and ran to the room; they were back in minutes. I told Sexy to leave the key inside the room so the manager wouldn't trip just in case they ever needed to rent a room again. We drove off and headed to the liquor store to pick up some Newports and some more drinks. The parking lot was full. I had to park the way down at the end of the parking lot.

I got out the car feeling great. I just knocked two fresh hoes. "What's up, playa, can I wash them windows for ya?"

I looked at him and said, "That's okay. What do you want to drink?"

"Wine," he said.

I said, "I gotcha. Don't trip." I gave him a few, and I got the wine for him. I always gave money to the homeless as long as they tell the truth. I don't care if they use dope as long as they keep it real. I was having a good day, and things were going my way. When I got back to my ride, I see a nigga pulling on my car door, hollering at one of the hoes.

"Get your ass out the mothafuckin' Cadillac. Get out, bitch, before I break this got damn window!"

I said, "Hey, man, that's my car you fucking with." I handed the bum his drink. "Hey, playa, you have to get away from my 'lac."

"Nigga, fuck you, that's my bitch in there," he hollered.

"That ho ain't trying to fuck with you anymore, that's why she's not getting out."

"Nigga, let my bitch out. I'll fuck you and that punk-ass bitch up."

I said, "You got me fucked up."

"Say, you faggot-ass pimp, I'll fuc—" As soon as he was about to say the last part, I took the cane from the bum I had just given wine to, and I cracked the mothafucka in the head till he fell to the ground. Then I slapped him like a ho. He said, "All right." I socked him in the jaw with a left and then a right. That ho-ass nigga damn near pissed his pants. I saw a few sports on his pants. He said, "Please don't hit me again."

I stopped and helped him to his feet. "Get your ass up, and your bitch chose up."

"Man, me and the bitch came here from LA." I went into my pocket and gave him five twenty-dollar bills.

"This should get you back where you came from."

He said, "Fuck that fat-ass bitch," and walked away.

I got in the car and told Sexy, "That's what happens when you fuck with a buster-ass nigga, ya dig?"

"Damn, thanks, Daddy. A bitch was scared than a mothafucka."

I gave the homeless man a twenty-dollar bill and said, "Thanks for the cane."

Sexy said, "Daddy, watch out for that nigga. I don't trust him."

"We're not going to work on this end of the track." I lit a Newport, and we drove off.

"What's up, P?" I was talking to AD on the phone.

He said, "Where you at?"

"I'm in Inglewood. I just knocked two fresh hoes. I had to whoop a nigga's ass about them."

AD said, "What the fuck?"

"He wasn't a pimp, he's a buster. He had trouble taking the bad news about the bitches. I let him know it was pimpin' with me. After, I got into some gangster shit."

AD said, "Come scoop me up."

"Where you at?"

"On Eighty-First and Alvon, at Mom's house."

"I'll be there in thirty minutes." I told my hoes, "My friends are not your friends. When he gets into the car, don't say nothing to him."

"Okay, Daddy."

I said, "When a pimp is riding with me, mind your business. You all are wife-in-laws, so just talk to each other or just listen to the music."

"Okay, Daddy."

"Always get into the back seat. My hoes ride in the back. I'm going to sit you guys down and spit some game to you and see how much you guys know.

"What's up, AD?" I said.

"Some more of it knocking hoes as slammin' Cadillac doors, ya dig?" I pulled away from the curb and turned up the music.

AD said, "If I had your hands, I'd cut mine off."

I said and pointed, "I named her Red Bone. I named the other one Sexy." They smiled.

AD said, "Vinnie's dream team, I see ya, man."

I said, "I'm going to the racetrack to play a couple of horses. After that, I'm going to take you girls shoppin'." They smiled. I pulled over to the gas station. AD and I got out.

AD said, "They look like some squares."

I said, "That's how they were dressed when I knocked them."

AD said, "I dig ya, man."

"I broke them for one hundred and some change. I gave it to that fool. It was the last trap, ya dig?" I said.

AD said, "You kept it pimpin'. A lot of niggas wouldn't have given that buster nothing."

"The game will bless me back. Look at the work in the car. Wait till I take them shoppin'. I'm going to add in the flavor to them, and they will look like top-flight hoes."

AD said, "They got some fly-ass stores in downtown Los Angeles."

"That's where I'm taking them to."

Me and AD ran into the racetrack, and I put my bets in.

*****

I pulled up to the meter and parked downtown. We all got out. Red Bone said, "Daddy, this is my first time in downtown and the first time I've shopped in the Alley." The Alley was a spot where all the players shopped for their hookers.

Sexy said, "I heard they got some bomb stores in there."

I said, "You bitches walk in front of me, and when you find something that you like, let me know. Don't buy nothing like you have on, find something short and low-cut to show off your boobs. Pick out two dresses, bra and panties, some boots and some flats, then we will pick up some makeup and whatever else you all need."

They said, "Thank you, Daddy." They walked and talked laughing and shopping.

AD said, "A happy ho is a good ho."

I said, "You better know it."

AD said, "What about your job?"

"I've got some vacation time, I'll use it. I'll take my time and lace them up on game, and then I'll put them down."

AD said, "Are you going to put them down in Hollywood and let them work the ho stroll?"

I said, "In a couple of weeks, I want to see how these bitches take to the game I teach them."

I ended helping them shop. I picked out some fly shit for them to wear. The girls liked my taste in clothing. I could hear them talking on the way back to the car. They were very happy, giggling and laughing. I heard Red Bone say, "Bitch, I can't wait to go to work in my new shit. I'm going to make all the money."

Sexy said, "You gonna have to beat me to it."

"It's on, bitch." Me and AD looked at each other and smiled.

I unlocked the Cadillac and told them to get in. I said, "I'll be right back. I'm going to leave the keys. Turn on some music and kick it for a minute. I'm going to get us something to eat." Me and AD walked down the street to the Church's Chicken.

AD said, "Pimpin', you gonna get paid."

"I'm the real boss with the hot sauce. When a bitch choose, she can't lose with the pimpin' I use."

AD said, "Them are some thick-ass fine bitches."

I said, "It's not in the beauty, it's in the duty, ya dig?" I added, "I'm a rich ho's king and a po' ho's dream."

"Pimp, son," AD said. "I'm gonna watch them and make sure that they stay in pocket." AD asked, "Are you gonna spot-pimp?"

I said, "I'm like poncho via. I'm gonna break them anytime I see them."

AD asked, "Are you gonna get a room?"

"Yeah, on Ocean and Cherry, at the beach motel, ya dig? I'm gonna show them that I do it like big Mac. Ya got that?"

"I'm too near ya not to hear ya."

I pulled up to the motel. I got two suites for a week; it cost $500 per week. It had a beautiful view of the ocean. It had stairs leading down to the beach. We stepped into the suite; one of the girls—I think it was Red Bone—said, "Daddy, this is the best place I ever stayed at or seen in my life."

I said, "You with the best, so fuck the rest, ya dig?"

Sexy said, "Come on, bitches, let's look at the rest of the place." They put their bags down, and they walked into the bedrooms. It had two bedrooms, two bathrooms, a living room, a den, a dining room, and a kitchen.

The living room had blue carpet, a TV, white leather sofas, love seats, and chairs with blue throw pillows to match the blue carpet drapes. It also had a coffee table and two end tables and lamps on them.

The dining room had a nice wooden table with six chairs. And it had a china cabinet full of dishes. The kitchen had a coffee maker, dishwasher, stove, and refrigerator. It had pots and pans and silverware. One bedroom had a king-size bed; the other had two twin-size beds, and both had TVs. The den had a futon in there and a chair to match and TV.

The bathrooms were nice also; one had a hot tub, and the other had a shower. The patio had matching tables and chairs and a barbecue pit; it had a sliding glass door, with a breathtaking view.

AD said, "This is real pimpish, Vinnie."

I said, "Thanks, P."

The hoes loved the place. I gave them the room with the king-size bed, and it had the hot tub room.

I told the girls to unpack and that I was going to the store.

Sexy said, "Daddy, me and Red Bone have food stamps, and we get checks next week."

I said, "Cool, give me the stamps, and I will go shoppin'. I'll wait for you and unpack."

We jumped into the Caddy and pulled off. I asked the girls how they felt.

Red Bone said, "I'm very happy. I'm glad I got with you."

Sexy said, "If I'm going to be hoeing, it will only be for you, Daddy."

8

Sexy said, "I was a fool giving that nigga my money. Oh, by the way, Daddy, I have some more money for you. I was stacking money so I would have money once I was gone from that punk-ass mothafucka."

I asked, "How much do you have?"

"Daddy, it's about $400."

I said, "That's cool, Sexy, thanks for keeping it real."

She said, "You're welcome, Daddy," and smiled.

"Daddy, can we get something to drink?"

"Sure," I said.

Red Bone said, "Daddy, I don't have any more money, but wait till tonight. I'll have plenty for sure."

I pulled up to the supermarket and told the girls what I wanted out of the market. I told them to get whatever they wanted.

I said, "By the way, you all won't be working tonight. I want to get to know both of you better. I want to tell you bitches the rules of the game and what I expect from you all."

They said, "Thanks, Daddy," and got out of the car and went into the supermarket.

AD said, "You got a winner right there. She could have kept that money she had stashed."

I said, "I know. Let's drive to the tracks and look at it. I want to go to the liquor store and pick up something to drink. They'll be done by the time we get back." I drove down Long Beach Boulevard and turned right, then I went down two more blocks on PCH to the liquor store. I pulled into the parking lot of the liquor store and parked. I asked AD to go into the store and get some Hennessey and Grand Marnier so we could make some French connections.

I said, "That's a pimp drink right there. Hennessey and Grand Marnier, half and half. And get some vodka, gin, and some beer—any kind." I counted my bankroll. I had $1,400. I gave AD $200 since he didn't have a hooker. I said, "If my horses hit, I'll give you some more."

AD said, "Right on, pimpin'."

I gave him money for the drinks. When we got to the super-market, the girls were standing out in front. I pulled up; they had a basketful of stuff. I popped the trunk. They put the bags in and closed the trunk back. When they got into the car, I asked how many food stamps they had.

Sexy said, "I had $240."

Red Bone said, "I had $160 worth of food stamps. We still have some left. Do you want them, Daddy?"

"No, just put them on the dresser in your room."

She said, "Okay, Daddy."

I said, "When you guys put the food up, I want y'all to make yourselves a drink then put the liquor and beer away. I will roll up some weed for you all, and after that, relax and enjoy yourselves."

"Daddy, can we go down to the beach?"

"Yeah, that's why we moved down here. Do your thang. I'm going to cook tonight."

Sexy said, "Daddy, you can cook?"

I said, "I can burn, baby." They started laughing. I said, "Later on tonight, me, you, and Red Bone will sit down and talk."

Red Bone said, "Okay, Daddy, would you like something to drink?"

I said, "Thanks, but I'll make the drinks this time so you will know how I like mine, then the next time, you can make them."

*****

Me and AD were sitting outside on the patio having a pimp's drink. We could see the girls out there on the beach. They seemed to be enjoying themselves.

I said, "Those girls even tried to give me the food stamps. I think they're going to be good hos. Just look at them laughing, running, and playing."

AD said, "Yeah, pimpin', you came up."

I fried some chicken, made some corn on the cob, potato salad, baked beans, and dinner rolls.

Red Bone and Sexy said that they really enjoyed their dinner. Me and AD did too. After dinner, they cleaned up the kitchen. I rolled up some more weed, and we had a couple more drinks.

We sat on the patio and took in the view; the sun was setting. It looked beautiful, orange and yellow, with a few clouds; it was picture perfect.

"AD," I said, "let me holler at you. I'm going to chop it up with the hoes. Do you want to take the Cadillac and roll so you can try and knock you some fresh work?"

AD said, "I was just going to ask you about that. Yeah, I want to try and come up with a new piece."

I said, "Cool—oh, I damn near forgot. Let me call and see what the horses did." I called the bookie. The phone rang. Robert Charles answered. I said, "What's up, playa? This is Vinnie Mac. Can you tell me what happened in the third race at Hollywood Park?"

He said, "Let me check and see. It came the 3 over the 5 and paid $75."

"Thanks," I said and hung up the phone. I had bet it twenty times. I had won $1,500. I was smiling like a mothafucka.

AD said, "Did you win?"

I said, "Hell yeah, it paid $75."

AD said, "That's all?"

I said, "That's all you need if you played it twenty times. Can you count, nigga?" I added, "That's $1,500, ya dig?"

AD said, "Yo pimpin' is on."

*****

I drove by Ms. Price's house and played with my son for a minute. I gave her $300 so she could get whatever she needed. I drove to where my mom was at. I gave her $400. I told her I had the third race at Hollywood Park. I had boxed it for a hundred; it paid $75. I gave her a hug and told her that I had two new girls and that they had given me over $500.

She said, "Nigga, give me a hundred mo' and go pay two car notes so you will be ahead by two notes. You hear, Vinnie?"

"Ya, Mom, I hear you." I kissed her goodbye. I jumped in my car and headed over to the car lot.

*****

"Mr. Jordan, can I help you?"

"I would like to pay two extra payments," I said.

"Sure, no problem," the woman said. I made the payments and headed to pick AD up from his mom, and we headed to Hollywood Park Racetrack. The money I spent I already had in my pocket, I didn't tell my mom; she would have asked for more.

We picked up the money and headed back to the room. AD dropped me off. I told him, "Pick me up later. I need to talk with my girls."

I walked into the room, and the girls were out on the patio. I poured myself a drink and pulled up a chair, lit a joint, and said, "I would like to take this time to get to know you guys better. Red Bone, you first."

"Well, my dad was a pimp, and my mom was his bottom bitch. I'm mixed with black, and my mom was white. I came from back east. I'm the only child. My real name is Stacy Flyer. My dad's name is Fly Macin—or was. He was from Boston. He got killed by a trick that was trying to hurt my mother. I heard that the trick had raped my mom and had stabbed my dad. My dad shot and killed the guy, and my dad died on the way to the hospital. I was one year old. My mom came here after that. When I was eighteen, I moved out. My mother's boyfriend had been touchin' on me ever since I was five years old. As I got older, he kept givin' me money and told me to keep my mouth closed. I did. My mom was in love with him, and he took care of us. He got me anything I asked for or wanted. So I guess you could say I've been hoeing all my life. I met Sexy at the county office." *Damn, that was fucked. I want to fuck him up. I need another drink.*

"Would you like another drink, Red Bone?" I asked.

"Yes, Daddy, I need one. Oh, I've been drinking since I was five years old. I just wanted to tell you, Daddy, don't worry, I'm a big girl. I know what I want, and that's to get paid and get out of this life by the time I'm twenty-five years old, so we got seven years, Daddy, to get this money. I'm as you say, Daddy, I'm digging you."

"Red Bone, I'm really digging you too, both of y'all."

I said, "Sexy, it's your turn."

"Well, I'm Michelle Jackson, I'm from LA, born and raised. My mom was—or is—a dope fiend. She shoots heroin and takes pills. I was a badass kid. My mother has a girlfriend named Jackie. My mother likes women. I was raised by them. I started smokin' weed and drinkin' when I was twelve years old. My mother let me do anything I wanted as long as I went to school so she could get that county check. I started fucking older guys for money when I was twelve years old. I've been doing it ever since. But I never worked the track till I came to Long Beach. That's been two months. I'm glad I met you, Daddy."

"I'm glad I met you too, Sexy."

When they were gone, I lit a Newport and said, "I'll do my best to take good care of you." I sipped my drink and said, "Let me tell you what I expect from you. Y'all pour another drink. I'm going to tell you the rules of the game." I said, "First, you should learn to respect me at all times. That means stay in pocket at all times. That means you don't look or talk to pimps. You don't look in their cars or dance to the music coming from their car. When you see a pimp coming, you put your head down and keep walking, or if you're posted on the corner, you turn your back to them as they drive by. And if you see a pimp walking on your side of the street, you put your head down and cross the street. Get out of their way. I mean run if you have to. Don't listen to what they have to say, and don't you laugh at them or look into their eyes. If you do, you will be out of pocket, and if you get out of pocket, they will break you. That means they will take all of your money, ya dig?"

They said, "We dig."

"We're with you, and we will respect you and stay in pocket."

"And remember, a pimp will break you by any means necessary."

Red Bone said, "Shit, a nigga ain't getting shit from me, Daddy. I like where I'm at. I'm going to stay in pocket."

Sexy said, "A mothafucka ain't getting shit from me. The only pimp that's getting my money is you, Daddy."

I said, "I want y'all to be dedicated. That means you do your best while you're out there getting money. Give me 100 percent, like I'm giving you."

"Daddy, we can't wait to go work and show you that we are down for you and only you," Sexy said.

Red Bone said, "I'm very happy to be with you, Daddy. You're really good to a bitch."

"Now for the rules. Number one: never tell the police that you have a pimp. Number two: always kiss your trick. The vice can't kiss you. You have to ask for a kiss on the lips—make sure it's on the lips. Number three: never let a trick take you more than a few blocks from the ho stroll—if you have to car date, but try not to car date. Number four: never drink or use drugs with a trick no matter what. Number five: never date a trick without a condom—never. I don't care how much money he tries to give you. Number six: never double-date with a ho that ain't your wife-in-law. A pimp can break you if you do. And never use another ho's room."

Red Bone said, "Daddy, you got game. We won't give you any problems."

Sexy said, "I like the way you are schooling us. I'm 100 percent down for you." I asked them if they had any questions. Sexy asked, "What if a trick tries to give me $200?"

"For what?" I asked.

"Not to use a condom," she said.

I said, "We have money, and no money's worth your life. And it's not worth your health."

"Thanks, Daddy, for caring," she said.

"It's morals and principles in my game. A lot of pimps don't have any. *Pimp* is a job title. It means a manager of hookers, hoes, prostitutes, or ladies of the night. Each pimp runs his business differently. No two are the same. The way I do things is a part of who I am. I'm a man doing my job. I'm a great boss, or I would like to think so. Some pimps dog their bitches out. He is an asshole boss and manager to say the least," I said.

Sexy said, "My ex-folks told me to date a trick without a condom if they had enough money. I mean offered me a lot of money like $200."

I said, "That $200 ain't shit. He didn't care about you. If a trick doesn't use a condom with you, he's not using a condom with any ho. He telling them the same thing." I added, "If he catches something, he's going to give it to everyone he dates. Ya dig?"

She said, "You're right, Daddy."

"You know what else he told me? And I'm not trying to be disrespectful talking about him, Daddy."

I said, "Go on and tell me."

"He told me to touch their dick, and if they let you, they're not cops, undercover vice."

I replied, "That's kind of right, but what he didn't tell you is that you have to ask them to take their dicks out of their pants, then you have to jack it off a little. That's called a lewd conduct, the undercover. Vice cop can't do that. That's breaking the law. The problem is that if you do that to a trick, he might cum, and you won't get paid. Most hookers just jump right into the car and rub the cop's pants or rub his pants where his penis is and think that's good enough, but it's not. When it comes down to it, you only rubbed his pants. That's why you see hookers going in and out of jail all the time. They think the cop is dirty for doing that.

"The prostitutes only know half of what they need to know. That falls on the pimp."

"Daddy, you are sharp," Red Bone said.

I said, "Without proper instruction, you're headed for self-destruction."

My hoes said, "That's what I'm talking about, Daddy, you got game for real." They gave each other another high five.

"I want y'all to remember this always. It's easier to walk to the driver's side of the car and ask for a kiss on the lips—the lips only—than ask a trick to unzip his pants and pull out his dick so you can stroke it, so you can tell if he's a vice cop or a date," I said.

"From now on, just watch the hookers as they work. You will see them just jump right into the cars. Those are the ones that go in and out of jail all the time," I stated.

"I want y'all to be like a sponge and soak up this game, ya dig?"

"Ya, Daddy, we dig."

We finished drinking, and I got in the car with AD, and I hit the gas.

"So tell me about it, pimpin'," AD said.

I said, "I was filling up their game tank, ya dig?"

*****

I called the job the next morning and requested a week's vacation. I told the girl about my job. They thought that was a good thing. Me being a manager at my age, Sexy said, "At least you have a hustle. That other nigga didn't do shit. He used to be a stickup kid before he met me."

I said, "That's the last time I want to hear about that Ray nigga."

She said, "Okay."

I said, "I'm going to quit once I get deep with hoes. Pimpin' is a full-time *job*."

Red Bone said, "You have to start somewhere, Daddy. At least you're starting from a job that you're a manager. If the white folks like you being manager, shit, then I know you will manage us better."

*****

The girls got up and took showers while I cooked breakfast. "Damn, Daddy, that food smells hella good," one of the girls hollered from the bedroom.

"I'm cooking bacon, eggs, and french toast," I said. "Let's sit down at the dining room table." I prayed over the food; they enjoyed their meal.

*****

AD said, "Man, those hoes look fly as hell, pimpin'. You gonna get paid."

I said, "We going to find out right now." I walked back to the room. We held hands, and I prayed, "God, please watch over them and bless us, for you know what we do."

I gave them their instructions, and we headed out the door to work. I fired up the Cadillac and got into the traffic. It was a beautiful day, not a cloud in the sky; it was eighty degrees. I drove straight down Cherry to PCH. I pulled into the parking lot, ran into the store, and picked up some condoms. I handed them the condoms and said, "Use the Super 8 Motel to date out of. They have rooms by the hour." I told them, "It's no more than five blocks, then cross the street and head back the way you came and split up." I gave them a couple of condoms and said, "Good luck." And they were off to work.

AD and I drove down the track and sweated some hoes and headed back the other way where I had set my hoes down. The hoes of mine were getting money fast. I saw Sexy getting into a car and headed to the motel.

I drove down the track and turned back around and went back down the track. Red Bone was getting out of a trick's car; she waved me over. I pulled into the liquor store. Another trick in a VW pulled over; she walked to the driver's side and kissed him and then got in. They went to the motel. Sexy came out of a trick's room and spotted me and headed over across the street to meet me at the store. I got out of my Cadillac and went into the store; she came in behind me.

She said, "Daddy, I'm out of condoms." She pulled out her trap and handed it to me.

"This is $160." I said, "You're halfway done." I got some condoms and handed them to her.

She said, "Daddy, it's poppin' out here today. I'm gone."

She walked out the store and went back to work. Red Bone was on her way over to the store. She gave me her money; it was $170. I gave her five more condoms. I said, "When you've used them up, you're done."

She said, "Okay, Daddy, I need something to drink, and I'm going back to work." She went back into the store and came out with an orange soda.

I got back into the traffic. I turned the music up and was filling myself. AD turned down the music and said, "How much did you check out of them hoes?"

I said, "$300 and some change. Ya dig?"

"Look at Vinnie Mac the Pimp," he said.

I gave him daps and said, "My hard work is paying off."

I turned the music back up. We bopped our heads to the music.

9

Kenny, Ray's cousin, asked, "What's up, Ray? You look mad. What happened to you? Did you get into a fight? You got knots on your head, looks like you're bleeding. Where's Michelle? Is she all right?"

"Man, fuck that fat bitch in her fat ass. I'm going to beat that punk-ass bitch up. That bitch had him do that to me. I saw her on the stroll, and she gave me a hundred. She gave me the money and walked down the street and came back in a Cadillac with some pimp-ass mothafucka. The nigga got out the car. I was standing in front of the liquor store. The nigga hit me with that cane till he knocked me on the ground. I can't wait till I see that punk-ass nigga. I'm going to fuck that nigga and that fat bitch up. The nigga told me that was his ho and not to fuck with her, or he was going to shoot me next time he sees me."

Kenny said, "Let me get this right. Michelle left you for a pimp, and he was driving a Cadillac. Did she have him jump you?"

Ray said, "I think he took the bitch or something. He must have done some funny shit. Anyway, that punk-ass bitch Michelle didn't say shit. The nigga said the ho chose up and not to fuck with her again. I just walked away. I didn't want to get shot."

Kenny said, "He pulled a gun on you?"

"Man, I don't want to talk about it. I want to get high. Do you know where to get some PCP from?"

"Yes, my friend has some down the street."

"Here's $20, bring my change back. I'm going to fuck that fat bitch and that pimp-ass nigga up if it's the last thing I do. Do you know someone that has a gun for sale?"

Kenny said, "My homie got a .38 for sale for fifty bucks."

"Go get him. I want to buy it—no, here you go, get it. Here's $65, you keep the change."

Kenny said, "You gonna shoot Michelle?"

"No, that pimp-ass nigga. He took my girl from me. And I'm going to use it to make me some money."

*****

"Did you get it?"

"I got the cherm (PCP)," Kenny said.

Ray said, "When can you pick up the pistol?"

"I'm going to get it now. I had to bring your shit. Wait till I get back before you fire up the cherm."

"Okay, nigga, hurry up, and make sure you get some bullets."

He came back fifteen minutes later. "Damn, you sure took a long time."

Kenny said, "His mom had him cleaning up, so he had to finish cleaning up first. His mom didn't play that shit. If she told you to do something, you better hurry up and do what she asked you to do."

"So did you get it?" Ray asked.

"Yeah, here it is. He made me pay extra for the bullets. You gonna give me back my money?"

"Nigga, I just gave you that money. Let me see the gun."

"No, give me my money back first."

"Okay, here it is," Ray said.

"Here it is, and here's the box of bullets."

Ray said, "Yeah, this is nice. Thanks, cuz."

Kenny said, "Fire up the stick so we can get high."

Ray said, "Let me test out the gun first."

"Nigga, the police department is right around the corner. The gun works. I know it does."

Ray said, "Okay, can you stash it for now?"

Kenny said, "I'm gonna take it into the house and stash it in my room."

"Let's smoke this in the backyard."

Ray said, "Before we smoke this cherm (PCP), let's go to the store an get something to drink. I've got a couple of…how much do you have?"

"You know I got the $15 you gave me," Kenny said.

"Okay, you buy the gin," Ray said.

"Come on, let's walk to the store."

Once they got there, Ray told Kenny to go into the store and get the drink. Kenny said, "I don't like that bitch in the store. She always thinks somebody is trying to steal something all the time out the store."

Ray said, "That's why I didn't want to come in with you. I don't like that bitch."

"Are her sons in there?"

"No, she's in there by herself," Kenny said.

Ray said, "Come on, let's get fucked up."

"Man, this shit is good, I'm feeling it," Kenny said.

Ray said, "Me too. It's like the shit from back in the days."

Kenny asked, "You want to put it out until later?"

"Yeah, pass me the drink."

"Man, I can't believe that bitch left me for that punk-ass pimp."

"Ray, I don't mean to get in your business, but I thought you were a pimp. That's what you were saying when you had Michelle."

Ray said, "Nigga, I'm a jacker and a robber. I was pimpin' when I had that fat-ass bitch Michelle."

Kenny said, "Man, you were fucking over her, running off with the money, not feeding her, and you called her fat-ass bitch all the time. Then you didn't even pay the rent on time. She just got tired of your bullshit."

Ray said, "Nigga, be quiet. You taking up for that fat-ass bitch?"

"No," Kenny said.

"Anyways, the nigga shouldn't have hit me with that cane, and he had a gun. Now we'll see what's up. I'm gonna take that nigga's car. Let's see how he likes that. That nigga ain't no pimp. He's a faggot-ass nigga, and I'm going to bust a cap in his ass after I take my money back," Ray said.

"Ray, do you know who he is?" Kenny asked.

Ray said, "I don't care who that muthafucka is."

Kenny said, "It's some nigga from Twenty-First. You don't want to fuck with them. I'm telling you, Michelle knows where his mom's house is. I don't want them niggas going over there."

*****

Ray said, "Shut up, bitch, get down on the mothafucking floor. Where's the rest of the money?"

"There's no more money," the clerk said. *Slap, slap.* He fired a shot, *blam.*

"Where's it at, bitch? Next time I'm gonna blow your head off."

"It's over there. Please don't kill me."

"You lucky I only shot you in the fucking leg. Now turn over." He pulled out his dick and made her suck it. Then he grabbed some liquor and ran out the store.

*****

"Hey, cuz, can you get some more of that shit from yesterday?"

"Yeah, I can get some," Kenny said.

Ray pulled out a bankroll and pulled off a $20 bill and said, "Get a whole stick of cherm."

Kenny asked, "Where did you get all that money from?"

"Man, I'll give you a dime to say out of mine," Ray told Kenny.

Kenny came back with the PCP. Kenny asked, "How much money is that?"

Ray was high and said, "$1,200." Ray just looked at him; he was higher than a motherfucka, and he was playing with the gun.

Kenny said, "You want me to get you a drink?" Ray handed him a $20 bill and didn't say anything.

When Kenny came back, Ray had come off his high enough to talk. Ray said, "Thanks, cuz, I was higher than hell."

Kenny said, "Yea, I could tell. I put it out. Can I light it up?"

"Yeah, you can have the rest, I'm still high." Ray took a gulp of gin. "Kenny, here's $100 for you."

"Thanks, cuz," Kenny said.

Ray asked him if he wanted a drink of gin. Kenny put out the rest of the PCP he was smoking. He said, "Man, give me a drink." Kenny took a swig. "Man, you came up, where you hit your lick at?"

"Mind your business," Ray said. They finished the gin. Both of them were higher than a mothafucka chilling out in Kenny's backyard.

Later on that night, Kenny asked Ray, "What kind of Caddy was the pimp driving?"

Ray said, "It was rust and tan. I think it was a Coupe de Ville."

"Why you asking me that?" Ray asked.

"I'm going to check it out and see if I can find out whose car that is," Kenny said.

*****

"On the got damn floor now, mothafucka, where the safe at!" He grabbed the clerk by the hair and smacked him upside the head. "Where's the safe, punk-ass bitch?" *Blam*, he shot the clerk. "Where's the money!"

"Okay, please don't kill me," the clerk hollered.

"Open the mothafuckin' safe." *Slap, slap.*

"Okay, okay." He opened the safe up. The robber pushed him to the floor and said, "Don't move." The robber took all the money out of the safe and knocked out the store attendant and ran out the store.

10

The track was starting to fill up. Me and AD were sweating all the hoes. We saw somebody's team; they were all wearing pink and white.

AD said, "Let me out on the corner. One of them bitches is lost."

I said, "I'm gonna go around the corner and then come back." So I drove around the block, and when I got back, AD had moved the ho around the corner. AD was smiling at the white girl with the pink minidress on. She had on white thigh-high boots and was carrying a white purse. There were several bitches with pink and white on. They were spread out along the track.

When I got back, this time AD told me to pull over; the bitch was out of pocket.

I pulled over. AD and the ho got in. She tried to talk to me as she was getting into the car. AD told her to lean over so nobody would see her. AD told her, "My friend's—aren't you friends? Don't speak to him, he's a pimp. Do you understand? Say 'yes, Daddy.'"

She said, "Yes, Daddy."

"How much do you have?" AD asked.

She said, "Here, you have to count it." He did; it was $320.

He said, "That's cool for now. How long have you been working?"

"About two hours. I got all that from one trick," she said.

We drove back down the track, and my hoes were on dates. I drove AD and his new girl to the room. We got out and went into the suite. Once we were in the suite, AD said, "Let's have a toast." We poured a drink and toasted some more of it; we downed all of the liquor. AD said, "This is my brother Vinnie Mac. This is Amber. He said you can speak now."

She said, "Hi, this is a nice place, it has a great view."

AD said, "I told you so. Let me show you the rest of the place and where the restroom is." He came back, alone. He said, "I told Baby to jump into the shower. We're going to walk down to the beach so I can tighten my game up, ya dig?"

"I dig. You and Baby can have the other room, and I'll sleep with my hoes."

He said, "Cool, Vinnie."

I said, "AD, since we will be living together, we will allow our hoes to speak to us—only us.

"I'm going back to the track to see if my hoes are done."

AD said, "I'm going to lace her up. I'll see you when you get back."

I jumped into the car and headed back to the ho stroll. I turned on some music and lit up me a Newport. I was glad for my brother; when I got back to the liquor store, the girls were waiting.

"Hi, Daddy, we're done." Sexy gave me her trap and said, "Daddy, there are some new girls out here working today."

I said, "I've been sweatin' them."

Red Bone handed me her trap and said, "Daddy, are you going to cook? A bitch is hungry than a mothafucka."

I laughed and said, "I'm going to grill some hamburgers and hot dogs. We will have salad and chips. Oh, my brother came up with a new ho, and I will be sleeping in the room with y'all. Him and Amber will take the other room. I want you guys to be nice to her. You can speak to AD since we will be staying together. You can only speak to him only. No other pimps."

"We understand, and we will be nice to her, Daddy."

I pulled over and called the suite. AD answered, "What's up, man?"

I said, "I'm on my way back. Do you need anything?"

"Yeah, bring me some cigarettes and some ice so we can have some more drinks. I talked to Baby, and I named her Star."

I said, "I told me hoes that they can talk to you. We're going to be one big family."

"That's cool," he said.

"I want you to start the grill so I can cook some hamburgers and hot dogs, and I'll make a salad, and we will have chips. I'm going to pick up some weed. Do you need some?"

"Yeah, pick me up one."

"I need to holla at you when you get back."

AD said, "Okay, playa," and I hung up the phone. I got back into the car and pulled off.

"Tell me about y'alls day. You first, Sexy."

"Well, Daddy, the day went by fast. I met a couple of tricks that I think will be my regulars. I didn't have any problems. I didn't see that nigga. He doesn't even come on this end."

I said, "You're smart. That's what I was thinking about when I asked you to go first."

"Red Bone, how was your day?"

"Daddy, I had a fun day. All my tricks were cool, and I kept you on my mind all the time. Me and Sexy are going to lose weight, so the burgers are cool."

I said, "Well, if you guys really mean it, I'll cook all the right foods. It's not what you eat, it's how much you eat. Red Bone, you're size 16, and if you get down to a size 10, I'll buy you anything you want. Sexy, you're a size 18, and if you get down to a size 12, I'll buy you anything you want."

"Daddy, even a car?" Sexy asked.

"Yeah, Daddy," Red Bone said.

"Yeah, even a car," I said. The girls had smiles on their faces. I pulled over to the store and sent Red Bone onto the smokes and the ice.

She came out the store and got into the car, and we headed home. I told the girls that each day that I drove them to work that they would take turns riding in the front seat. It was a warm evening; the sun was just about to set. It looked fantastic. All the yellow and orange in the sky. You could smell the ocean as we drove closer to the room. I parked. I told the girls to take the things out of the refrigerator and put it on the counter. They did and went to take a shower.

The fire was burning on the grill. I patted out some burgers and added seasoning and put them in the icebox. And I also put the salad in there along with the pickles.

*****

AD's girl was fine—5'5", 36-C breasts, twenty-six-inch waist, thirty-inch hips, red wavy hair, freckles, and green eyes.

"Star."

"Yes, Daddy."

"Come over here and make me a drink. The ice is in the freezer."

"What would you like, Daddy?"

AD said, "Pour me some yak. Make it two, one for my brother."

"Okay, Daddy."

AD said, "When Vinnie's hos get out of the shower, y'all will have a chance to talk and kick it. Do you know how to roll?"

"Yes, Daddy." I pulled out a bag of weed and handed a bag to AD; he handed it to Star and told her it was a shoebox top under the couch with papers in it. She walked over into the living room to roll a joint.

I asked AD, "How's everything going?"

He said, "Things are great. Baby's from Ohio, and Max-a-Million had picked her up two days ago at the Greyhound bus station in downtown LA, and her clothes are in a room in LA." He told her that she didn't need them and that he would buy her new clothes in the morning.

I said, "We will go shopping at around 10:00 a.m."

AD said, "He needs to serve pimpin' for the bitch. Vinnie, all them bitches in the pink and white were with him."

"How deep is he?" I asked.

"The bitch said he got four other hoes. Star said that the other hoes acted like they didn't like her. She told me that Max spent the night with her, and his main bitch was talking shit, and he had to slap the ho," AD said. He asked her if she had ever worked before she met Max-a-Million. AD said, "She was a turnout. It was her first time working last night. Star didn't mind hoeing, but she didn't like the other hoes he had. She felt unwanted. That's why she chose me, ya dig? I told her she was my bottom ho, and we would build our team up. The bitch was real green. I will teach her the game right, you know what I mean?"

I said, "I feel ya, pimpin'."

"Vinnie, after we finish our drinks, I need to call pimpin' about the bitch," AD said.

I said, "Cool. I saw those other hoes still working."

AD called Star; he told her we would be right back, and he asked her for the phone number to the room. I walked back to the room and told my hoes that I would be back in a minute. I told them what had happened with Star and her wife-in-laws and to be cool with her and get to know her so she would feel welcome. They said they would and not to worry about it. I told AD, and we headed out the door to the car. I let him drive.

He said, "The nigga's in a white Cadillac. He won't be hard to find." We drove down PCH and Cherry and turned left on to the ho stroll and drove down the track. When we got to PCH, we spotted a white Cadillac at the Jack in the Box. AD pulled into the parking lot. We got out. Max-a-Million was dressed in a white suit with a pink silk shirt, a white brim, and white snakeskin boots. AD said, "Ey, what's up, pimpin'?"

I said, "I'm Vinnie Mac."

"I'm Max-a-Million."

"I'm AD," AD said. "Say, pimpin', I got that Amber ho, she chose up."

Max said, "I was looking for that ho. She seemed not to be getting along with my other hoes. I met the bitch at the Greyhound. The bitch didn't give me that much dough, to keep it real."

AD said, "The bitch gave me $340. She said she got it from one trick."

Max said, "Well, happy pimpin', AD. I'm going to scoop up my team and bounce."

I said, "Max, it's a pleasure. We'll have a yak next time we meet."

We watched Max as he pulled off in his white Eldorado Cadillac. AD said, "Pimpin' was cool. He didn't even sweat losing the ho."

I said, "He knew when we pulled up what time it was. You're looking just like a pimp with that silk shirt, slacks, and snakeskin shoes on. You driving a Cadillac, ya dig?"

AD said, "I got respect for the pimpin'. Just for the record, I'm going to give him action back at the ho in Hollywood, ya dig?"

I said, "You sure?"

"Man, I count on my pimpin'. Star is new to the game. She will stay in pocket. She's happy."

I asked, "When are you going to Hollywood?"

"Not right away. Maybe in a week or two. I still got some more pimpin' to do." AD started up the Cadillac, and we drove back to the room. We pulled up and parked; as we headed to the suite and got closer, we could hear the hoes laughing their asses off. They were on the patio having a drink and blowing a joint.

"Hey, what's so funny?" I asked.

Red Bone said, "Star has been having us rollin'. She is funny as hell."

"Cool, I see things are going great."

"Daddy, we would have put the food on the grill, a bitch can ho, but I can't cook worth a damn."

"That's cool. I'm going to finish cooking right now." The girls went back inside. The food was good. Sexy and Red Bone only had one hot dog and some salad. I was proud of them. They meant business; they were going to lose that weight.

The girls cleaned up, and we had some drinks. After that, we called it a night. Sexy and Red Bone were glad to be sleeping with me. AD tapped the door and asked me to come out to the patio. We poured ourselves a drink of Hennessy over ice.

"What's up with it, P?" I asked.

He said, "I just wanted to chop it up with you for a minute."

"I was going to come and get you in a minute anyways. I was just kickin' it with my hoes, telling them that I was happy with them for making Star feel at home."

AD said, "Yeah, man, she was having a good time with your hoes."

I said, "They like her too."

AD said, "Let's have a pimp's toast." We raised our glasses and clinked them together. Our toast was to the game. I pulled out some weed and lit it up; we smoked and chopped it up for an hour, then we went into the living room, and my hoes were knocked out. AD said, "Star went to sleep with all her clothes on. And her shoes." Me and AD went to sleep in the living room.

I got up and cooked breakfast—turkey bacon, eggs, wheat toast, orange juice, and coffee. Me and AD jumped into the car and went to the store to pick up some Newports. When we got back, I rolled up some weed, and we smoked. After that, I had my hoes run us some bathwater. I told both of them to get in with me; the bathtub was huge. Six people could have got in there. The girls were excited to take a bath with their Daddy. The water was hot and had plenty of bubbles.

My hoes washed me up; they liked washing me up. I hadn't had sex with them yet; they needed to give me $2,000 each—that was their chosen fee. Once I got that, I was going to fuck them real good. I let them play with my dick while they washed me up.

After we were done, Red Bone dried me off while Sexy laid out my underwear, T-shirt, socks, blue sweat suit, and blue snakeskin shoes. Both of my girls wore sweat suits also. AD and Star took showers in the other bathroom. AD had on some brown slacks, multicolored shirt, and brown snakeskin shoes. Star had on one of my girls' sweat suits; she didn't have any clothes yet.

We had some drinks and smoked some more weed then headed back downtown LA to the alley. My girls knew exactly what they wanted and where to go. Star fit right in. They walked ahead of us; they were high and laughing. The hoes were having a great time.

AD said, "I told my ho to pick out four minidresses and another pair of boots and a pair of flats. Then I'm going to let her get a week's worth of panties and bras and some makeup and something to sleep in."

"Damn, P, you gonna make my pimpin' look bad. I'm only letting my hoes pick out a couple of things."

AD said, "Your bitches were just down here. My ho doesn't have anything."

I said, "I'm just fuckin' with you pimpin'."

The next couple of weeks went by fast. AD bought a burgundy Cadillac, and I was stacking my dough, and my hoes were staying on their diets.

I told my bitches where I worked. I had them bring my trap to my job. I let them have dinner there so I could talk to them and see how things were going. AD and Star came with them so it wouldn't look like they were with me, but it didn't look like that at all, it was just me thinking that way. AD was stacking like a mothafucka. The game was good. After I got off work, I met my bitches at the room. We talked all about their day. I did that all the time so I would be on top of them at all times. And it showed that I cared about them. Barbershop Mac told me that pimps didn't give a fuck about how their hoes' day went, they just wanted their money, and that's it. He said that was the difference between a pimp and a great pimp.

Sexy said, "Daddy, I'm doing good on my diet, Red Bone too. In another month, we will be done losing the weight you wanted us to lose."

I said, "I've noticed that."

Red Bone said, "Daddy, I want a VW, and Sexy wants a Ford LTD."

I said, "I know. I be hearing y'all talking about it all the time. You know what I want?"

"No, Daddy."

"I want both of you to run us some water so we can get into the hot tub."

"Okay, Daddy."

"And I want both of you to give me some head."

"What did you say, Daddy? I thought you said you want us to give you some head."

I said, "That's what I said."

They both smiled and said, "Daddy, don't play like that."

I said, "You know I don't play. Fix me a drink. I'm going to fuck both of y'all real good. Tonight is the night, so you might as well get ready for it. Y'all ain't too tired?"

"Shit, a bitch ain't ever tired for you, Daddy. We have been waiting for this a long time. I still can't believe it."

Red Bone said, "A bitch like me can't too."

We had a couple of drinks and headed to the hot tub. They pulled off my clothes, and I got in first. Sexy was next and then Red Bone.

I started kissing Red Bone. I told Sexy to suck my dick. She took her time; she gave head well. She licked it up and down and in and out her mouth. I started sucking on Red Bone's titties, around her nipples; she started moaning. "Mmm, Daddy, that feels good." She started rubbing the back of my neck. I had those nipples harder than a mothafucka. I told them to switch, and they did.

I started kissing Sexy, then I started sucking her boobs. Red Bone sucked my dick very slow, up and down, in and out. Damn, she could suck a dick. Sexy's big-ass breasts were lovely. I really got into it. I had her nipples hard as hell. I put my fingers inside her pussy, in and out, nice and slow. I told Red Bone to sit up so I could put my fingers inside of her too. I had both of them on both sides of me, playing with their pussies. They had their hand on my hard-ass dick. Their pussies were soaking wet. I moved faster and faster.

Sexy said, "That's it, Daddy, just like that."

Red Bone said, "Yes, Daddy, yes." They both moaned.

"Ah. Ah. Mmm, mmm. Shit, I'm cummmin'," Sexy said; after she came, she started sucking my dick again.

I started sucking on Red Bone's breasts; she moaned as I played with her pussy. "Faster, faster," she said, "yeah, yeah, I'm cummin', I'm cummin'."

After she came, I put my dick inside of Sexy. I kissed Red Bone. I drove my dick deep inside of Sexy and pumped faster and faster; she yelled louder and louder, and she came again and again. I pulled it out and put my dick in Red Bone. I stroked it in and out, round and round, back and forth. She moaned. "Yes, yes, yes, Daddy, that's it, that's it. Oh yeah, just like that, Daddy, that's it, oh, oh, yeah,

yeah, I'm cummin'." She came a couple of times. I pulled it out, and I nutted on their faces.

"Damn, Daddy, that was good," Red Bone said.

Sexy said, "Daddy, you damn near made a bitch pass out."

I laughed. We washed up and got out of the hot tub. The girls went to bed. I went into the living room, made me a drink, and rolled a joint. I got high then went into the bedroom and got in the middle of them and fell asleep.

11

The next morning, I got up and cooked ham and eggs, hash browns, and wheat toast. I made a pot of coffee, and we had orange juice. The girls were happy, and they enjoyed every bite of the food.

Me and AD went to see Mac at the barbershop. "What's up, players?" Mac said.

"Just some more pimpin'," I said.

AD said, "Breaking hoes and slammin' Cadillac doors."

We got our hair done and headed to downtown LA.

AD asked, "What are we going to buy?"

I said, "I'm going to buy some silk fabric to have some robes and boxers tailor-made by Tony on Eight and Los Angeles."

AD said, "Man, that's some cool-shit pimpin'."

We parked and got out in the garment district. We walked and chopped it up. I told him I had fucked my hoes last night. He said, "I heard y'all in there. Damn, man, y'all keep it down in there next time. It almost made me want to fuck my ho." We laughed. I spotted some silk fabric with gold dollar signs on it. I got royal blue, black, brown, red, and white. I was having five pairs of boxers made. AD got some fabric to have a suit made. We looked around some more, then we headed to the tailor shop.

*****

"Hi, my friend, what can I do for you today?" Tony said.

I said, "I want to have robes and boxers made out of this fabric." Tony took my measurements and asked me how long I wanted my robes made. He said it would take a couple of weeks to be ready. I gave him a deposit, and we headed back to the car; we got in and drove to Arthur Williams Tailor Shop on Broadway. AD was having a suit made with his name on it. He gave Arthur a deposit. Arthur said that his suit would be ready in a week.

AD said, "Cool, I'll be back next Thursday."

Me and AD stopped to have some lunch.

AD said, "Pimpin', when are we going to Hollywood?"

"Man, I'm going to rent a limo in three weeks and have a driver bring us to Hollywood. That way I can school my hoes on the way how the hoes work the track and how the pimps sweat the hoes while they're working, ya dig?"

AD said, "That's a good idea, P. I'll do the same with Star, and we will see what's poppin'."

We finished lunch, and then we drove back down Broadway to the jewelry district. We parked on Eighth in a parking lot. I lit a joint, and we smoked. AD said, "My boy Jerry makes some fly jewelry. His store is down the street."

I asked him, "What are you going to have made?"

"Man, I'm having a crown medallion and ring with diamonds in them. I'm going to show them niggas how some real pimpin' does it."

I said, "I'm going to have my name made in my medallion, and then I'm going to have a three-finger ring made with diamonds encrusted in them."

"Hi, Jerry, what's happening?" AD said.

Jerry said, "The same old, thanks, just making the best pimp jewelry in the city, ya dig."

AD said, "That's right, player. This is my brother Vinnie Mac, so if he comes in, give him the pimp discount."

Jerry said, "No problem, my friend."

AD said, "I'm here to have those pieces made I was telling you about, and my brother wants to have his name and a ring made with diamonds encrusted in both of them."

The jeweler gave me a book of different rings in it. I saw a ring of the United States—the whole map with all the states outlined on the ring. I asked if he could do the outline in diamonds. He said, "No problem, Vinnie, I'll have you lookin' real fly." He smiled.

Jerry was cool as hell. I spotted a gold chain that I wanted to put my medallion on once it was made. We gave him our deposit, and he told us to come back in three weeks.

AD said, "Man, we really going to be fly with our new jewelry on, ya dig?"

I said, "Pimpin', I can't wait to flash my game on those hoes."

AD said, "Vinnie, I got one more place I want to go," as he started up the Caddy.

"Let's roll, baby."

He drove down to Eleventh and Soto. We parked and walked into a store that had some of the coldest minks I've ever seen. AD said, "What's up, Frank? I came to look around. This is my brother Vinnie Mac."

"Hi, Vinnie, it's nice to meet you," Frank said.

"It's all good and well, my friend." We looked at all kinds of mink coats. I saw a waistline mink, and I thought I had to have it. Frank gave me a great deal. I paid $1,700 for it, and I put a $1,000 deposit for a full-length mink coat. I told Frank that I would be back in a couple of weeks to give him some more money on my other mink coat.

Frank said, "Take your time, friend."

"Thanks," I said. He gave AD some mink spray for our coats and special bags for the coats. When we got back to the car, AD told me that the minks we just bought cost at least $2,500 anywhere else. I said, "Damn, that was a pimp's discount." I lit a smoke and headed back to the LBC. I slid down Figueroa; we sweated the local hoes that were on the track. I spotted a fine-ass bitch.

I parked the car and told AD, "Man, I need that ho on my team. I'm going to work on the bitch." I got out and walked down the street to get at the ho. She didn't run or cross the street. I said, "Damn, lil momma, you need to take a chance to advance. What's up with you?"

She said, "Trying to get me rent money. You want a date?"

I said, "I want you. Who are you with?"

"I'm with my girlfriend. We just got here from Texas."

"Where is your friend at?" I could see AD was walking my way. She said, "On a date."

I asked, "Have you ever been to Long Beach?"

She said, "Can my friend go to?"

"Yeah, she can come. Is she fine as you?"

"Yeah, she's pretty, and she's white. I need to get our stuff out of that room. It's checkout time."

"Do you need some help?"

She said, "Yeah, it's a lot."

Just then her girlfriend walked up, and so did AD. "Bitch, that mothafucka only had $15. I took it and got out. Fuck, that was wasting my time."

I said, "Hi, my name is Vinnie Mac."

"I'm Rebecka."

The other one said, "I'm Toni. They call me Tee."

I said, "This is my brother AD. AD, this is Rebecka and Toni, they're going with us."

"We are," Rebecka said.

"Yeah, they've got a room on the beach."

AD said, "Hi, where's your room at?"

Rebecka said, "Down the street." We walked to my car and got in and drove to the motel and got their stuff. I knew AD wanted Rebecka. I wanted Toni. As we drove to Long Beach, we had a chance to get to know them. They had come from Texas with a guy, and he went to jail for robbery. They were left there by themselves.

The guy's name was Stone. They drove to Las Vegas on the way to Cali; he lost their money gambling. Once they arrived here, he tried to hit a lick and got himself busted.

I asked Toni if she had just started working the track. Toni said, "No, I've been hoeing for over six years. My friend Becky has been hoeing for over two years."

She told me that Stone let them date black guys. "Stone told us that we were going to Hollywood, but we never made it." I told her I was a pimp. She told me that she thought so. We had a good understanding of what it was. AD and Becky were getting along great.

I fired up some weed, and we smoked on the way to the beach. Toni was 5'5"; she had small boobs and a nice ass. She was brown-skinned and real cute. Toni was twenty-one years old. Becky was about 5'3", with black hair and hazel eyes. She had a nice shape.

I called the girls and told them that me and AD had knocked some hoes from Texas. When we pulled into the motel, AD showed Becky his Cadillac. The other hoes came out to help carry their suitcases into the suite. Toni and Becky loved the place. Star and Becky got along good. Sexy, Toni, and Red Bone carried Toni's stuff into the room. The rest of the day went smooth.

Red Bone said, "Daddy, your mother called, and she wants you to come over to the bookie joint. She said you knew where she was."

"Thanks, Red Bone, I'll go see what she wants."

*****

"Hi, Mom, what's up?"

"Baby, Momma needs a few till I get paid. Those horses been fucking me up. All long shots today."

AD said, "Hi, Mom," and handed her $100. I gave her $200.

She said, "Damn, you niggas got a lot of money. Pimpin' must be paying."

I said, "We just got two new girls from Texas. AD has two hookers, and I got three."

She said, "Vinnie, give me another hundred."

I gave it to her and said, "I have to get back to the room. We came as soon as Red Bone told me you called. We just got the other girls, and I want to make sure everything is all right."

Mom said, "That girl Red is very nice. Don't worry about them. Things are going to be all right. I need to go to the store and pick up a couple of things."

"I'll go. What do you need?"

"I need a racing form and some cigarettes." I drove to the store and back. I honked the horn, and she came out to get her things.

"Vinnie Mac, are you still working?"

"Yeah, Mom, I'm still there."

"That's good, keep your job."

"I know, Mom."

"And, AD, how have you been?"

"I'm good, Momma, just stacking money," he replied.

"That's right, baby," she said.

"Mom, you like my new wheels I got on the car?"

"Yeah, baby, they look good.

"Vinnie, drop your momma off at your aunt's house. Let me run in and get my purse."

I dropped her off and said, "Mom, I'm going to buy you a car for your birthday." I kissed her and said, "If you need anything, just let me know."

"Oh, baby, Momma loves y'all."

I pulled from the curb and drove back to the motel. I lit a Newport and said, "My hoes are doing great on their diets. They've lost a lot of weight. I'm going to buy them a car, ya dig?"

AD said, "You doing pimping right, ya dig."

"Thanks, P, that means a lot coming from you."

AD asked me how much money I had stacked. I told him about $10,000. "That's cool. I've got $7,000 stacked. I need to stack the money back that I spent. Vinnie, how much did you spend?"

I said, "$9,500. I can't wait till my jewelry is ready. I'm going to fuck them niggas up in Hollywood, ya dig?"

We pulled up to the motel, parked the Caddy, and headed to the room.

*****

We could see the girls down on the beach having a wonderful time. I asked AD what he was going to name the new girl. He said, "Pimpin', I'm still thinking about a name for that ho."

I said, "Me too. She said they call her T. I don't know who gave her that name, but if the nigga did, I'm changing it."

"I feel ya, P, I would too."

"I've got to take some time to get to know the bitch. We've been running around. I like how they're getting along. Those hoes look happy, don't they?"

AD said, "You right, pimpin', we do need to get to know them. I've been trying to come up with a name. I need a drink. Don't you?"

"Yeah, let's have one, player."

We made a drink and sat on the patio and checked out the hoes as they ran and played and splashed water on each other. I said, "AD, those new hoes have been hoeing longer than our other hoes. Star is still your bottom?"

AD said, "If the ho is real, she will respect that fact and will help school her wife-in-law, ya dig?"

"I feel the same way. I'm going to tell what I want her to do. The first thing is she is not going to date niggas. And then I'm going to sit down with all of them together and fill up their game tank, ya dig?"

"I feel ya, P, I'm going to do the same thing. No bitch of mine is going to fuck a nigga at all, ya dig?"

"A pimp's job is never done. You have to keep your game tight." We had a toast to pimping.

"To the pimpin'," AD said.

"To the pimpin'."

12

The girls came in and had a couple of drinks. I rolled up some weed for them to smoke. Red Bone said, "Daddy, are we going to work today?"

I said, "No, you guys can kick back today. You've been working hard and staying on your diets."

Sexy said, "Daddy, a bitch is working hard on getting her shape together. You can tell, Daddy?"

"Yeah, I can sure tell. You were a size 18, and now you're what, a size 14?"

"That's right, Daddy, you amaze me. You notice everything."

"That's why I named you Sexy, because I could see you being a size 12 with that sexy walk." She walked over and kissed me on the side of my face. "Red Bone, come over here and kiss your Daddy."

She said, "Daddy, you okay? You never asked me to do that before. I like my new Daddy. You fucked the shit out of me. I still cum when I think of you putting that good dick on a bitch."

I smiled and said, "Red Bone, you're down to a size 12. In another month, you guys will be ready for your cars and new clothes."

Red Bone said, "A bitch will be good and ready by then."

Sexy said, "Daddy, can I say one thing? You really look out for us, and I'm glad I chose you."

I said, "Thanks, I'm glad you did too. I'm going to fry fish and make coleslaw, corn on the cob, and baked beans."

Toni walked in. She had taken a shower first. She said, "Who's cooking that food?"

"That would be me," I said.

Toni said, "That sounds gooder than a mothafucka."

Sexy said, "Bitch, Daddy's cooking. I told you he can burn," as she headed to the room to get ready to take a shower to wash that saltwater and sand off her.

Red Bone said, "Daddy, I'm going into the bedroom and take off these wet clothes then come back and vacuum this sand off the carpet."

I said, "Okay, that's cool." And she left the room. I asked Toni, "How are things going on so far? Are you and the other girls getting along with each other?"

She said, "Vinnie, everything is good. I'll call you Daddy once I give you my chosen fee. The girls are very cool with me. They talk very highly of you. They told me how you met them and that you brought them to this beach to have a talk with them. That you gave them a choice to choose, or you would drop them back off where they had come from. And you're not mean. You don't talk like you would slap a bitch and shit. Sexy told me that you sat them down and told them what you expected out of them, and you found out that they were turnouts. You took time to explain the game. That you didn't want them to date black men and that they had to use condoms. That you want to be respected at all times, and you wanted them to stay in pocket. That they were not to look in a pimp's car or stare at their cars or dance to the music coming out of a pimp's car. You also told them not to date with another ho or use their room. Only to double-date with her wife-in-law. Pimps play all kinds of tricks, and to stay on top of your game at all times. You also taught them how to spot the undercover vice cop. You told them to kiss all their tricks on the lips, that a vice cop cannot kiss a hooker on the lips, that's entrapment. You told them that hookers try rubbing on a vice cop's pants and think that they can't go to jail. The only problem is that it is only half true. In order not to go to jail, you need to tell the trick to pull his dick out of his pants, then you have to rub his dick. That's called lewd conduct, and that's against the law. Plus it takes too long."

I said, "A ho will suck a dick, but they won't kiss the trick. Most pimps tell their hoes they better not kiss a trick. That's why hoes go to jail all the time." I said, "I'll sit down and chop some more game with you later. That way we will be on the same page. Would you like a beer or a shot or a mixed drink? I've got all kinds of drinks."

Toni said, "I sure would. You don't mind if I help myself?"

I said, "Make yourself at home, do whatever you like. You don't mind sharing a room with your wife-in-laws, do you?"

"No, Daddy, that's the biggest bed I've ever seen. It's plenty of space for us. You and five other people." She laughed and said, "See, you already got me calling you Daddy. I've got a little money, do you want it?"

I said, "If you're going to choose me, of course I want you too." I smiled. She went to the room where she had put her things. She came back with $120 and handed it to me.

She said, "Daddy, do you need some more help?"

I said, "No, you kick back. I got it I love to cook."

She said, "The girls told me you are a manager of a large restaurant. Down on Ocean Drive. I hope you're not mad at them."

I said, "Of course not. You don't mind that I work, do you?"

"No, I feel like the other girls. If you can manage the white folks' money, then you should do real good with ours."

I said, "I'm going to be there for another year, while I build our family, and then I want to travel and work different states."

Toni said, "By then I will get to know my way around here. Daddy, when are we going to Hollywood?"

I said, "You know your wife-in-laws are turnouts, and I want them to get used to working the ho stroll here in Long Beach and a couple other tracks.

"Mainly Long Beach because this is home. After that, we will go there. There are over five hundred hoes on the stroll, so a bitch better be on her A game, or a pimp is going to starve to death."

Toni said, "You're right, Daddy. If you don't mind me saying, you got some fine-ass bitches on your team, me being one of them. We will make a lot of money for you, Daddy."

I said, "I'm going to talk to you later, and we will talk in more detail then. For now, I want you to enjoy yourself in your new home, okay?"

She said, "Okay, Daddy, I'll do that. I'm going out on the patio and enjoy this cold drink and look out at this beautiful ocean, Daddy. Thanks." She hugged me around the waist then headed out to the patio.

I said, "What's up, P?"

AD said, "Man, some more pimpin', ya dig? Let me make a drink, and we will chop it up." After he was finished making his drink, he said, "Those hoes are getting along great, pimping. I schooled them on things I expected out of them. I had no problems with them. They'll be out in a minute. They're getting dressed.

"Yeah, P, I named Becky *Snow*, ya dig?"

I said, "I dig, that fits her. Pimp on, player."

AD said, "I'm going to make the coleslaw and put the corn on the cob in a pot with some butter, salt, and a little sugar and fill it up with water. Mom always cooked it like that."

I said, "That's cool. I'm almost finished frying the fish, and the baked beans are in the oven."

"Yeah, P, my hoes are getting along cool. Sexy and Red Bone schooled Baby on what I expect out of her and some of the rules to my game. It will be Easter to game her up like I want."

I said, "Toni, come here please."

She came in and said, "Yes, Daddy."

I said, "I'm going to call you Baby Face from now on. You tell your tricks that's yo name."

She smiled and said, "Daddy, I like it. I'm going to tell those hoes." And she headed to the room.

AD said, "P, that's the right name for her. She has a baby face." The girls came out of their room and made mixed drinks. Then they walked out to the patio. AD turned the music on, and we finished eating. I sat my team down and had a talk with them. I informed Sexy, Red Bone, and Baby Face that in three weeks, I was going to take them to Hollywood so I could show them around and lace them up on how to work the track. Then show them around where the pimps hang out so they wouldn't walk on that side of the street. After I finished talking to them, I told Sexy and Red Bone to go to their room so I could talk to Baby Face.

I said, "Baby Face, tell me something about yourself so I can get to know you."

She said, "What do you want to know?"

"Anything you want share with me."

"Oh, okay, the girls told me you would want to talk to me about how and where I grew up at."

"You don't mind, do you?"

"No, Daddy, not at all. I grew up in Dallas, Texas, and when I was nine years old, we moved to Washington, DC. My dad was in the Army, so we moved around a lot. When I was thirteen, my dad was killed while he was in the Army. It broke my heart. We were having hard times, so we moved back to Texas. When I was fifteen years old, I met a guy named Danny P. He was twenty-four years old. He turned me out. By the time I was seventeen, we had worked all over Texas and the South. I was with him for a year and a half, and he died from an overdose of smack.

"He showed me how to get into a trick's pocket while I was dating. I would be sucking their dick, and I would put my fingers in their pockets. If we fucked, I got on top and made as much noise as I could, and I would take their wallet out of their pockets, take the money out, and put it back. I can take the wallet out with my toes too.

"The trick called the police. I went to jail for six months. When I was in jail, Danny overdosed. After that, I mostly worked on my own. I would help my mother pay the bills. She only got a welfare check. She needed the help.

"I went to jail a couple more times for prostitution. I ran into Stone a month ago, and he told me he was going to Hollywood. He said there was a lot of money out there. I had talked to some hoes that had worked out there, and they said the same thing. I always wanted to go there anyway, so I decided to go with him. He seemed cool.

"We went through Las Vegas on the way to Cali. That's when I met Becky. We worked that night, and I hit a lick for $500. Becky made $300. Stone had fucked off almost all of the money, and he didn't tell us. He took us to Figueroa, and he said he would be right back, but he never returned. He called and told us to bail him out. His bail was $5,000 and that he needed $500 to get out. I asked him what he did with all the money, and that's when he told us that he had fucked off the money. I was pissed. Becky and I were stuck till you came along.

"I liked the Cadillac that you were driving, and once you came up to me, I liked the way you carried yourself. I made up my mind right then I wanted to be with you. Once you said you had a room on the beach, I thought that was enough."

I kissed her and said, "I'm going to send your mother money every week."

She said, "You knew. How?"

"I pay attention, that's my job. So you're a thief?"

"Yeah, Daddy, a pretty good one too."

I said, "Let's get it cracking." We both started laughing.

She smiled and said, "I see why the girls talk so good about you." We finished our drinks, and I walked her to the bedroom. She hugged me and said, "Daddy, I'm drunk, I'm going to sleep."

I said, "I'll be in later, I'm going to chop it up with my brother."

"Okay, Daddy, I've got something I want to ask you in the morning, okay?"

"Okay, Baby Face."

She got into the California king bed with her wife-in-laws.

AD was in the living room kicking back with his hoes, when I walked into the room; his girls were on their way to their room.

I said, "What's up, AD?"

He said, "You know I was making sure my team is ready to go to work in the morning, ya dig. My folks are getting along real good, pimpin'. I'm gonna stack a bank."

I said, "I feel ya. My new bitch knows how to steal money from tricks. She dips in their pockets with her fingers and toes, takes out their wallets, gets the money out, and puts the wallet back without them knowing anything."

AD said, "You really came yo, Vinnie Mac."

I said, "We will see what's up in the morning, ya dig?"

"I dig, P."

Me and AD poured another drink and gave each hand daps.

AD said, "I can't wait till our jewelry is ready. Did you tell your girls about our day?"

I said, "I've been so busy I didn't say anything."

AD said, "Cool, let's wait until we rent the limo, then we will wear our new jewels and our mink coats."

"That sounds like a plan. I'm off tomorrow, so I'm going to work the ho stroll and see just how good my new thief is, ya dig?"

AD said, "Yeah, I can't wait to see my team down for my crown."

I said, "If my new bitch hits a good lick, I'm going to take them to Inglewood by the race track and see how the action is."

AD said, "Me too. I need to show Star and Snow a different ho stroll so they will be used to working all of them." We finished our drinks, and we smoked a joint and a Newport. AD turned on some music. We talked for another hour then called it a night.

13

The next morning, I cooked breakfast—french toast, turkey bacon, eggs, juice, and coffee. Baby Face wanted to talk to me. We walked outside. I lit a Newport for me and her. I took a drag off my smoke, and she said, "Daddy, I want to ask you something, okay?"

I said, "Okay."

"Do you mind if your hoes had a blow of cocaine?"

I said, "You like to blow?"

"Yeah, from time to time. I have some. I was going to give it to you last night, but I forgot to, I was drunk."

I said, "I don't care if you do, but I don't want you to use that shit with no trick, ya dig?"

"Okay, Daddy, can I share it with my wife-in-laws?"

"How much do you have?"

She said, "I have about $400 worth. I got it when we were in Las Vegas."

"Does Becky use it?"

"She does sometimes."

I said, "Go get the blow, and I will put some out for y'all, and I will save the rest."

I called AD and told him what it was. He said, "I asked Star and Snow if they used any drugs, and they said coke once in a while."

All the hoes sat at the dining table. I sat a plate down on the table and poured out the cocaine. I made some lines. My hoes said, "Daddy, I didn't know you blew coke."

"You never asked me either."

AD told his hoes, "It's okay as long as you don't blow with no mothafuckin trick." They agreed.

The hoes had their blow and a drink, and we headed out the door to the ho stroll. I said, "It's like this: each of you hoes will ride in the front seat. Y'all will take turns. I'm saying it to Baby Face. You two already know." I told Baby Face to ride in the front with me. I said, "Y'all know that Baby Face is a thief, don't you?"

"Yes, Daddy."

"Baby Face, you gonna need a couple of different wigs, aren't you?"

"Yeah, Daddy, I was going to tell you that. I have one more at the room. If I hit a lick, can you take me home to change?"

I said, "Of course I will."

I said, "Red Bone and Sexy, I'm going to buy your cars next week."

"You are, Daddy, for real?"

"Yeah, I am, and if Baby Face hits a lick, one of you take her home so she can change."

"Okay, Daddy, we will." I pulled into the liquor store parking lot and gave my hoes $10 each.

Baby Face came back to the car and said, "Daddy, are you going to be around here?"

I said, "Yea, me and my brother are taking his car to the car wash down on the other end of the track. I left my car unlocked. In case you hit a lick, you just get into the back seat and wait till I get back. Take that wig off once you get in the car."

She said, "Yes, Daddy, I see you are on top of your game." She turned and walked down the track. Sexy and Red Bone caught dates as soon as they hit the track. I got into the car with AD; he drove down the ho stroll about five blocks and turned the corner to let his hoes out.

He said, "You guys can double-date if you want to, and be careful."

"Okay, Daddy." AD gave them some money to buy condoms; they walked down the street to the ho stroll.

I said, "Pimping them hoes are looking good. You gonna stack a bankroll."

AD said, "Pimping, them hoes of yours were dressed fly as hell. That bitch Baby Face is a jazzy ho. You can tell she's been around for a minute."

We drove down the ho stroll on the car wash. AD's Caddy was cleaner than a mothafucka. He said he was going to get his rims and Vogue tires next week. After the car was finished, he gave the guy a tip, and we got into it and drove off. He put on some music. Johnny "Guitar" Watson's "A Real Mother for Ya." That was my favorite jam.

As we drove down the track, we saw some hoes, and we sweated them. I said, "If you know better, you would do better," to one of the hoes. She held her head down and kept walking. I said, "I like a ho that stays in pocket, just keep me in mind all the time. When you get tired of your Daddy, you can get into my Caddy," and AD drove off.

We headed back down the track. We had been gone for an hour. AD spotted his hoes. They gave him the sign, and he turned the corner and found a spot to park. He kept the music on. I was feeling myself. AD got out the Cadillac. His girls handed him some money and headed back to work.

AD got into the car and smiled. He said, "It's just some more of it, ya dig?" He counted his first trap; it was $180. Then he counted the other one. It was $260. AD said, "That Snow bitch is a real prostitute, ya dig? She gave me the biggest trap so far. Star is doing her thang too."

We got back in traffic and drove on down the ho stroll. I saw Red Bone getting into the car with a trick, and Sexy was talking to a trick. I didn't see Baby Face. Me and AD turned around and drove to the Jack in the Box to get a bite to eat. We laughed and chopped it up for a minute. After we were done eating, we drove to the VIP Records on PCH. We walked in.

I said, "What's up, Calvin?" He was the owner of the VIP.

He said, "Nothing much, brother, how about you?"

I said, "You know me, just trying to be like you when I grow up."

"Shit, I want to be like you," Calvin said, smiling. We looked around for a minute and picked out some new music. We paid Calvin and headed out the door.

AD put on some Rick James, started the car, and we got back in traffic. When we got back down to where his hoes were working, we didn't see them. Both of them had caught dates. We drove on down to where my hoes were working at.

Red Bone was talking to Sexy as we drove up. They gave me the sign. AD pulled over and said, "I'm going back down the track to break my hoes, are you cool?"

I said, "Yea, pimpin', I'm cool." I got out and walked into the store. My hoes followed me.

Red Bone gave her money and said, "Daddy, this is $180. I need some more condoms." I gave her $10 back. Sexy gave me her money. It was $150.

She said, "Daddy, have you seen Baby Face?"

I said, "No, I haven't."

Red Bone said, "Daddy, a trick asked me if I had seen a girl that was dressed just like her. I think she hit him for a lick."

I said, "I'll meet y'all in the car. Let me just see something." I walked over to my Cadillac, and I spotted Baby Face lying in the back seat.

I got in, and she said, "Daddy, I got a trick for his bank. He only had $560," and handed me the money.

Red Bone and Sexy said, "Bitch, we were worried about your ass."

Baby Face said, "Bitch, I hit a lick. Daddy left the car open for me."

I said, "Baby Face, stay lying down in the seat till I drive off." And she did.

Red Bone said, "A trick was asking for a ho dressed just like you. I knew you had it. I told Sexy that you was in the car because Daddy never leaves his car there. I didn't come and check. A bitch was getting her money."

Sexy said, "Daddy, are you going to drop us back off? I got a trick coming."

I said, "Yeah, I'm just taking Baby Face to change clothes." I pulled down the street from the store and let them out. I said, "I'll be back in a little bit. Y'all stay down and stay safe." They walked away, and I drove off.

Baby said, "Daddy, can I have a blow of coke once we get to the room and I change clothes?"

I said, "I'm going to drop you off. You change clothes, and we're going to another track."

She said, "Okay, Daddy, that's cool." She got out. I told her where the coke was. She said, "Daddy, where are you going?"

I said, "To pick up yo wife-in-laws."

She said, "Okay, I'll wait till y'all get back, and then I'll have my blow." Baby Face walked in and closed the door to the suite.

I headed back to the hoe stroll. I saw AD parked by the store. I parked and got into the car with him.

I said, "My bitch just hit a lick for $560. I'm going to pick up my other hoes and go back to the room. I'm going to let them take a break, then I'm off to Inglewood to put them down."

AD said, "Cool, I'm going to meet you at the room." He fired up his Caddy and headed to pick up his hookers. Sexy and Red Bone came to the car. I told them to get in.

Sexy gave me her trap and said, "Daddy, that trick is still looking for Baby Face."

Red Bone said, "Here, Daddy," and gave me her trap.

I said, "We are going to Inglewood to work on Century by Hollywood Park Racetrack."

"That's cool, Daddy. It's starting to slow down anyways," Red Bone said.

Sexy asked if they could have a blow and looked at Red Bone. I said, "That's why I'm picking y'all up so you can take a break, ya dig?"

Red Bone said, "Thanks, Daddy, you seem to know what a bitch needs."

Sexy said, "What a bitch *wants*, not what a bitch *needs*. Bitch, all I need is my Daddy."

"Bitch, you know what I mean. Daddy, you know."

I smiled and said, "That's hoes' business," and laughed.

I turned the key and pulled off into traffic. I said, "Since Baby Face knows how to steal, we will stay on the move to keep her safe, ya dig? I'm going to send you hoes to self-defense classes."

Red Bone said, "You mean judo classes?"

"Yeah, that's what I mean."

Sexy said, "I always wanted to learn how to fuck a mothafucka's ass up." She started laughing, and so did we. I pulled into the parking lot of the suite. AD was already there.

We got out and went into the suite. Sexy and Red Bone went into the room with the other girls. I pulled out the money that Sexy and Red Bone had given me. Just then Sexy walked into the living room where me and AD were sitting. She asked if she could fix something to drink for her and the other girls.

I said, "Sure, no problem, Sexy."

She said, "Thanks, Daddy," and headed into the kitchen.

One stack had $135, and the other had $120 in it. Sexy walked by smiling on the way back into the room. AD said, "How did you do, pimpin'?"

I said, "Baby Face gave me almost $600. She hit a lick, and that was her only date. Sexy and Red Bone gave me about $300 each." Baby Face came into the living room and asked for the blow. I said, "Baby, you didn't get it already?"

"No, Daddy, I waited for you to come back."

I said, "It's under the table in that magazine."

She picked it up and said, "Daddy, I'll get the plate so you can put some on it." She walked into the kitchen and got a plate. I poured some on it. She said, "Thanks, Daddy," and went back into the room.

AD said, "Vinnie Mac, can I have some for my hoes too." I handed him the blow. He got a plate, and then he called his hoes and gave it to them. I called Red Bone; she came out of the room. I asked her to pour me and my brother a drink.

She did as I had asked and said, "If you need anything else, just call me, Daddy." She gave me a quick hug and disappeared back into the room. Me and AD were finishing our drinks when Sexy appeared. She asked me how much longer before we were leaving.

I said, "In about forty-five minutes."

She said, "Okay, Daddy, we will be ready."

*****

"Daddy, there's a lot of hoes out here. It must be poppin'," Red Bone said.

Sexy said, "I can't wait till we park so we can show these bitches how Vinnie Mac hoes do it."

I pulled into the racetrack and parked. AD pulled next to me. I said, "You know how we do it." We held each other's hands, and I prayed for my team. After I was done, I said, "You hoes work together out there. It's a lot of money out here, so stay focused and be careful. How many condoms do you bitches have?"

Baby Face said, "I've got three, Daddy."

Sexy said, "I've got two. I'll buy some more once I break luck."

Red Bone said, "I got four, Daddy. I'm good."

I gave them each $10. As they were getting out, I said, "Baby Face, it's the same thing: if you hit a lick, the car will be parked right here. Make sure nobody sees you getting in."

She said, "Can I get my change of clothes out of the trunk?" I popped the trunk; she got the stuff out. She had a pair of black boots too. She said, "Daddy, I'm going to try to hit two licks, okay?"

I said, "Cool, Baby." They headed to the ho stroll. I had my hoes looking fly. Red Bone had a pink minidress, white thick belt, white boots, and white purse. Baby Face had on a black minidress, yellow thick belt, and yellow boots and purse. Sexy had a red minidress, black thick belt, black boots, black purse. AD talked to his hoes and let them out after my hoes were out of the parking lot.

I said, "Pimpin', let's ride in your car and sweat some of these hoes."

AD said, "Get in, pimpin', and let's roll." I got in; he turned up the sounds and pulled out of the parking lot.

There were a lot of pimps riding around. We saw New York T, E-money, Pimp Jerry, T Mac, Big Pimpin', and all kinds of other niggas.

I said, "Pimpin', I can't wait till we get our jewelry out. I'm going to fuck niggas up. They better be pimpin'. Ya dig?"

AD said, "Yea, my tailor-made suit will be ready in a couple of days."

The day was going smooth. We saw Max-a-Million riding around; he was sweating the hooker AD had knocked him, for the ho stayed in pocket. AD said, "I'm glad to see my pimping is on. That bitch is about my business, ya dig? I'm going to knock him again if he ain't pimping on those other hoes right." I rolled up some weed; we smoked and pimped. All afternoon, our hoes were getting money. Baby Face had a lick for $900 and another one for $750. My pimp was on and here to stay, so those pimps better watch out for Vinnie Mac the Pimp, ya dig?

14

"Be quiet, bitch, on your mothafuckin' knees." He pointed the gun at her and shot. *Blam!* "Open that got damn safe. If you don't, I'm going to shoot you in your fucking head."

The clerk screamed, "Please don't shoot, please."

"Shut the fuck up, bitch. Shut up." *Slap. Slap. Slap.* "Open the got damn safe. I'm not going to ask you again."

The woman said, "Okay, okay, I'll open the safe." Her hands were shaking.

"Hurry up, bitch." He pulled her by the hair.

"Please, please, I'm trying." She finally opened the safe.

The robber said, "Damn, look at all that money. Hurry up." Then he slapped her again. She filled up the bag.

"Please don't hurt me," she cried.

He said, "Suck my dick, bitch." *Blam!* He shot her in the arm. She screamed. Then he pulled her by hair. "That's right, suck it, bitch, suck my dick."

The store clerk did as he said. She had blood all over her. Once he was finished, he hit her over the head with the gun. She was knocked out cold. He put his penis in his pants. He grabbed a pack of Kools and a bottle of gin. He said, "Have a nice day." He jumped over the counter and ran out the liquor store.

The whole thing took less than four minutes; to the clerk, it seemed like a lifetime. Once the police arrived, the ambulance rushed the clerk to the hospital. This was the seventh robbery in the last two months. The crime scene unit didn't find any fingerprints.

The detectives questioned the clerk. The law enforcement had no clue who the crook was.

*****

My sister said, "Welcome, Eddie," and gave him a hug.

"Hi, Lizz, how have you been?"

Lizz said, "Just working and going to school. I stayed busy so I wouldn't miss your brother so much."

"Well, he's home now, I know you're glad." Peaches and all the Twenty-First gangsters gave him a coming-home party. I hadn't seen my brother in over two years. The last time he was with me, he was taking me to the airport and I was off to Job Corps.

"What's up, EJ? Man, I know you're glad to be home," Pee Wee said.

"Nigga, your lil brother been pimpin' for real."

Eddie said, "Vinnie Mac, how many hoes do you have?"

I said, "I've got three hoes. One of them is a thief. That bitch is like four hoes by herself." Babs, Charles, Peter Humphry, Wayne, and Dale Oden gave EJ hand daps.

"What's up, EJ?" Glen said. He gave him hand daps. Jimmy came over and gave him daps to. Jimmy had just got out of jail too. The rest of the gangsters came over and gave him daps.

The party was jumping. All the girls from Twenty-First were there. Eddie's girlfriend Lizz was holding on to him. She made sure the other girls kept their hands off her man. I told Eddie I had a surprise for him tomorrow. We partied till 2:00 a.m. After everybody left, I helped my sister clean up. Eddie and Lizz were in the room getting their groove on. My sister said Kevin (my younger brother) called and talked to Eddie. He was in jail too. He's getting out next year.

The next morning, me, Eddie, and my sister went to breakfast. We had to drop Lizz off; she had something to do. My sister paid for the meal. I left the tip. Once we got back into the car, I gave Eddie $2,000 so he could buy himself a car and get some new clothes.

Eddie said, "Thanks, lil brother, you must be getting a lot of money."

I said, "I'm stacking as much as I can." We took my sister home and dropped her off. Eddie had asked if I would take him shopping. I said, "I will take you to downtown LA after you see your probation officer." We went back to pick up Lizz. Once she got in, I started up the Caddy and drove Eddie to the probation office. After he was finished, we headed to LA.

Eddie said, "Why do we have to go to Alley? We can go to the mall."

I said, "You will see why as soon as we got there."

Eddie and Lizz said, "Damn, I've never seen so many people shoppin' at the same time." Eddie got Lizz some clothes too. Once they were done, I paid for everything.

Eddie said, "Damn, baby brother, you got it like that."

I said, "I want you to save your money so you can get a car." We had lunch at Denny's. I dropped him and Lizz off at my sister's house. I headed back to the suite. The girls were on the beach having fun. It was Sunday. I always gave them that day off. AD was inside watching football. It was October, and it was still nice and warm.

AD said, "How's the family?"

I said, "They're all doing okay."

*****

Once my hoes saw me, they headed up the stairs to the suite. Baby Face said, "Hi, Daddy, did you have fun with yo brother?"

I said, "He had a good time. I just came home to have a drink. I'm going to meet my homies. He told me he would be in pocket in an hour."

She said, "That's cool, I'm going to take a shower."

I said, "Okay."

The other girls came in. They asked, "How did things go with yo brother?"

I said things went great with him. After that, they headed to the room. I said, "AD, let's go."

AD said, "Let me talk to my hoes real quick, then we will bounce, pimpin'."

Once we were in the car, AD asked what time were we going to Hollywood. I said, "The limo will be there in a couple of hours. You didn't tell the hoes?"

He said, "I didn't tell them." I got out of his car and got my jewelry out and put it on. AD got out his and put it on too.

I said, "We're going to the gambling shack to meet Babs. I told him what we needed."

AD gave me $150 and said, "When we get to the gambling shack, pimpin', let's put our mink coats on before we walk in."

I said, "That's cool. Them pimps better keep their game together, or I'm going to knock their socks off."

AD said, "Sounds like some pimpin' to me." I drove up and parked in the front of the spot. My jewelry was fly, and my mink was killing them niggas. AD looked like a million bucks. I knocked on the wrought iron door. Skateboard opened the door. Baby was on the dice. I waited till he hit his point after we came out the back from handling our business. I gave him daps.

I said, "Take a good look. This is a pimp at his finest." I pulled out $3,000 and said, "I'm down and around. If any one of y'all shoes get out of picket, I'll be back to give you some news you can use."

Hollywood Snake said, "What they hit for?"

I said, "I'm already a winner. I don't need to gamble. I'm out. My hoes are waiting for me. I'm headed to Hollywood, ya dig?"

Pimping Shine said, "Put them hoes down, nigga."

I said, "You couldn't knock me if you had a knocking stick." Everybody started laughing. Me and AD headed out the door to the car. Once we got in, I put on Johnny "Guitar" Watson and turned up the music real loud. AD pulled out into traffic.

AD said, "Vinnie, you let him have it."

I said, "I like the bitches he's got. He needs a knockin'." We took off our coats and jewelry before we drove back to the room. I stopped at the liquor store and picked up some Newport; we were almost at the motel. Once I pulled into the parking lot, the limo was already out there. I pulled alongside of it and handed the driver a $100 bill and told him to come back in an hour.

We walked inside the suite, and Sexy said, "Daddy, did you see that limo outside? I think there were some tricks in it." Red Bone was in the shower. I told Sexy and Baby Face to put on something nice and told Red Bone too.

"I'm taking y'all out to dinner and drinks." I split the coke in half and gave AD his. I gave the rest of it to my girls. I told them to be ready in an hour. AD came out of his room, and we went out to the car and put our jewelry back on.

AD said, "My hoes are going to see this real pimping, ya dig?"

I said, "I dig." We put on our mink coats and headed back into the suite. We walked outside to the patio, poured a drink, and fired up some weed. Red Bone came out and started screaming. The other hoes came out to see what was going on.

AD's hoes said, "Daddy, let me see you. Damn, you look good. Daddy, can we touch your mink coats?"

AD said, "Touch it. It feels so soft."

AD's hoes were rubbing all over it, and then they spotted the jewelry and said, "That shit is fly as hell, Daddy, I'm scared of you." My hoes spotted my ring and said, "Daddy, that ring is the shit." Baby Face, Sexy, and Red Bone came over and rubbed my mink coat.

I said, "You looking at some real pimpin', ya dig?"

My hoes said, "Daddy, you're looking real good. A ho better watch out, my Daddy is some real pimpin'." They were smiling from ear to ear.

I said, "You hoes better hurry up. Our limo—that limo out there is for us."

AD said, "Yeah, we taking y'all to Hollywood."

Star said, "Daddy, for real? Thank you."

Snow said, "I gonna hurry up and get dressed."

My hoes ran back to their room to finish getting dressed.

15

The limo driver knocked on the door. I opened it and said, "We will be out in about five minutes."

He said, "Okay, sir. I'll be out in the car."

I said, "Okay," and closed the door.

AD said, "My hoes are dressed and ready to go."

Sexy came out from the room and said, "Daddy, we're almost ready, can I get something for you?"

I said, "I'm cool."

"Okay then, I'm going back to finish up my makeup. Baby Face is ready, and so is Redbone."

After a couple of minutes, we all walked out to the limo. The driver was very nice. He got out and opened the doors for us. Once we were in, the girls said, "This limo is fly as hell, Daddy."

I said, "Only the best for my dream team."

Red Bone said, "That's right, we're the dream team."

AD's hoes said, "Daddy, how many people can fit in the limo?" The limo was a stretch. It was filled with liquor, ice, and crystal glasses.

The driver asked, "Where would you like to go first?"

I said, "Drive down the coast and get on the 710 Freeway and take us to Hollywood. Once we get there, I'll let you know our next move."

He said, "No problem, sir. All the controls are in the top panel of the car. You can control everything from there."

I said, "Thank you very much." He rolled up the partition window and headed out into traffic. The shore of the beach was beautiful, and the weather was great.

AD told Star to pour some drinks for them, and Sexy poured our drinks. I turned up the music, and we partied our ass off. The girls were smiling and talking big shit, dancing and singing; before we got to Hollywood, we told our hoes to sit on the other side of the limo with each other so me and AD could talk.

AD said, "Pimpin', we should do this once a month."

I said, "That sounds good to me." We drank while the driver drove us all over the coast. We pulled over in the hood. I had to stop and talk to my homies.

After that, we headed on to Hollywood. I fired up some weed, and the hoes had a blow of cocaine. "Baby Face, pour Daddy another drink please."

"Yes, Daddy, anything for you."

AD called up front to the driver and said, "Once we got off on Sunset Boulevard, pull over at the Denny's. We will be having dinner."

The driver said, "Okay, we will be there in about five minutes. Is there anything else, sir?"

AD said, "No, that's all for now." The hoes freshened up their makeup, and we finished our drinks. Once the limo exited the freeway and pulled up to the light on Sunset Boulevard, we saw hoes everywhere.

Baby Face said, "Daddy, can we drive down the track one time before we eat?"

Red Bone said, "Bitch, I got to use the restroom first."

Snow said, "Daddy, can we run in and go to the restroom and then drive down the ho stroll?"

AD said, "Let's take a vote and see."

Sexy said, "Daddy, I want to look at the track."

Red Bone said, "Once I use the restroom, we can go."

Baby Face said, "I'm not hungry right now."

Star said, "Daddy, can we eat later?"

AD said, "Fuck it, let's go and check it out."

I said, "Well, if y'all want to go, then let's go."

The driver asked, "Where to now, sir?"

AD said, "Drive down Sunset Boulevard to Vermont Avenue, then turn around and go the other way."

"Yes, sir," he replied.

AD told his team to move over and let him sit next to them so he could show them what he expected from them. I told my hoes to let me sit next to them so I could tell them and show them where I wanted them to work at and which motel rooms to use. The track was on full; we could hear the sounds of hundreds of heels clicking like hammers on the sidewalk on both sides of the streets. After we passed Western Avenue, I told my hoes to look on the corner. I pointed somebody's hoes; they were dressed alike. There must have been seven of them.

Red Bone said, "Daddy, can we dress like each other?"

I said, "No. Because if the vice is out, they will know you guys are together. That's not smart."

Baby Face said, "Bitch, I'm going to hit me a lick, and we don't want to dress alike."

Sexy said, "Yea, y'all can, so you can watch each other's backs."

I said, "Once you guys learn how to drive back out to Hollywood. Sometimes I will let you hoes drive your cars."

Baby Face said, "Daddy, I can't drive, and I don't want to."

I said, "Don't worry, you will ride with your wife-in-laws."

She said, "Cool." AD was schooling his hoes too.

We passed by the tricks' hotels and the corner known as the Thieves Corner. I told my hoes that on the corner of Hobart Avenue and Sunset Boulevard, the cops found 115 wallets. "I want y'all to stay away from there."

They said, "Okay, Daddy." The driver turned around and headed back the other way. We talked, laughed, and smoked and drank. We had a great time. We only rented the limo for six hours, so it was time to head back to Long Beach. We drove down the shores on the way back. It was a beautiful sight to see. We pulled into the parking lot of the motel, and the girls saw two cars with ribbons on them.

Sexy said, "Somebody is lucky, Daddy. I wish it was me."

Red Bone said, "Me too."

The driver pulled over and let us out. I told Red Bone to go to the office and ask for a key because I had left mine in the room. Once she got into the office, the clerk gave her two keys; before Red Bone came back, I tipped the driver another $100.

He said, "Thank you, sir, you guys have a good night."

I said, "Sexy, go and unlock the door." She went to stick the key inside the door, but it wouldn't fit.

She said, "Daddy, this key doesn't work."

I told Red Bone to use the other key, and she said, "Daddy, did you pay the rent? This key doesn't work."

I said, "Well, try them in those cars over there." Sexy started screaming, and Red Bone too. They ran to the cars to see if the keys worked.

Red Bone said, "Daddy, this key don't work."

Sexy said, "Yeah, Daddy, mine don't work either."

I said, "Well, switch keys and try it again." The keys worked this time; my hoes were very happy. I told them to look in the trunk. Once they opened up the trunks to their cars, they found brand-new clothes in there. I told them I was proud of them and to keep up the good work.

They ran over and hugged me and said, "Daddy, thank you. A bitch can't wait to drive to work and make some money for you, Daddy." Me and AD walked into the room, and the hoes jumped into their cars and took them for a test drive.

Baby Face got in the car with Red Bone. Snow and Star got into the car with Sexy. I got Sexy a Ford LTD, and I got Red Bone a VW bug.

AD said, "Vinnie, them hoes are happy as hell. You gonna make that money back in no time."

I said, "Them hoes are down for me 100 percent, and I'm down for them 100 percent too. A good ho is a happy ho, ya dig?"

16

The next few months went by fast. My hoes were driving themselves to work, and they were doing great in their self-defense class. Those hoes could whoop the shit out of a trick if it came to that. I always told them to only use judo on a trick as a last resort.

Baby Face said, "Daddy, can we go to work early? I have a regular that gives me a hundred."

I said, "Yeah, you can go."

She said, "Sexy and Red Bone wants to go also."

"Cool, I see y'all when you get back."

*****

"Michelle, is that you?"

"Shit, that's Ray's aunt."

Red Bone said, "Are you going to talk to her?"

"Yeah, I'm going to see what she wants. She was always nice to me."

"Okay, girl, I'm going to keep on walking. I'm trying to catch another date."

"Hi, Aunt Tina, how have you been?"

"Girl, look at you. I haven't seen you in almost five months. You have lost a lot of weight, and you're looking fine as ever."

"Thank you, Aunt Tina."

"Have you seen Ray?"

"Tina, not since I left him."

"Well, he got a car, and he's doing better for himself."

"Well, I'm glad to hear that. Seems like we're both doing better. You know, sometimes people do better without each other."

Tina said, "You're right about that. Me and Kenny's Daddy didn't have shit together, but he's working every day. Some people just aren't good for each other."

Michelle said, "That's my car over there," pointing to the LTD. Aunt Tina said, "That's my car over there."

"Thank you, Aunt Tina. Please don't tell Ray that you've seen me. He doesn't like my man, and I don't need any trouble, okay?"

"Okay, girl, I won't. Well, let me get on my way to work. It's nice to see you again."

"You too, Aunt Tina."

*****

Baby Face walked up and said, "Bitch, let's go. I hit a lick for $1,000."

Sexy said, "Damn, bitch, you gonna have to teach me how to dip on a trick's pockets too."

Baby Face said, "Okay, I'll start teaching you, but let's go before that mothafucka finds his money's gone."

They jumped into the LTD and pulled into traffic. Red Bone was just coming back from her date. Sexy yelled out the window, "Bitch, I'll be right back. I'm going to drop Baby Face off at the house."

Red Bone said, "Oh, okay, I'll be out here getting all the money while you're gone."

*****

I had moved my hoes into a plush penthouse suite in the tower apartments right across from my job. It had five bedrooms, four on one side of the apartment and the master bedroom on the other side; it also had four bathrooms, a den that had a beautiful view of the city, a stepdown living room with a fireplace, and a fantastic view of the ocean. The carpet was pure white; it had a black playpen couch, set with white pillows. There was a big screen TV. The suite also had a black marble bar with five barstools. It also had pure white drapes. The penthouse was a pimp's dream.

"Hi, Daddy, I hit a lick for $1,000. Do you want me to change clothes and go back out?"

"No, that's good for now. I want to go to the mall in downtown Long Beach. Come with me."

"Okay, Daddy, I'm going to take a shower. I'll be ready in a minute." Sexy said, "Daddy, I ran into Ray's aunt on the track. I talked to her for a minute. You're not mad, are you?"

"No, Sexy, I'm not mad. Where's that nigga at?"

"She just said that he was doing good, and I didn't ask any more questions about him. I showed her my car, and then she had to go to work."

I said, "That's cool. How's it going out there?"

Sexy said, "Oh, Daddy, here's my trap." She handed me a hundred and some change.

I said, "How's Red Bone doing?"

"She had a couple of dates, Daddy. I'm on my way back to work. Do you need anything?"

"No, I'm okay, thanks." She gave me a peck on the side of my face and headed out the door. Baby Face came out from her room, and we headed to the mall.

*****

"Daddy, pull the car over. That's that nigga's car right there." Rohda jumped out and stabbed all four of my tires, making all of them flat.

Mac Ton, Rohda's man, said, "I can't wait to see that mothafucka. I'm going to rob him just like he did you."

Rohda said, "Daddy, let's just go. It's too many people out here for that. He can't drive that car nowhere. Until he gets new tires." Both of them started laughing as they pulled off.

*****

My son's birthday was coming up, and I planned on giving him a party. He will be two years old. His mother didn't give me any problems; she knew it was over, and she got herself a white boyfriend. I was cool with that. She needed someone in her corner, and he was there for her.

Me and Baby Face grabbed a bite to eat as we shopped for my lil Vinnie's birthday present. Baby Face said, "Daddy, let's go to Toys 'R' Us after we find his baby clothes and shoes."

I said, "Yea, okay, let's do that. I don't like the toys in here." I paid for my boy's clothes, and we left the mall and headed for my car. I was having a good time with Baby Face. We were laughing and talking until we got to the car.

Baby Face said, "Daddy, look at your car."

I said, "Ain't this a mothafucking bitch. Who in the fuck stabbed my got damn tires out?" I looked around, and I didn't see anyone. I called a tow truck and had my car towed to Mike's tire shop. It cost $845 to have new tires put on and $105 to have it towed there. I was mad as hell.

I said, "I know that Debbie bitch didn't do that shit. I wonder who did. Sexy said she had seen Ray's aunt, but she didn't know we were coming to the mall."

Baby Face said, "Daddy, that's fucked up. Some jealous-ass mothafucka did that shit."

I smiled and said, "Yeah, them niggas are jealous. I've been staying down for my crown."

Baby Face said, "Daddy, you not mad anymore?"

I said, "No, but if I find out who did it, that's their ass. Ya dig?"

I paid the man for the tires, and I headed back to the house to pick up some more cash. Once we got there, I told Baby that we would wait for her wife-in-laws to come home, and all of them would go together and buy lil Vinnie some toys.

She said, "Daddy, you're not coming?"

"No, I'm going to meet Babs and my homies."

"Okay, Daddy," she said. Red Bone and Sexy came home and gave me their traps. It was about six hundred and some change. I told them what had happened to my car at the mall's parking lot. Sexy asked if I thought it was Ray.

I said, "No, I don't think it was him. It was some jealous-ass nigga. Don't worry about it." After I gave them some instructions, I was off to meet my homies.

*****

"Hey, Kevin. What's up with you?"

"I'm okay, thanks for the money, what's happening out there?"

"The same old things. Niggas still hanging on Twenty-First selling weed and gambling."

"I'll be out in two more months. I can't wait."

"I know you can't. My son is getting big. Momma's doing okay. Eddie is working in the store with Peaches."

"Yeah, I know, I just talked to them." I said, "When you get out, I'm going to take you shopping."

"Okay, Vinnie, I'll talk to you later," and he hung up. I haven't seen my little brother in over two years. His voice was changing; he was growing on up and sounding like a man.

*****

I was heading over to the bank to put my workmen's company check into my account. I kept my ho money at home in the safe. I took some time off work from the Copper Penny. I slipped and fell and hurt my back. I was going to a therapist once a week. When I was coming from there, I would always drive down the ho stroll on my way back to the penthouse. I spotted two white hoes out there working. I pulled over on the side street and parked. I watched them for a while after they turned a few tricks. I went to sweat them. One of them had just jumped into a car with a trick, and the other had just talked to one but didn't get in. I pulled over and blew my horn and waved my hand for her to come over to me. She looked and started walking real slow to my Caddy.

I said, "Hi, what's your name?"

She smiled and said, "Candy."

I said, "Get in," and she did. I pulled off and into traffic, turned down the music, and turned the radio on to the news. I had played a couple of horses in the fifth race.

"This is Chuck Henry of KNX Radio. There's been a string of robberies in Long Beach. The bandit has robbed over fifteen liquor stores and small markets. The suspect has shot nine of the clerks and assaulted six others, taking an unknown amount of cash and items. If you have any info regarding the suspect, please call the Long Beach Police Department. There is a $50,000 reward out on the robbery suspect."

Candy said, "Damn, is it hot out here?"

I said, "No, the police are busy trying to catch that robber." I also asked her where she was from.

Candy said, "Pasadena, me and my wife-in-law came out here yesterday. It's been a little slow out here."

I said, "How much have you made?"

She said, "I made $700 yesterday, and I only made $300 so far today."

I said, "You know it's pimpin' with me."

Candy said, "I knew that when I got in your car."

I said, "You know what to do then." She handed me the money that she had on her.

I said, "What's up with the other ho?"

Candy said, "She's not going to leave her man. She acts like that's her boyfriend."

I said, "Where's the rest of that money you said, and where's your room at?"

She said, "It's a couple of blocks from here. I'll show you." We went and got the rest of the money and her clothes. I told her to leave the key and that other hoe's money and ho clothes in the room. Candy was about 5'10" with those clear stilettos on. She had strawberry-blond hair, and she was wearing a fuchsia-colored dress and had a purse that matched. I drove to the beach motel and got my favorite suite. I helped Candy bring her things into the room. She asked if I had any other hoes. I told her, after she was done unpacking, I was going to take her to meet her wife-in-laws.

Candy said, "Daddy, what's your name? You were moving so fast that I didn't get a chance to ask."

"My name is Vinnie Mac. We will get a chance to talk. I want to get to know you and tell you what I expect from you."

Candy said, "Okay, Daddy." We jumped into my car and were on the way to the penthouse. I told her that all my hoes had to earn their way to the penthouse. Candy said, "That suite is very nice. I've never stayed by the beach. I love the sounds of the ocean, seagulls squawking, and pigeons cooing." Candy had been with five pimps, and she told me that she had been in the game for six years. Her mother was in prison for stabbing her boyfriend; the judge gave her fifteen years for attempted murder. Candy had been in and out of foster homes and had been raped a couple of times by her foster brothers. She was a runaway until she turned eighteen years old. That's when she met her first pimp at the bus station while on the way to see her mother. G-Money was her pimp; she ran off because he beat her all the time. She ran into Vicky on the stroll in Hollywood. Candy chose up with Vicky's folks; his name was New York D. She was with him for three weeks. Vicky was jealous of Candy. Once she chose up with me, I schooled Candy on my game, and my hoes welcomed her into the family.

17

"What's up, Vinnie Mac?"

"Some more of it. How have you been pimpin'? Where are you at now?" I asked.

AD said, "I'm in Phoenix, Arizona. The ho stroll is on full. There's a pimp here called New York D. He said you knock him for a white bitch in Long Beach."

I said, "Yea, I got the bitch, and she's staying down for my pimping, ya dig?"

AD said, "I dig ya. Once he said Long Beach, I knew it was you that that got him for that white ho."

I said, "When are you coming back this way?"

AD said, "I'm going to the east coast first, and then I'm going down south. I'll be back on the West Coast after the summer ends. I ain't fucking with winter over there, it's too cold."

I said, "I feel ya, man, I hate that shit too. I had enough when I was in Job Corps in Utah."

AD said, "Okay, pimping, I'll holler at you later." And he hung up. It was good hearing from him; my brother put me in the game, and now I'm playing to win. I was becoming one of the biggest pimps on the West Coast.

*****

"Fuck you, bitch, I'll whoop your ass out here if you keep talking that shit to my wife-in-law. That's why my man broke your sorry-ass bitch. Because you're always out of pocket," Sexy screamed.

Rohda said, "That's why I stabbed his tires out, bitch, and my man is going to take care of his ass. Fuck y'all."

Red Bone was walking up, and she heard what Rohda said. Sexy and Red Bone walked up to her and started whooping her ass right on the ho stroll, and everybody was looking. Mac Ton drove up and parked his car; he jumped out and slapped Candy, my white bitch, and she fell onto the ground. He kicked her in the ribs. Baby Face ran over and gave him a roundhouse kick right in the face. Once he hit the ground, she kicked and kicked until he was out cold. After that, all my hoes jumped on Rohda. They fucked that bitch up and took her money. They jumped in their cars and drove to the suite at the Long Beach motel and called me.

"Are you guys all right?" I said.

Baby Face said, "Daddy, I knocked Rohda's man out, and then we all fucked that ho up too." I could hear them talking loud; they were hyped up. It was the first time they got to use the judo on someone. I told them to stay put until I got there. Baby Face handed Sexy the phone. I talked to each of them one at a time; they were excited about the fight. Candy was the last one that I talked to.

I said, "Candy, are you all right?"

She said, "Daddy, my ribs are hurting, and my face is swollen."

I said, "I'm on my way. I'll look at you once I get there."

"Okay, Daddy, I'm going to lie down," and she hung up.

"Damn that mothafucka. He fucked my bitch up." I banged my hands on the steering wheel. I had to calm down. I was driving too fast. I pulled into the motel, parked, and ran to the room.

"Daddy, Daddy, the nigga kicked Candy, I think she needs to go to the hospital," Sexy said. I walked back to her room, and she was sleeping. I asked Baby Face and Red Bone to take my car and go to the store and get some Zig Zags and something to drink. After they got back, we smoked, and they told me everything that happened. Candy's ribs were cracked, and she had to take some time off to heal up. I moved her into the penthouse, and my mother came and stayed for a while to help me out with the girls. I looked all over the place for that nigga and that bitch. They were gone, and I didn't know where. I was going to fuck that punk-ass nigga up for putting his hands on my bitch and letting that ho stab my tires out.

I had to keep it down low because everybody knew what happened. I didn't want anybody to snitch on me and tell them I was looking for them.

*****

I drove my hoes to work from then on; if a mothafucka wanted to fuck with them, I was going to be right there. I was working hoes in Hollywood, and Baby flagged me down. I pulled around the corner, and she ran and got in.

She said, "Daddy, Stone is out here, and he's sweating me so hard that he's fucking up my money."

I said, "Where's the nigga at?"

She said, "He's riding around in a brown car. With some bitch in there with him."

I said, "Okay, you work on this corner, and I'm going to pick up your wife-in-laws so they can watch your back. I'm going to be looking for him too." He never showed up again.

Two months had passed by. Candy was back to work, and she was clocking a lot of money. Baby Face hit a lick for $9,000 last night, so I let her stay home for a couple of days. Things were going great. My pimping was back on track, and I was out to peel another pimp for my next ho. Them niggas better watch out; if they slip, I was going to be there and give them some news they could use.

18

I pulled over to Pioneer Chicken to get me some wings and some mashed potatoes and a biscuit. There was always a lot of pimps there; it was the headquarters for a lot of them. Pimpin' Rico and Slim P were having a Mac out. The players obviously relished verbal fencing. Once their joust ended, the other pimps were laughing their asses off. I finished eating and got back into traffic. I spotted a fine-ass bitch with a voluptuous body. I had to have that hooker. I parked and got out; she saw me and started walking real fast. The ho turned the corner away from the ho stroll.

I said, "Say, ho, let your next move be your best move." She crossed the street, and I was right behind her. She was Asian with long black hair. She was about 5'3". She crossed the street, and I did too. I had on a white captain's cap, a white silk suit, and a gang of jewelry on. She turned the next corner and slowed down. I walked up to her and said, "I'm Vinnie Mac, sexy, and what's your name?"

She said, "Naomi."

I said, "You're just what I need in my life—a piece of rice." Naomi started laughing. I knew I had her. She was nervous. I said, "You know you're out of pocket."

Naomi said, "I'm choosin' up," and reached into her purse and pulled out the money when a tampon fell out. She handed me a knot and picked up the tampon and said, "I'm sorry about that."

I said, "Don't worry about it. You stay right here. I'm going to get my car and pick you up."

She said, "Please hurry up. I don't want him to find me."

I made it back to my car, got in, and fired the Caddy up then drove and picked up my new bitch. Once she got in, I drove to Santa Monica Boulevard and pulled into the gas station so she could change her tampon. While she was in there, I counted the money she gave me. It was $585. Naomi got in, and I pulled off into traffic. I asked if she was Korean.

She said, "Filipino."

I said, "Where are you from?"

Naomi said, "I'm from Albany, New York." I asked who her folks were. She said, "His name is Billy Mac, and he's driving a white Mercedes 450 SL with New York plates." I told her to lean over in the seat until I leave the ho stroll. I pulled back onto Sunset Boulevard and scooped up my other hoes. Once Candy and Red Bone got in, I headed to the freeway.

Candy said, "Hey, bitch, I see you chose up. You made the right move."

I said, "You know her?"

Candy said, "I was trying to bring her home, Daddy. That's the one I was telling you about."

I said, "So this is the bitch."

Naomi said, "That's one of the reasons I got with you. Candy was telling me all about you and where you guys live and that you're the best pimp she ever had."

Red Bone said, "She's right about that. My Daddy is the best."

I said, "I'm going to take y'all to Inglewood so you can work with Baby Face and Sexy. Naomi, I know you're on your period. Are you bleeding heavy?"

She blushed and said, "I'm almost done. I can work."

I pulled off the freeway and into the Hollywood horse racing track and parked like I always did. I always tipped the attendant very well, and he watched out for me. He was Red Bone's trick. Candy gave me $380, and Red Bone gave me $240 and got out and headed to work with Naomi. I told her to tell Baby and Sexy to come and drop their traps off.

"Hi, Daddy." Sexy was the first one there, and she gave me $190 and was off back to work.

Baby came minutes later. "Hi, Daddy, I'm glad you came out here with us." She gave me her money. It was $170. She said, "Daddy, it's kinda slow right now, but I'm staying down. You know I'm going to get my money."

I said, "I know, Baby. Okay, I'll see you later. I'm going to be driving around. Have you met Naomi?"

"Yeah, Daddy, she's nice." She got out of the car and went back to work.

*****

The weather was changing. It was foggy and cold on the beaches. I decided to take Naomi to the penthouse. She and Candy shared their room. The nigga Billy Mac had left town, so I didn't get to service him for the ho. I got word that he had gone to DC, but I kept my eye out for him.

19

"Hey, Kevin, jump in."

"What's up, Vinnie? I'm glad to be home."

I said, "I know you are. Do you want something to eat?"

Kevin said, "Yea, can we go to Jack in the Box?"

"Yeah, we can go there." I pulled in to the parking lot; we got out and went inside to order. "So, Kevin, what are you going to do now that you're back home?"

Kevin said, "I'm going to get me some weed to sell and get me some hoes too."

I said, "You ain't no pimp."

He said, "I will be once you teach me."

I said, "No problem, lil bro."

After we finished eating, we went to see Mom. "There's my baby. Come here and give your momma a kiss, boy."

"Hi, Mom, I missed you so much, I love you," Kevin said. We all got back in the car and headed over to my sister Peaches's store.

Momma said, "Kevin, are you going to work in the store with your brother?"

Kevin said, "Yeah, Momma, I'm going to work in the store." I pulled up to my sister's market and parked; we all got out and went into the store.

"What's up, brother?" Eddie said while swinging a punch at Kevin. Eddie was always trying to play fight.

Momma said, "Stop that shit, Eddie."

"I was only playing with him, Momma."

Peaches gave him a kiss and said, "Look at you, boy, you've gotten big."

We hung out for a while. After that, I dropped Mom off at the bookie joint and took Kevin shopping. I gave him $1,000 and paid for his clothes. After that, we went to the hood. I dropped Kevin off at his girlfriend's house and headed back to the penthouse. I told Kevin I would pick him up tomorrow.

*****

I blew the horn, and Kevin came out of the suite I got for him on the beach. It wasn't the one I always rented; it was upstairs. It was a one-bedroom but was just as fly. He had been staying there for a couple of months. Connie, his girlfriend, was staying with him. Kevin was selling a lot of weed on Twenty-First and Lemon. Kevin told me that a nigga he met last night told him where Mac Ton and Rohda were staying at. I asked him if he told him why we were looking for them.

Kevin said, "Man, I know better than that."

I said, "We will move on that nigga later. I want them to think everything is all right."

Kevin said, "Yeah, that's a good idea, Vinnie. That way that nigga won't know if we did something to them or not."

"That's right, lil brother, that's why we're waiting."

Kevin said, "Vinnie, when are you going to take me with you so I can start learning the game?"

I said, "I'll start taking you in the next couple of weeks."

Kevin said, "Yeah, that will be fine with me." We drove over to meet our homie Babs. I needed to pick up some more cocaine for my hoes. Kevin said, "Vinnie, do you get high with your hoes?"

I said, "No, I don't. That's not a good thing to do. If I did blow some cocaine, I would do it by myself. But I don't, ya dig? I want my hoes to have total respect for my pimpin', so I would never blow with them."

Kevin said, "I just wanted to know if you did, so I won't either."

I said, "Don't ever do that, okay?"

He said, "Okay." After I was done scoring from Babs, I dropped Kevin off on the set.

The following week, Kevin went and got a Cadillac. It was clean as brown with brown interiors. Kevin picked me and Eddie up, and we went out to get something to eat. I asked Eddie and Kevin what's up. I knew they didn't just want to go out for breakfast.

Eddie said, "Vinnie, me and Kevin want to start selling cocaine. Everybody's asking us do we know where to cop some blow at." I asked what they needed from me. "We need a loan from you so we can get started."

"No problem, when do you need it?"

Kevin said, "I called our cousins Shawn and Shannon, and they can score it for us."

"Damn, I haven't talked to them in a minute. What's up with them?"

"They got the projects on lock," he said. My cousin lived in a Jordan Downs projects in Watts, the home of the Grape Street Crips.

"Let me meet you guys in an hour at the store, and then we will roll out. I need to talk to them."

*****

"What's up? Damn, look at y'all, you niggas must be having a lot of money." Me, Eddie, and Kevin had on brims, slacks, fly shirts, and Stacy Adams. I had some fly jewelry on too. We looked more like players than gangsters. We gave both of our cousins hand daps. They were dressed in white and khakis, with Chuck Taylors on. Eddie gave them the bag filled with money to cop the cocaine. Shannon counted it, and Shawn weighed out the blow. It was a half kilo, eighteen ounces. We had a few drinks, smoked some weed, and talked for a couple of hours. We hadn't seen our cousins in years.

"Shawn, I need you and Shannon to take care of something for me." I tossed another bag of money. It had $15,000 in it.

Shannon said, "What's up, Vincent, you need us to put in some work?"

I said, "Yeah, I need you to whoop this nigga and his bitch. Don't kill them. I want you to break the bitch's arms and break that punk-ass nigga's legs and arms. That mothafucking punk-ass nigga cracked my white bitch's ribs and slapped her in the face. She had to take off work for a while. I missed over $25,000, if not more, ya dig?"

Shawn started laughing. I said, "What's so mothafucking funny?" Shannon looked over at his brother.

Shawn said, "It's Vincent. He sounds like a pimp. The last time we saw you, we were shooting marbles. Plus this fuckin' weed has me doing that shit."

We all started laughing. I told them how they looked and where they lived—on 108 and Fig. I informed them that they lived in that motel on the corner and what kind of car that nigga drove. Our cousins told me they would call once it was taken care of. We all walked out to the car. We gave them daps one more time, and we peeled off out of the projects and headed back to Long Beach.

*****

"Daddy, here's $150," Rohda said to Mac Ton.

"Okay, lil momma, stay down," he said as he slapped her on the ass. Rohda smiled as she headed back to work. There was a car parked down the street from their room. Rohda walked up to the car.

"Hey, you want a date?"

"Yeah, get in," the trick said. They pulled around the corner. He parked, and Rohda started sucking his dick once he gave her the fifty she had asked for. Once she was done, she jumped out and headed back to the stroll. A nigga was walking on the same side of the street as she was. The bitch didn't cross like a real ho would have. As she walked by the nigga, he grabbed her ass. She started talking shit to him. She ran to the room and told Mac Ton. Mac Ton and Rohda headed out the door.

Rohda said, "Daddy, there, that nigga is right there." Mac Ton pulled out his knife as they walked close behind him. He turned the corner.

Mac Ton said, "Come on, bitch, I'm going to cut that moth-afucka's ass up." The guy started walking fast, and they were right behind him. Three other niggas were walking in the same direction as they were. Mac Ton said, "Hey, grab that nigga, and I'll pay you guys." They ran and grabbed him. Mac Ton and Rohda ran up. One of them had a bat. Instead of fucking him up, they grabbed Rohda and Mac Ton. It was a setup. One of them slapped Rohda, and the other one hit Mac Ton with the bat. *Crack, crack, crack* was the sound of the bat. Mac Ton screamed, "Here, here, take my money. Don't kill us." *Crack, crack*, he hit him again. Mac Ton's legs and arms were broken; one of the others was choking Rohda.

The other guy with the bat walked up and said, "Let that bitch go." Once he did, the guy hit that bitch with the bat. *Crack, crack!*

She screamed, "Please, please don't kill me." One of them kicked her in the ribs. Another one took Mac Ton's money out of his pockets. They took off running.

Rohda's arms were broken; her ribs were cracked. Mac Ton's legs and left arm were broken.

Rohda screamed, "Daddy, Daddy, are you all right?"

He said, "Bitch, go get the car and call the police."

20

Kevin and Eddie were selling blow and weed out of the store. Bennie, our brother-in-law, didn't mind as long as they worked in the store for free and only sold it to people they knew. Eddie called me and told me that the business I had my cousins do for me was done. I talked to Eddie for a few more minutes. Then I ended the call. I never told my hoes what I had done to the bitch and her punk-ass nigga. One thing's for sure: if you put your hands on one of my hoes, payback was a mothafucka.

The first thing I learned that you don't ever do is put your hands on another man's ho; if you did, it was open season on your ass. Other pimps would lose respect for you and give you a roasting for being out of pocket. In fact, that's the only way a pimp could be out of pocket. The term only applies to hoes or a ho-ass nigga.

*****

I was five deep with some of the finest bitches a nigga could want, but I was staying down for my crown. I had quit my job at the Copper Penny. I had over $100,000 stacked in my safe, and I was on my way to pick up Diane from the airport. She was finally ready to come to Cali. My other hoes talked to her all the time on the phone. I named her Goldie. It's one thing for sure: Goldie fit right in. She was fine as hell. It took over an hour for me to make it to the airport.

*****

On my drive to the airport, I was thinking about how Candy was a great knock, and so was Naomi. Those two were getting a lot of money. Naomi was a perfect ten; her hair was down past her waist, and she had a bomb shape. Cars would damn near crash if they were watching her. She loved to dress in some shade of pink. I got her pink thigh-high boots, pink skirts, pink dresses, pink purses; sometimes she would mix it with black or white.

Naomi had given me over $50,000 in the last few months. Cars would line up for her; pimps would sweat her every day, but she stayed in pocket. One of Billy Mac's pimp friends told him that I had the ho. Billy came back to Cali and tried to take the ho back, but she ran from one side of the street to the other side. I flagged the nigga down, and we had a Mac out. The nigga has two other pimps with him. I told him that bitch chose up and to give the ho some room so she can get my money.

Billy Mac said, "Nigga, who the hell are you? I've been pimping on the bitch for over two years."

I said, "I'm Vinnie Mac the Pimp. I knocked you for the bitch, but you left town, so I couldn't serve you for the bitch."

Billy said, "Nigga, you from the itty-bitty committee, you ain't no pimp. You're rest haven for hoes."

I said, "Nigga, I've got some of the finest bitches on the ho stroll. I'm five deep with no sleep, nigga, and I've stacked a bankroll on them hoes." I opened up my silk shirt. I had on seven gold chains. I pulled out my ring of the map and four other gold and diamond rings and put them on. "I pulled out over $10,000 on that, nigga." He couldn't take it; he tried to steal on me, and he missed. I side-stepped that punk-ass nigga and kicked him under the chin. That nigga fell like a wet rag. I pulled out a chrome-plated .38 caliber.

The other pimps said, "Pimpin', we ain't got nothing to do with that shit." I put my gun back in my pants pocket. I smiled when I thought about it. I looked at the clock in my car, and I was running late. I still had another twenty minutes to drive before I got there.

I started thinking about candy; she was tall and walked just like a professional ho. She kept her hair curled up; it took her damn near two hours to get ready to go to work, but once she was done, she made traffic stop. You could see tricks trying to pull over nonstop. She always had a good attitude, and I really liked that. I felt that we could talk about anything. She could sing like a mothafucka. The girls always sang. She was great for my family. Candy loved to get money. She worked day and night. I had to make her leave the ho stroll. She would have at least ten dates in the morning and another ten at night. On good days, she would pull in $1,000; and on a slow day, at least $700. I looked up, and I was at the airport parking. I locked my car and hurried over to meet her.

"Goldie, over here!" I ran up and helped her with her bags; she had three of them.

"Daddy, I've been here for thirty minutes."

"The traffic was heavy," I said. I gave her a hug, and we loaded the bag into the car.

"Daddy, I love your car. It's just like you told me." My Caddy had the fifth wheel on it, rims and Vogue tires. It looked just like some pimpin'. I pulled over into the Denny's out by the airport. Goldie and I stopped to have a bite to eat. We had a good time talking while having our lunch. Once we were done, I tipped the waitress and paid the bill. After we got into the car, I turned on the music. I passed Goldie some weed to roll up. As we headed back to the house, Goldie asked me if she could go and see her brother that lived in Compton. I told her once we get to Long Beach and she unpacked, Sexy, her wife-in-law, would take her to see her brother.

Diane was looking fine as hell. I stopped at a motel and got a room. I had to fuck her. It's been a long time since we made love. After a couple of hours, we checked out, and I decided to take her to meet her brother. He turned out to be a cool-ass nigga. We had a few drinks and dinner. Diane told her brother that she was going to be a ho; he didn't care and told her that she was a grown woman and that she knew what she wanted but to be careful. His name was Donald; he was a hustler. He sold cocaine and weed. Diane gave him a hug. I gave him daps, and we headed home.

*****

That next day was going to be Diane's first day working; she was nervous about going out, but she was ready. The girls took time out to explain everything to her. Baby Face told her not to spend more than fifteen minutes with a trick and to only use a trick's room. Sexy told her about the first time she had worked the track and how she felt. The other girls told their stories about when they had turned out. Goldie was dressed in a lime-green minidress with a black belt, and she had on black thigh-highs; she had a black and lime-green purse. That bitch was looking fine as ever. I was rolling up and down the track watching my hoes. I saw a blue truck pull over, and Goldie walked over to the driver's side window and gave him a kiss. Then she got in and rode across the street to the trick's room.

After that, it was on. She was hoeing up alongside her wife-in-laws. The first time I broke her for her trap, it was $220. I asked her how she felt.

Goldie said, "Daddy, I'm good. Can I hit the weed real quick so I can get back to work?" I was proud of her; she was down for me 100 percent, and I was down for her too. Pimps sweated her. She would turn her back to them. If they walked on her side of the street, she would run to the other side and keep on getting my money. The next few months went by fast. Goldie took to hoeing like a duck to water. She and my other girls got along great. I was stacking a lot of paper. Diane went to see her brother on Sundays. I gave all of them that day off. I would let Diane buy cocaine for her wife-in-laws from her brother Donald. Goldie didn't use coke. She liked to drink yak. It didn't bother her that some of my hoes used coke. She knew a ho needed something to get them ready for work. I don't care what a nigga says. A ho is going to drink or use some kind of drug, or she is a nympho that just loves sex. To me, anybody that fucks all kinds of strangers for money will need something to get them ready. "Daddy, this is Janet. She wants to come home with me," Goldie said.

"Let me talk to her." Goldie handed her the phone. "Hi, what's up with you?"

"Nothing much, how are you?" Janet asked.

"I'm fine. So you want to choose up?"

"Yeah, but I've never done it before. Diane says she will teach me?"

"Are you sure?"

"Yes, I'm sure!"

"Well then, let me talk with Goldie." She handed Goldie the phone back.

"Yes, Daddy?"

"How does she look?" I asked.

"She's about 5'4", and she's mixed with black and Mexican blood. She has long curly hair, and she's about a size 16 with big breasts. I told her we had some clothes for her to wear. Daddy, Sexy and Red Bone have some clothes that will fit her too, and she can sleep in the room with me, if that's okay with you?"

"Does she use?"

"Yes, Daddy, she likes to drink and smoke weed."

"I'll be there in about twenty minutes."

"Daddy, my brother told me to tell you, you owe him one." I could hear him laughing in the background. Janet was from Bakersfield. Her boyfriend went to jail for shooting a gangbanger in front of a store in Compton. His bail was $100,000. His name was Jerry. He and Janet were staying next door to Donald, at Jerry's aunt's house. Once he went to jail, his aunt told Janet she had to leave, and she stayed with Goldie's brother for a couple of days. Donald had a lot of bitches, but he wasn't taking care of any of them. He called Diane and told her to come and meet Janet and to take her home with her. Donald got all the pussy he wanted from her, and it was time for Janet to move on. Sexy and Red Bone shared rooms, Candy and Naomi shared rooms, Goldie and Janet roomed together, and Baby Face had her own room. I had my pimps room. Baby Face made more money than any of my hoes; that's why she had her own room, and it was going to stay that way. If I knock any more hoes, they would have to sleep in the den. I was working Hollywood every day now; my team would work day and night. I was seven deep with no sleep, and I loved every minute of it. My mother would come by on Sundays and cook for us. She would ask my girls to help her pick out her horses to play with the bookie. I didn't mind as long as they didn't want to gamble on the horses on their own. My hoes loved Mom, and Mom loved them.

*****

Christmas was coming up in the next few weeks. I let my hoes decorate the penthouse. They bought a seven-foot tree. It had snow on it. The girls wrapped lights on it also. They added all kinds of ornaments on the tree and placed an angel on the top. My hoes also added pictures of them cut out like Christmas tree ornaments. Each girl cut out five pictures of themselves with different outfits on. I had to admit they had the tree looking really good. They also hung up Christmas stockings over the fireplace.

21

It was a sea of prostitutes on Sunset in Hollywood. The closer it got to Christmas, the more pimps brought their hoes to town. Cali has great weather, and that's why the ho stroll was so full. The rest of the country was cold. Niggas from New York, Milwaukee, Chicago, Boston, Denver, and a lot of other states were in town. The track was also full of rich tricks, dope boys, hustlers, and robbers. I stayed in traffic; they had some niggas breaking into tricks' cars. My hoes used the same motel, and I didn't want anybody breaking into the tricks' cars my hoes got out of. Baby Face peeled tricks for their wallets, and she was teaching Sexy how to dip in a trick's pockets. The last thing I needed was somebody breaking into their cars. Last week, I ran this nigga down that had broken out the window of one of the cars. I didn't catch him, but he knew not to try that shit again. As I was rolling down the ho stroll, Sexy flagged me down. I turned around the corner and parked. She was walking fast.

"Daddy, Daddy, I just hit a lick. I don't know how much it is. Here, Daddy, count it."

"Say, bitch, lie down in the back seat." She climbed over the seat of my Coupe de Ville. I pulled off and looked in the bag she had given me. "Shit, bitch, there's thousands in here!"

"Yeah, Daddy, that's the only reason I flagged you down," she said. I pulled over to Western Avenue.

I pulled out some of the money and counted. "One, two, three thousand. Damn, Sexy, give me a mothafuckin' kiss. Bitch, it must be $15,000 in here," I said.

"Yeah, Daddy, damn, I did good."

"Yes, bitch, you sure did." That was Sexy's first big lick. I was very proud of my bitch. I rounded up the rest of my team, and we headed back to the penthouse. Naomi gave me $900. Candy had $700. Red Bone had $650. Goldie gave me $480. Janet, whom we named Velvet, gave me $380, but she was improving all the time. She was my latest turnout. Baby Face gave me $1,800 the first time, and the next lick she hit was for $950. I could tell Baby didn't like Sexy making more money than her.

Sexy said, "Bitch, I did just what you told me. I fucked him in his car. I had seen where he put the bag of money. I started making all kinds of noise. 'Yes, fuck me. Ohh, that dick is good. Fuck me.' That silly mothafucka thought his little dick ass was doing something. He closed his eyes, and that's when I grabbed the bag of money. I had him drop me off, and Daddy was coming down the track." My other hoes started laughing. I had all my hoes in martial arts class. All of them hoes could whoop a mothafucka's ass if it came down to that.

*****

It was a week before Christmas, and me and Candy were on our way to see her mom in prison. Her mom was at CIW. It was about a two-hour drive. I was driving my Lincoln Continental, which I got with some of that money Sexy hit the lick for.

"So how do you feel seeing your mother after all this time?"

"Daddy, I feel good. I can give her money for Christmas, and I'm coming to visit her. Thank you, Daddy."

"It's all good," I said.

She gave me a kiss on the side of my face. I turned up the music and put the pedal to the metal. Candy had a great time with her mother. She told me all about it on the way back home.

As I exited the freeway on PCH, I saw a couple of new hoes. I drove around the block a couple of times and sweated them hoes. All of a sudden, a police car was behind us. "Damn, the fucking cops are behind us." The mothafucka pulled me over. One of the cops walked up to the car and instructed me and Candy to get out.

"Put your fucking hands on the car, pimp." It was Boline. That asshole mothafucka was a dirty cop.

"Officer, why did you pull me over?" I said.

"You know why I pulled you over. You and this white bitch were trying to recruit those hoes, and don't say you weren't, or I'll run your ass in, Mr. Vinnie Mac. I know who the fuck you are," Boline said. The other officer was running our names, and Boline went into my pockets and pulled out the money I had in there. He said, "Now what do we have here?"

"Damn," I said.

He bent down and pulled a little bag of cocaine out his pocket and said, "You're going down, boy, felony, possession of a controlled substance."

I said, "That's not mine!"

"Shut the fuck up!" He kicked my legs apart as far as he could. Then he walked over to Candy and felt on her tits then ran his hands up her legs. "I'll tell you what, Mr. Pimp. I'm going to take this money and let you go, unless you and this bitch want to go to jail. Either way, I don't give a fuck," he said.

"What money?" I said.

The other cop came back and said, "They don't have any warrants."

Boline said, "You can go now. Have a nice day." The officers got another call and left in a hurry.

"That bitch-ass mothafucka took $1,800, but it's nothing to a boss like me," I said.

"Daddy, fuck that asshole, are you all right?"

"Yeah, Candy, I'm all right. A nigga needs a drink," I said as we pulled off. I turned up the music and headed home.

*****

We had less than ten days before Christmas. I pulled into the parking lot in downtown Los Angeles, locked the car, paid the parking attendant, and headed to the jewelry district. I had seven gold and diamond rings made that said "Vinnie's Dream Team." To pick up the tailor-made outfits, I had to go to Arthur Williams down on Broadway. My suit was light blue with dark-blue stiches in it, and it had my name on the pockets. After I was done, I drove down the stroll on Figueroa. Then I jumped on the 110 Harbor Freeway to the 405 Long Beach. I got off on Pacific Avenue. I didn't get on PCH like I normally would. I didn't want to run into that asshole cop Boline. My mother was waiting on me at my sister's store on Hill Street.

"Hi, Momma, sorry it took so long, it was a lot of traffic out there."

"That's okay, baby. Momma knows how that traffic is. As long as you're safe, that's all I care about." I told Mom about Boline. And she told me that I should drive one of my other cars while I was in Long Beach. I listened to her; she knows best. My brothers Kevin and Eddie were on the way to the store. We all pitched in and got our mother a car.

"Eddie, you got a new car?" Mom asked. We all smiled at each other.

Peaches said, "Momma, that's your car."

"What! That's for me?" she asked. She ran over and said, "Thank you, guys, very much. I need that car to drive back and forth to work."

Kevin said, "You thought that was Eddie's car. We had you fooled."

"You sure did." Eddie gave her the keys. She took it for a test drive. I went with her.

"This car sure is nice, baby."

"We're glad you like it, Momma."

Once we returned to my sister's store, Peaches handed her an envelope with $1,200 in it. My mother started crying. She was so happy. I had to hurry home to put my hoes' gifts under the tree.

*****

Sexy asked, "What shoe size does Daddy wear, Red, did you look?"

"Yeah, bitch, I looked. He wears a seven and a half," Baby said. "He wears a fifteen-and-a-half shirt." Goldie and Velvet got my pants size: thirty inches for the waist and thirty-two inches in length. Candy and Naomi were in charge of getting my ring size. It was a seven. I had given them $1,000 each to go Christmas shopping. Red Bone's mom and stepdad, Sexy's mom and her women, my mother, and my sister and her husband were all coming to dinner along with my brothers and their girlfriends. I cooked all night. We were having baked ham, turkey and stuffing with cranberry sauce, yams, greens, potato salad, dinner rolls, along with cakes and pies. Three sweet potato pies and two white cakes with frosting and a german chocolate cake. I already had plenty of liquor and beer. I had a surprise for Baby Face. I had her mother flown in on Delta Airlines. She had a suite at my favorite spot, the beach motel. All the other girls already knew about her mom.

"Baby Face, come with me to the store, I forgot something. It's Christmas Eve, so we better hurry up."

"Okay, Daddy, I'll be with you in a minute," she said. I decided to take my Caddy. Once we were in the car, I asked Baby what would make her Christmas complete. She said, "Daddy, it is complete. I have you and my wife-in-laws, and we sent my mom some money. So I'm very happy." I backed the car out and jumped into traffic. "Daddy, what store are we going to?"

"We're going to Von's, but first I need to stop by my brother's room." Once we got there, I told Baby Face to go and knock on the door and tell him to come out so I can ask him something.

"Daddy, which room is it?"

"It's 218, the one upstairs." She ran up and knocked on the door. The door opened up real slow.

Her mom said, "Merry Christmas!"

Baby Face screamed, "Momma, Momma, it's really you!" Then she started to cry. They hugged each other. She kissed her mom then hugged her again, and they headed down to the car. "Daddy, thank you, thank you." She and her mom jumped in, and we drove back to the penthouse; we had a great time with our families. We really enjoyed ourselves; it was one of the best holidays I've ever had. I let

Velvet go to Bakersfield to visit her family. She wanted to give them their presents in person. She only stayed overnight. She was back home to have Christmas dinner with the rest of us.

22

I dropped Baby Face and her mother back off at the motel. "Momma, did you have a good time?"

"Yes, baby, the food was great. Vincent seems like a very nice guy. Is he?"

"Yes, Mom, he's very nice to me."

"So why are you still seeing Eric?" That was Stone's real name. Eric Stone Mason. "Toni, did you hear me?"

"Yes, Momma, I heard you."

"Well, tell me why you're messing with both of them at the same time?"

Toni said, "Vinnie is slim, brown skinned, with long hair, and he dresses very nice and takes care of me very well. But Stone is tall and has a muscular body with a bald head—that's what I like about him. He went to jail trying to make sure we were taken care of. He messed up the money we made, and he is very sorry about it. Vinnie was so nice to me that it's hard to leave him. I like all the other girls also, Momma. I called Stone, and he's going to meet us here in twenty minutes or so. He's on the way right now. He has a present for you."

"Toni, I hope you know what you're doing. You have a good man, you should stay with him. Does Vinnie hit you?"

"No, Momma, he doesn't."

"Somebody knocking on the door?" She looked through the peephole. "It's Stone." She opened the door.

"Hi, Ms. Parker, Merry Christmas, this is for you." He and Toni got her a dozen roses, a card, and a couple hundreds were in it.

"Momma, let me talk to Stone for a minute. We'll be right back." They went into the bathroom to talk.

"Hi, baby, I missed you," Stone said.

"Yeah, I missed you too!" She had $1,000 stashed. She pulled out her pussy. She got on her knees and gave him a blow job. After they were done, they went back in the living room with Toni's mom.

"Eric, how's your mother?"

"She's fine, Ms. Parker. I talked to her this morning. She told me to tell you Merry Christmas."

"Thank you."

"Momma, me and Stone are going to take you out and show you around Los Angeles."

"Okay, baby, let me shower and get dressed."

"Okay, Momma." Her mother left the room.

"Tee, what's up, baby, are you ready to leave that nigga and come back home?"

"Stone, I told you that I would help you out. I'm not leaving Vinnie Mac."

"So how long is this going to last? We doing all this fucking, and you giving a nigga head with your mother in the next room."

"Stone, don't say that shit. As a matter of fact, I'm not going to keep on doing this shit. You got a bitch at the room. I'm not going to keep taking care of you and that bitch."

"Tee, I'll leave her right now for you."

"No, you better keep her."

"If that's the way you feel, I'm going to leave right now."

"Nigga, fuck you. I don't need you, mothafucka. You got my mom thinking you're gonna take her out." *Slap!* Stone hit her so hard that she fell on the floor.

"Bitch, don't you ever talk to me like that." As Toni was getting up, she kicked him in the nuts. "Ooh," Stone said.

"Mothafucka, get the fuck out right now." Stone swung at Toni. She ducked and elbowed him in the ribs then chopped him in the throat. The nigga couldn't breathe. Toni opened the door and kicked that big-ass nigga in the ass.

As he was leaving, he said, "Bitch, you and that nigga gonna get fucked up. I'm going to rob him and your bitch ass." Toni ran and jumped on his back. She scratched his face and bit him in the back. That ho-ass nigga started to scream. "Bitch, get off of me." She pulled his shirt. He broke away and ran to his car. "You dead, bitch," Stone said as he peeled out of the parking lot. Toni's mom watched the whole thing.

Once she got back upstairs to the room, her mother said, "Baby, what's going on?" Toni started crying.

"Momma, you was right. I don't know what I was thinking."

"That's okay, baby, you're going to be all right."

"Thanks, Momma."

"Girl, where did you learn how to fight like that?"

"Vinnie sends us to self-defense classes."

"Damn, girl, I'm telling you, you whooped that boy's ass."

"Did I, Momma?"

"Girl, you had the boy running for his life."

Toni smiled and said, "That bitch-ass mothafucka."

Toni's mom said, "Did he teach you how to cuss like that?"

"I'm sorry, Momma, please forgive me."

"Baby, I'm sorry that happened, but that boy is crazy."

Toni said, "Momma, I wanted to show you around so you could enjoy yourself."

"Baby, just being with you makes Momma feel good." Toni hugged her mother. "Toni, you have a beautiful home and a good man that cares about you. I know what you do for a living, I've always known. So I'm saying if you're going to do that, be with somebody that cares about you."

Toni said, "Thank you, Momma, that means a lot to me. Vinnie is very good to me. He makes sure you get money every month. I don't even need to tell him. He just sends it."

"Baby, you know you have to tell Vinnie what happened. I don't trust Eric, so y'all be careful." *Knock, knock, knock.*

"Momma, somebody's at the door. See who it is." Baby Face's mom looked in the peephole.

"Toni, it's Vinnie!"

"Oh, shit, the manager must have called him."

"Vincent, is that you?"

"Yeah, Momma, it's me." Ms. Parker opened the door; to her surprise, my brothers were outside both sides of the door. "Baby Face, what the f—— is going on? Excuse me, Ms. Parker, I don't mean to cuss in front of you."

"Momma, I'll be right back."

"Daddy, can we go somewhere and talk?"

"Yeah, we can go to the park across the street, or we can walk down on the beach, whichever you prefer." We walked and talked. Baby Face told me everything that had happened. I was mad as hell, but I knew Baby Face made too much money for me to fire her, but I did tell her to fly back home with her mother, and I would send for her in a couple of weeks.

She cried and said, "Daddy, I'm very sorry. I didn't mean for all this to happen. I told him I was done with that shit." She had already told me on the beach.

I thanked my brothers for having my back. I sent them on their way; it was Christmas, and they wanted to get back to finish Christmas with their girlfriends and their families. Kevin and Connie had moved into their new apartment on Seventh and Cherry. It was only a few blocks away. Eddie and Liz lived on Fifteenth and Cedar.

"Vincent, don't make Toni go back home. I'm asking, please let her stay."

"Okay, Momma, I'm going to do that for you."

"You are, Daddy, for real?" Toni said.

"Yeah, I'm going to let you stay, your wife-in-laws really have respect for you." I kissed Toni on the side of her face. Every time I thought about her sucking his dick, I got mad. That's the part of pimping I didn't like. One thing's for sure: I was going to stay on the lookout for that nigga Stone. We have unfinished business. Baby Face's mom stayed for a few more days; she wanted to be with her boyfriend for New Year's. Me and Baby drove her to the airport, helped check her bags in, and we kissed her, and we boned out after that. On our way home, I had Baby Face show me where Stone's people lived. I called my cousins and told them what happened and paid them once again to take care of that problem.

23

"Six, five, four, three, two, one. Happy New Year's!" Horns were blowing, people were shouting. Me and my team had rented my favorite room at the beach motel. The beach motel was packed. We could see the fireworks from the Queen Mary. Everybody was on the beach having a ball. It had been a great year for my pimping. I have some of the baddest bitches a nigga could want. I got five cars; one of them was a Rolls-Royce. I bought it for myself, and I had it delivered on Christmas. It was pure white with peanut butter-colored interior with bamboo wood grain. I only drove it out of town. That motha-fucka Boline would never have a chance to catch me in that. I gave my hoes the next day off; we all got fucked up last night.

My phone started ringing early in the morning. "Hello."

"Say what's up, pimpin'?" It was AD.

"Man, I'm hung over from last night," I said.

"Well, get on up, I'm downstairs."

"Nigga, stop playing."

"For real, man." I jumped up and put on a sweat suit and headed to my private elevator. Once I was downstairs, I could see AD's Cadillac. I walked out of the glass door and met him.

"Man, why didn't you tell me you were back?"

"I told you I was coming back. I spent the day with my family." I gave him daps. "Vinnie, I need some blow for them hoes."

I said, "No problem." I called Goldie's brother Donald and told him I was on my way. I didn't buy cocaine from my brothers because I didn't want them in my business. I jumped in the car with AD, and we rolled toward Compton.

"Vinnie, I knocked a bad bitch in Texas on my way back to Cali. I named her Sugar. She sure is sweet." We both laughed. AD has three snow bunnies. He always said, "If it ain't snowing, I ain't going." We rolled up Long Beach Boulevard. On our way there, there wasn't a ho in sight; it was early.

"AD, where are you staying at?"

"I got a room in Hollywood."

"Oh, okay."

"Vinnie, your name's been ringing. Niggas from Oakland were talking about you."

"Was it good or bad?"

"They said you got some badass hoes and that them hookers were always trying to knock another pimp's ho."

"That's because they send their hoes at mine, ya dig?"

"I dig ya," he said. I had to stop and get something to eat. I was hungrier than a mothafucka. He pulled over to the Golden Burger. I ordered just a hamburger and a Coke. AD didn't eat; after that, we pulled up in front of Goldie's brother's house.

"Donald, this is my brother AD. AD, Donald."

"What's up with it, Donald?" AD said.

"Nothing much, just getting this paper." Donald weighed out a quarter ounce of blow. AD paid him, and we were out the door, but not before I asked Donald if AD could come by if he ever needed anything else. Donald said it was cool.

"So that's Goldie's brother?"

"Yeah, that's him."

AD said, "He looks just like her."

"He sure does," I said.

"Vinnie, can you roll with me back to Hollywood? I need to pay for them hoes' rooms, and I'll drop you back off."

"Sure, why not?" I said. AD jumped on the 110 North to the 101 Hollywood North, and we exited on Sunset Boulevard. The track was on full; there were at least one hundred hoes out there. That was more than any other track. Sunset Boulevard usually has over three hundred hoes. I saw that a lot of pimps gave their hoes the morning off. We drove down a couple more lights and then turned up into Sunset Motel. AD parked, jumped out, and went into room number 17. Then he came out and then went into the office and paid the rent. Next he went to room 35; he stayed in there a couple of minutes. Next he went to room 35; he stayed in there a couple of minutes. Next he went to room 5, and he called me to come in. Star and Snow were in there. AD called them in to the bathroom. AD came out, and they stayed in there.

"Pimpin', I'll be done in a minute," he said.

"I'm going back to the car," I told him.

"Okay, Vinnie, here's the keys to the car." I jumped in and turned the key to listen to some music. AD came out a few minutes later. "Say, pimpin', you got them hoes in pocket?"

"Yeah, man, that's what happens when you take them cross-country, ya dig?" AD fired up the car, and we headed back toward the freeway.

*****

"Baby Face, pass me that fork."

"This one, Daddy?"

"Yeah, that one," I said. I was cooking breakfast for my hoes. A late breakfast. It was about three in the afternoon. AD had dropped me back off, and I had taken a little nap. "Tell your wife-in-laws they can come to the table so we can eat." After we were done, everybody went back to sleep. I woke up again about 6:30 p.m., ordered pizza for everybody; we ate and lay around and watched a movie. After that, we all called it a night. The next morning, we were back at it.

Sexy, Baby Face, and Red Bone rode in one car; Candy and Naomi rode in a car with me; and Goldie and Velvet were in another car. We followed one another as we drove to Hollywood. I dropped Velvet and Goldie off by the trick motel. My other hoes parked their cars inside the motel. They all headed to work. I was driving my Coupe de Ville. The ho stroll was super full. Baby Face, Goldie, Velvet, and Candy caught tricks as soon as they had made it out to the front of the trick motel. Naomi, Sexy, and Red Bone were talking to some johns. I was driving up and down the track sweating hoes.

"Hey, pimpin', pull over and let's ride together." That was AD; he was driving on the side of me. We pulled into a McDonald's parking lot. I looked to the left of me, and I saw twenty vice cops just finished having a meeting. They got into their car and rolled down the track.

"AD, did you see those police?"

"Yeah, pimpin', I saw them."

"Let's go tell our hoes to be careful," I said. "AD, let's drive your Cadillac. My Cadillac is too flashy."

"Come on, let's roll," he said. By the time we made it back down to where my hoes were, they were all gone.

"Man, I hope them hoes are on dates," I said. We turned around and headed the other way.

"Say you bitches go in the room now," AD hollered to his hoes. They ran into the motel. We headed back toward where my hoes worked at. I spotted Candy and Velvet.

"Say, bitch, y'all stay inside the motel, the vice is out. Tell your wife-in-laws to go to the ho stroll in Long Beach."

"Okay, Daddy. We'll tell them." The vice had picked up Naomi, Goldie, and Sexy. Red Bone, Baby Face, Candy, and Velvet made it back to Long Beach. I had to bail out the others. They were picked up for loitering with the intent to prostitute. The vice had picked up over two hundred hoes that day. The police had passed a new law so it would be easier to bust hoes. They could go to jail for just standing on the corner. The shit was in the newspaper. I didn't read it on New Year's Day.

*****

That mayor in Hollywood was on one. He's got the police tripping on pimps and hoes. A nigga better watch his ass, or he's going to jail. They've been having women vice cops posing as hoes. The last sting they had set up busted eight pimps. Them niggas were facing sixteen months to two years. AD called.

"What's up, Vinnie, where you at?"

"I'm in Bakersfield. The track is on Union," I said.

"How many hoes are out there?"

"There are about eighty or ninety hoes on the track."

"Man, as soon as I get my hoes out of jail, I'm on my way." AD's hoes had been to jail at least ten times each. The Hollywood Police would round up hookers at night and hold them until 5:00 or 6:00 a.m. So a nigga was missing his money; the track still had a lot of hoes working, but they were going back and forth to jail. It was election time; the mayor was trying to get reelected. The polls opened today. After the election, things would go back to normal. The hookers had a lot of tricks and money coming to Hollywood, and nobody wanted that to change. The prostitutes were good for the economy. The police always tripped at that time of the year. If you put your hoes down after 2:00 a.m., they didn't trip at all.

"AD, why you keep putting them hoes down in the daytime?"

"Vinnie, all the good tricks are rolling in the day. You know that. Besides, them tricks late at night are all coked up, and some of them be tripping on the hoes. I would rather have a bitch take a chance of going to jail than me having to beat up a trick or one of them hurting my hoes, ya dig?"

"Yeah, that's why I left until elections are over," I said.

"Well, I'm on my way. I'll see you in the morning?"

"Okay, AD, I'll see you then." I ended the call.

*****

"Has anybody seen Velvet?"

"No, Daddy. The last time I saw her, she got in a red truck."

"How long ago was that?"

Goldie said, "Daddy, that was over an hour ago."

"Okay, keep your eyes open for her. Tell her to call me once she shows up again." I rolled my window back up and turned my music back up. "Hey, y'all, what's going on?" I said.

"Not you, you're a pimp," one of those square bitches said.

"Not a pimp. A great pimp."

They got back into their car and pulled away from the liquor store on Union. Bakersfield was popping; my hoes were getting a lot of money, but I was worried about Velvet. Was that ho out of pocket?

She had no reason to be. I was good to all my hoes. I kept them happy. A happy ho is a good ho. My phone started to ring.

"Hello."

"Daddy, it's me Velvet. You were looking for me?"

"Yeah, I haven't seen you in a while. Is everything all right?"

"Yeah, everything's all right. I was on a date."

"I didn't see you at the trick motel."

"I went to his house."

"What, you know the trick?"

"No, but he gave me $300," she said.

"Look, Janet, don't ever go anywhere with no mothafuckin' trick but to the trick room. Do you understand me?"

"Yes, Daddy, I'm sorry, I won't do it again."

"I don't like getting mad, Velvet, but you have to do what I tell you."

"Do you want to break me for this money?"

"Yea, meet me at the liquor store on Eighth."

"Okay, Daddy, bye."

I hung up.

*****

We were finally back home. I missed the penthouse. Hollywood was back on. Me and my team of hoes traveled up and down California. We worked Bakersfield, Fresno, San Jose, Oakland, and San Francisco. We were on the road for three months. I knocked Jap Black for a badass Mexican bitch. I named her Spicy. She was 5'9" with 38-C breasts with long pointy nipples. She had long blond hair. The hair on her pussy showed through her panties. I was in San Diego at that time; the niggas followed me to Hollywood. They wanted that ho back bad, but my pimping was on, and the next nigga better be pimping, or his ass is mine—his ho anyway.

<<image>>

24

"What's up, pimpin', so you heard about the knocking I put on that nigga Jap Black?"

"Yeah, man, every pimp is talking about it."

"AD, what are they saying?" I asked.

"Man, they're saying Jap Black had that bitch for five years, and you had your hoes move that bitch."

"Yeah, man, my hoes put me up on the bitch. She was tired of that nigga. She said Jap was fucking off all the money on square bitches. While she hoes all day and night," I said.

"Vinnie, you're getting deeper than a mothafucka."

"Somebody's got to do it, ya dig?"

"Yeah, man, I dig. Well, pimpin', I'm still in San Diego. I'm coming back on the weekend."

"Okay, I'll see you then." I hung up the phone.

*****

"Hi, Vincent, it's me, Beverly. Where have you been? I called your job, and they said you quit?"

"I didn't want to tell you I'm looking for another job," I said.

"Well, I don't know why you stopped working there, but you know better than me."

"I'll tell you about it later on," I said.

"Well, Vincent, I need to talk to you in person," Beverly said.

"I know it's been months since I've been over to your house, but I've been getting money."

"Vincent, you know I don't mess around with that stuff."

"Well, I might as well tell you. Beverly, I've been pimpin'."

"Pimpin', who?"

"Well, I got eight of the finest hoes in Hollywood."

"Vincent, I just don't know what to say. But I'm not going to see you anymore. I'm not into that shit, no sirree."

"Beverly."

"Vincent, I love you, but that's not the life for me. So don't call or come by, I mean that. Goodbye and good luck." I could hear her crying as she hung up the phone. Damn, that's fucked up, I had finally made love to Beverly. That was the first time for her. Damn, damn, I felt fucked up about it. But I had to tell her. I couldn't keep on making up shit I was doing. I had to tell her the truth. Now she's gone. Well, what can I say? I couldn't keep on fucking with a square bitch. I loved her—that's why I had to tell her.

*****

"Bitch, on the floor now. Get down now, bitch, or I'm going to bust a cap in your ass," the robber said.

"Please don't shoot, don't shoot." The clerk's hands were shaking. "Please take the money, take the money."

"Shut up, bitch, shut the fuck up," he said as he kicked her on the side of her head. Blood spurted out of her mouth. The man took all the money he could put in the bag. He even took the change. "Now, bitch, on your knees now."

"Please, please don't hurt me."

"Where's the condoms at?"

"No, no, please. Take all the money," the clerk said as she begged for her life.

"I'm going to ask you one more time."

"Okay, okay, there, right over there."

The robber put a condom on and made her suck his dick. Once he was done, he shot the clerk in the leg and said, "Have a nice day," before he knocked her out with the gun.

*****

"Hey, Kenny, what's up?"

"Man, I haven't seen you in months. Where have you been?"

"I've been in Los Angeles, at the house. Is your man still in pocket?"

"Yeah, he got some good shit. You can only take a hit, and you'll be fucked up," Kenny said.

"Well, get a half of a stick of cherm (PCP)." Ray handed him a fifty-dollar bill off his bankroll. He got over $4,000 from the liquor store robbery.

"Man, where did you get all that money from?"

"Man, stay out of my business." Ray had parked his car in front of his aunt's house. His aunt Tina was looking out the window.

"Boy, get in here and say hi to me," his aunt Tina said. Ray hopped out the car as Kenny was on his way to cop the cherm (PCP).

"Hi, Aunt Tina, how have you been?"

"I've been fine. Where did you get all that money from?"

"I was gambling and won it."

"Well, your aunt needs a loan."

Ray said, "No problem," as he peeled off a couple of hundred bills. "Here you go, Aunt Tina, you keep that, you don't owe me nothing." He gave her a kiss on the side of her mouth.

"Thank you, baby, your aunt needs this money. Are you going to be here for a while?" she asked.

"Yeah, I'm going to be down here for a couple of days if that's all right with you."

"Boy, you don't even have to ask. You can stay as long as you want. I'm going to the store. Do you need anything, Ray?"

"No, I'm fine, thank you," he said.

"Boy, I saw Michelle. She's doing good for herself. She's lost about seventy pounds. She's looking fine as ever. She got a black Ford LTD. It's nice!"

"Where did you see her at?"

"I saw her up by Cherry Avenue and PCH, by the liquor store." Ray said, "Was she with that nigga?"

"No, boy, I was just letting you know, that's all. The girl is doing well for herself. You're doing better by yourself, boy, you don't need her." Kenny was walking back from down the street. "Well, boy, I'm on my way to the store."

Ray said, "Take my car," throwing her the keys.

"Thanks, Ray, I'll be back in a bit."

"Okay, Aunt Tina." Tina got in the car and drove off.

"Ray, I'm telling you this shit is the bomb. Just take a couple of hits. That shit creeps up on you."

"Man, don't worry about me. You take your time," Ray said.

"Man, fire that shit up. Mom is gone. Let's smoke it out in the backyard."

"Here, man, break it in half. I'm going to save mine until I take care of some business," Ray said. Kenny opened the foil paper that the cherm (PCP) was wrapped in. He tore a piece and handed the rest to Ray. Ray walked out back with Kenny as he fired up his piece of the cherm. "Damn, Kenny, that shit smells strong."

"I told you this shit is the bomb," Kenny said as he put the cherm out. Kenny said, "My homie Tommy took off all his clothes and ran down the street butt naked after smoking a half of a stick of this shit."

"Man, you bullshitting."

"No, I'm for real." Kenny was high as hell off a couple of hits of that cherm. They walked back in the front of the house. Kenny said, "Ray, the nigga in that Cadillac was Vincent, Eddie's brother. They're from Twenty-First. You better leave that shit alone." Kenny could hardly talk.

"Man, fuck him and that bitch, I don't care about them," Ray said. But truth is he couldn't wait to see them.

*****

My team was working the morning in Long Beach on PCH. Goldie and Velvet worked on the Westside. Candy and Naomi worked on PCH and Chestnut. About ten blocks from Goldie and Velvet. Spicy worked Long Beach Boulevard and PCH, by the car wash. Sexy and Red Bone worked on Cherry and PCH, and Baby Face worked on Myrtle and PCH. I worked them from 5:00 a.m. till 7:30 a.m. I always moved them to another track about that time so that schoolkids wouldn't see them.

The school bus ran down PCH about 7:45 a.m. There would be at least a hundred of them out there. Those little assholes would fuck with my hoes if they were working out there at that time. Those badass kids would call them hoes and bitches, and the boys were the worst. They would yell, "Bitch, how much to suck my dick?" and laugh. It didn't really bother my hoes; they wanted to kick their asses. One morning about six thirty, I was rolling down the track. I saw Rohda's punk ass out there working. She didn't know the car I was driving in. I was driving Sexy's black LTD. I liked to drive that car; it was clean as hell. I was at the light. I blew the horn at the ho and kept it moving.

I gave my hoes Sundays off.

"Daddy, my regular trick called, and he wants to date. He gives me $150 for an hour," she said.

"What times does he want to meet you?" I asked.

"At noon at the liquor store on Cherry and PCH."

"Okay, I'll drive you and drop you off. I need to drive your whip."

"Okay, Daddy, I'll be ready in about thirty minutes."

"Okay, Sexy," I said.

*****

"Kenny, come roll with me. I'm going to eat breakfast," Ray said.

"Man, I'm hungry. What time is it?" Kenny asked.

"It's about eleven thirty, so hurry up. I want to get to the Burger Shack before breakfast is over."

Kenny said, "Do you have that piece of cherm left?"

"Yeah, but you can't have none. You smoked yours already," Ray said.

After Kenny was dressed, they jumped in Ray's Ford and headed to the restaurant. It was packed; breakfast was over at twelve thirty, and it seemed like everybody in Long Beach was there for the $2.99 special—two pancakes, two pieces of bacon, two eggs, and coffee. After Ray and Kenny were done with their meal, Ray drove Kenny home.

"Say, Ray, where are you going?"

"I've got to take care of some business," he hollered as he was driving off. Ray was thinking as he pulled out his gun, *I wish I could see that bitch and that nigga*, as he drove up and down the ho stroll. He decided to rob the liquor store on Cherry instead. He drove around the corner and parked in the alley. He fired up that half of a cherm and swallowed a huge drink of gin as he planned to hit the liquor store.

*****

"Good morning, Daddy. My regular wants to see me again," Candy said.

"Damn, Don's been seeing you every day. How much is he spending this time?"

"He wants to see me for three hours."

"What is he up to? He's trying to steal my piece of Candy?" I asked.

"Daddy, he can't take me from you. He's always asking me how much it would cost for me to stop working."

"What do you tell him?"

"I told him to give me $25,000, and then you will let me go with him."

"Not for all the tea and china."

Candy smiled and said, "Daddy, I'm not leaving you and my wife-in-laws for Don. He's a trick, and he's always going to be a trick."

"I'm just checking, Candy. That mothafucka's been seeing you every day for the last month. Shit, he's given you over $9,000. You be careful, Candy. Familiarity breeds danger," I said.

"Daddy, Don's only 5'6", and you've sent me to judo classes. I'm not worried about him," she said. "I'm telling you to just take it easy with that trick. What kind of work does he do?"

"He works in construction, Daddy."

"I'm going to drop you off this time so I can see who this Don person is. What time does he want to see you?"

"He wants to see me at 1:30 p.m. He meets me at the liquor store on Cherry and Tenth Street."

"Okay, I'll be there. Are you dressed?"

"No, I'm going to start getting ready," she said.

"Once I pick Sexy up, I'll be on my way," I said as I was hanging up the phone. I've been having nightmares; it was so often I'm going to be careful myself.

*****

Man, this cherm is good. I better put this shit out for now. Let me drive around the block one more time to make sure no police are by the store, Ray thought to himself. He pulled out of the alley and on to PCH; as he drove around the corner, he spotted Michelle getting out of a trick's car. She headed into the store. Ray pulled into the gas station across the street.

"Daddy, I'm in the store, do you need anything?" Sexy asked.

"No, I'm cool. I'll be right there in ten minutes."

"Okay, Daddy, I'll be standing on the side of the store."

Man, this is my lucky day. The bitch must be waiting for somebody. Ray fired up his car and drove back into the alley. He fired up the rest of the cherm. He took a big puff of the PCP, then he downed the rest of his liquor. *I'm going to bust a cap in that ho's ass.* Ray checked his gun, rolled his window up, locked his car, and started creeping up the alley. *Man, this shit is stroooooong.* The cherm had Ray fucked up. *Mannnnn, I'mmmm going to fucccck up that*—He couldn't finish what he was thinking. All he knew was that Michelle was on the side of the store, and he was out to get her.

*****

Sexy waved as I pulled to the stoplight. She was looking good. I was very pleased with her. She lost weight and was doing great. She had planned on staying that size. She kept up with her diet. The light changed. I pulled into the liquor store parking lot and parked.

"Sexy, go into the store and get me some Newport," I said.

"Okay, Daddy. Here's my money that the trick had given me. He gave me a tip too," she said, smiling. She walked into the store. I got out and lit my last smoke. I left the car running. A bum came staggering out of the alley.

"That mothafucka is drunk," I said to myself. I turned my back to him. Sexy came walking out of the store smiling. All of a sudden, her face changed.

"Daddy, watch out! Ray's got a gun!" As soon as she said that, Ray threw the gun at me. *Blam. Blam.* The gun hit the ground and went off. I felt a burning in my legs. I stumbled back and fell to the ground. I hit my head on the side of the building. I felt blood running down the back of my head. Sexy ran into the store. "Help, help! My man has been shot." Ray jumped into Sexy's car and stomped on the gas; he flew out into traffic. A beer truck was on the way to the liquor store. *Scrrm!* You could hear the brakes from the truck.

It slammed against Sexy's car. It knocked the car into a telephone pole. The car and Ray were crushed. The last thing I remember was the sound of firetrucks and police cars after the violent altercation and freak accident. The ambulance came; the fire department had to use the Jaws of Life to cut Ray's still body out of the wreck. He was dead. I was taken to the hospital by the ambulance. The doctor had to shave my head so that he could put fifteen stitches in. The doctor said that I slipped in and out of consciousness. Sexy called her wife-in-laws. She had a sense of urgency in her voice. My hoes came running to the hospital.

25

It had taken over an hour to cut Ray's dead body out of Sexy's destroyed Ford LTD. The truck driver only had minor injuries. The Long Beach police had a press conference. It was on every news station.

"The man hunt came to an end yesterday. The robbery suspect was killed in a robbery and carjacking of a local man and his girl-friend. The suspect was in the car when it was struck by a beer truck head-on, then slammed into a telephone pole. The truck driver was treated and released from the hospital after giving a statement to the police. Meanwhile, the victim is still hospitalized. He's being treated after being shot twice and sustaining a head injury. The man is being questioned by the Long Beach police. There is a fundraiser being set up to help with medical bills. For more information, call LBPD or Victims of Crime Organization."

*****

My mother, brothers, and sister stayed with me at the hospital until I was released. After that, I told them to go home.

"Daddy, can we get something else?" My girls took turns taking care of me.

"No, I'm fine. Has anyone heard from Baby Face?"

"Yeah, Daddy, she called Red Bone and Sexy. They went to pick her up," Goldie stated.

"Daddy, Velvet ordered some pizza, would you like a slice?" Naomi asked.

Velvet said, "Daddy, Candy is with Don. She said she would be home in thirty minutes. Candy said that she's going to stop and pick up your prescriptions."

"Naomi, I would like a slice of pizza."

"Okay, Daddy," she said as she headed to the kitchen.

"Hi, Daddy, how are you feeling?" Spicy asked.

"I'm feeling pretty good." Spicy took it the hardest; she cried while I was in the hospital. The nigga Jap Black was still sweating her. A lot of pimps saw what had happened on the news.

Some of them niggas got the story wrong. They said I was the robber and that I was killed. I stopped working Hollywood after pimps were trying to force my hoes to choose up. My bitches had to whoop a nigga and his bitches' asses. I told them to only work Long Beach and date their regulars. I couldn't wait till I was better; every pimp that told lies was going to get knocked for their hoes. I was mad as hell that the doctor had to shave my head to put those stitches in.

"Hi, Daddy, here's your sterile pad, tape, and bandages. I also got your prescriptions filled. They gave you two kinds of pain pills and antibiotics," Candy said while handing me her money she got from Don.

"Give those things to Baby Face. She's going to change the pads on the back of my head." My other hoes didn't like the blood. My head would be bloody every time she changed the bandages. The doctor said that my leg would keep bleeding for a while. Sexy and Red Bone took care of my leg and washed me up. Each ho did something to help me. The doctor told me to rest for a couple of weeks. After that, I would be going to rehab for my leg.

After three months, I was ready to go back to Hollywood with my team. I rented a limo for me and my team; we took a lot of pictures. The girls didn't mind me keeping my haircut. We all had a good time.

"What's up, Vinnie Mac?" It was AD.

"Man, some more of it," I said.

"Where are you at?"

"I'm in Hollywood, by the donut shop."

"Okay, I'll be pulling up in a minute." AD ended the call. He would come by every day and check up on me. He was a real friend and a brother to me.

"Vinnie, what's up with that nigga Jap? He keeps running his mouth about the bitch."

"Damn, that nigga still mad that I knocked him for the bitch? Man, that's why I only work the ho in Orange County or Long Beach. Out of sight, out of mind, ya dig?"

"I dig ya, man."

"AD, let's go and get a pimp's drink."

"Let's roll," AD said. The track was on full; there were hoes from on the top end of the ho stroll to the bottom of the ho stroll and on both sides of the street.

"AD, you know my ho Candy got this trick that's been dating her every day for the last few months. I'm thinking about telling her to stop seeing that prick. He's trying to buy the bitch."

AD said, "Vinnie, watch out for that mothafucka. Don't trust him with your bitch."

"Yea, I'm going to tell her to stop dating him. I've broken him for over $50,000. That's a lot of money, ya dig?"

*****

The next few months went by fast. The nigga Jap Black had left town finally. I had my whole team down and dirty in Hollywood. I had gotten Sexy another car; she was driving some of my hoes to work. Sexy, Goldie, and Velvet in one car; and me, Baby Face, and Spicy would ride together in another car. My hoes didn't mind riding with their Daddy. We were in Hollywood, and all my hoes were on the same corner when Candy called.

"What's up, Candy?"

"Daddy, me, Red Bone, and Naomi want to go to the other end of the track."

"Okay, y'all can go. I'll call later to see how things are."

"Daddy, this is Red. Can I get us a drink?"

"Yeah, Red Bone, it's okay." I ended the call.

A couple of hours had gone by. I decided to drive up on the other end to see what was going on with my team. My phone started ringing.

"Hello, what's up, Naomi?"

"Daddy, it's slow up here. Have you heard from Candy?"

"No, I haven't heard from her," I said.

"She's been gone for about an hour and a half."

"How much money do you guys have?"

"Daddy, I got $325, and Red Bone is on a date."

"Well, when you see them, have them call me."

"Okay, Daddy, I will." She hung up. My phone started ringing again.

"Hello."

"Hi, Daddy, it's Baby Face. I hit a lick for $850."

"Okay, where are you at?"

"I'm on Hollywood Boulevard and Western," she said.

"Stay right there. I'm on my way." I ended the call. My phone started to ring again.

"Hello."

"Daddy, it's Spicy. I've got $530. You want to come and get it?"

"Where you at?"

"I'm on the corner of Western and Sunset."

"Okay, I'm on my way." I hung up. My phone rang again. This time it was Candy.

"Daddy, I'm back. I got $800. I'm here with my wife-in-laws."

"Okay, you guys head back down this way. No! As a matter of fact, start heading back to the house. I'll meet y'all there." I hung up.

My team was in full swing. I was checking a lot of money. I kept having bad dreams. I couldn't figure out why. I was staying on top of my hoes just in case something happened, but them bitches could whoop the average person's ass. My mind kept telling me to watch out.

"Vinnie, this is Roach. I need to meet with you so we can talk."

"Roach, I'm in Inglewood right now. Let's meet in the morning," I said.

"All right. You want me to meet you at the store?"

"Yea, what time?" I asked.

Kevin said, "I'm going to Peaches's house so we can go to the bank and get some change for the store. Come about 10:30 a.m.?"

"Okay, I'll be there."

Kevin and Eddie were selling a lot of cocaine out of my sister's store. It was the only market that sold beer and wine in the hood. I grew up in that store. All the homies would come and hang out with us after school. Back then I worked from 4:00 p.m. till the store closed at 9:00 p.m. My brother-in-law let me and Roach sell weed to our friends. Bennie was his name; he bought us our first pound of weed. He was cool as hell. He really loved my sister. Peaches was pregnant with her second baby; that's why Eddie and Kevin worked in the store now, so they could help Eddie out. Bennie worked at the oil plant. The Shell oil company. He got a loan and was able to buy the store and two houses from Mr. Green. He kept the name Green's Market. My mother would help her out when Eddie and Kevin needed to cop some more coke or just wanted some time off. That's the good thing about owning a family business. You could do that without getting fired.

"Vinnie, what's up with you, boy? You don't come to the ghetto anymore. Are them girls keeping you that busy?" my sister asked. Peaches looked like she's going to pop.

"When's your baby due?" I said, smiling at her while pointing at her huge stomach.

"I'm due in two weeks. I'll be glad when I have this baby. I've gained sixty-five pounds."

"Yeah, I can tell."

"Be quiet, boy," she said.

"Peaches, where's Kevin and Eddie at?"

"They went to get me something to eat from Jack in the Box. They should be back anytime now." I started helping at the store. It had gotten busy.

"Hi, Vincent, how have you been? I haven't seen you in years," Ms. Hunter said.

"I've been fine, Ms. Hunter. And yourself?"

"I'm good. How's lil Vinnie and Debbie?"

"Ms. Hunter, lil Vinnie is fine. Ms. Price keeps him while Debbie's going to school." Ms. Hunter was Debbie's mom's first cousin. She lived down the street from the store. That's how I met Debbie, while I was working in the store. Peaches and Bennie had split up back then, and we moved out from his house. Then back in with my mother. That's when we got evicted out of the apartment and moved in with Ms. Williams. That's when I found out Debbie was pregnant, and I decided to go to Job Corps.

"Vinnie, here they come now," Peaches said.

"What's up, Vinnie?" Kevin said. His nickname was Roach; we started calling him that because he would steal our weed roaches.

"Man, so what's going on? Y'all called me."

Eddie said, "One of your hoes is buying dope from T. Powell and dating him. Your ho stole an ounce of cocaine and about $7,000. We need that shit back, Vincent."

Roach said, "Vincent, fuck that nigga. You should whoop that punk-ass nigga up for fucking with one of your hoes. You know that's G-code. Nobody fucks with the homie's bitch even if she is a ho."

"Kevin and Eddie, I'll meet you on Twenty-First in an hour."

"Okay, we'll be there."

I raced home. *One of them hoes is in trouble. The only way I'm not going to fire the bitch is if she comes clean. No, fuck that, them hoes know better than to date that nigga, plus the bitch has been spending my money on cocaine.* My phone started ringing. "Hello, who the fuck is this?" I said.

"Daddy, you must know."

"I must know what, bitch?"

"Daddy, please let me tell you what happened."

"Okay, bitch, meet me in the front of the apartments." I slammed the phone closed. It was Baby Face. *I should have known. That bitch has been buying coke from my homeboy.* I pulled up to the apartment building; she was standing in front. "Get in, ho, you better start talking now!"

"Daddy, please, let me tell you what happened," she said.

"Bitch, where's that dope at? That shit was my brother's."

"Daddy, it's up at the house. That nigga was talking shit about you. He was saying that he would take care of me and that you ain't shit. He said that he would whoop your ass. Daddy, he had been coming around and trying to sell me cocaine. I would tell him, 'No, I don't fuck with drugs.' He kept pulling out his money and coke. When I first talked to him, he asked where you were and if you all were from Twenty-First. After that, he would always try and talk to me. Daddy, that's why I robbed that trick-ass nigga. Daddy, I'm sorry, please don't whoop me."

"Bitch, I ain't going to whoop you, but I'm going to fuck his ass up."

I called Kevin and Eddie. We set a trap for that disrespectful-ass nigga. I had Baby Face call and tell him that she was sorry and that she would meet him and give him the money and coke back if he promised not to tell. He wanted to fuck her bad. She told him to meet her on Chestnut and PCH, in the alley behind the restaurant. I, Eddie, and Kevin hid behind a big screen trash can; she was standing in the front of it. We spotted his blue Nova coming up the alley.

"Hey, get in," T. Powell said.

"No, you get out, and let's talk first," she said.

"Come on, baby, I'm not going to do anything to you. I've always wanted you since the first time that buster Vincent brought you on Twenty-First. The nigga's always bragging about how good your pussy was and how great you head game is. A real nigga wouldn't tell how his woman's sex was."

Baby Face said, "Look, here's the money. Get out and count it. I've got the cocaine across the street at the poolside motel."

T. Powell said, "You got us a room? Damn, lil momma, you're really making me want you."

"Well, at least get out and count the money. It's all here. The only thing I did was pay for the room," she said. He pulled his car closer to the trash can, turned it off, and got out.

"Now give me that money so I can count it," he said as he walked up closer to her. She acted like she was going to give it to him, then she chopped him in the throat. Eddie, Kevin, and I came from behind the trash can.

"Yeah, muthafucka, you trick-ass nigga." I had a bottle in my left hand. *Crack. Crack.* I hit that punk upside his head. He stumbled back; that hat he had on stopped the bottle from knocking his ass out.

T. Powell said, "Put the bottle down, nigga, let's fight." I threw the bottle down and gave a roundhouse kick to his chest. It knocked him down.

"Get his ass, Daddy, fuck that bitch up," Baby Face yelled. He grabbed my legs and tried to trip me. I socked him in the jaw. He grabbed my shirt. I knocked his hand, tearing it. He swung; it landed. I shook it off. I hit him with a left then a right; he stumbled. I kicked him under the chin; he fell back. I landed another left. That knocked him out.

"Baby Face, take that nigga's shoestrings out and pull his shirt and pants off." Once she finished, I told her to pour the lighter fluid on his shoes. Once she was done, I poured some on his hat. I lit his ass up, then I poured water in his face; he woke up, jumped up, and ran. We laughed our asses off. "That nigga was running like a mothafucka. Did you see how he tried to kick his shoes off? That stupid nigga started patting his head to put it out. That will hold his ass. He thought he was running shit. It turned out that the only thing he was running was his mouth," I said.

"Vinnie, that's what he gets fucking with your girl," Kevin said.

"Yeah, bro, fuck that punk ass. He's lucky it was you he fought. I would have knocked his teeth out if it was me," Eddie said. I gave Eddie and Kevin their money and cocaine back once we got to Eddie's house.

"All right, y'all, I'm gone." Baby Face and I jumped into my car and pulled off. On our way home, Baby Face apologized again. "Baby Face, I thank you for standing up for me." I kissed her and rubbed her hand as I drove down PCH.

26

"That punk-ass nigga ran fast as hell down that alley," I told my cousins Shawn and Shannon. We all started cracking up.

"Damn, cuz, you fucked his ass up," Shawn said.

"Yeah, he broke the G-code. You don't fuck with the homie's bitch," Eddie said. Shannon gave me my money back; they couldn't find Stone's ass. After they were done handling their business, we all drove to the fish market—"you buy, we fry." I told my cousins that if I got some more information on the nigga Stone, I would let them know. I think he must have gone back to Texas. If he knew what was good for him, he would have gone home. My cousins were going to bust a cap in his ass. After we finished with lunch, we drove back to the Jordan Downs projects so Eddie and Kevin could pick up the cocaine they had bought from our cousins.

"All right, cuz, we'll see you later."

We gave them daps and drove off. It had been two weeks since we had heard anything about T. Powell. He had a couple of brothers, but we didn't give a fuck. We'll fuck them up too. Their brother was out of pocket doing that punk-ass shit. Fuck all of them.

*****

"Get out the car now," the police said. It was that fucking, ass Boline. "Keep your hands where I can see them." He pulled me out and led me to the police car. I was driving my Cadillac. My mother told me not to drive that car in Long Beach. I didn't listen. Now this mothafucka police was all over my ass. He was driving by himself. "Mr. Fuckin' Jordan, how the fuck are you?"

"I was fine until I saw your punk ass."

He slapped me right across my face. "Asshole, give me a reason to shoot your black nigger ass." He put handcuffs on me and put me in the back of the police car. That muthafucka tore my car up. He had taken $2,000 out of my pockets. He came back to the police car. "I heard you and you brothers robbed a man in the alley and then set him on fire. You're lucky that asshole didn't call the PD. I'd love to lock your nigger pimp-ass up. How many whores do you have? Where's that pretty little thing that was with you the last time I saw you?" he said. I didn't say anything. He jabbed me in the ribs. "You heard me, Jordan."

"Where's your momma at, mothafucka?" He hit me in the back with the billy club.

"You're a smart-ass. You think that I don't know where you live, don't you, pimp? I know you live on Ocean across the street from the Copper Penny. You're living high on the hog. I bust my ass busting mothafuckas like you, and you're making all that money selling bitches' asses. Well, I'm going to let your sorry ass go for now, but if I hear anything else from that black-ass nigger you and your brothers set on fire, I'll be at your fucking front door. I'm going to bust your ass." He took the handcuffs off. The muthafucka kept my money. "Have a nice day, Mr. Jordan," he said as he drove off. The asshole threw my keys; it took ten minutes to find them. I didn't give a fuck that, that asshole cop knew where I lived. My bitches were solid; they weren't going to tell them anything. Fuck the LBPD.

*****

"Get off me, get off!" The mothafucka was dragging me by my hair. "Let me go!" I kept swinging at him. He ripped off my shirt. I started running. I could hear glass breaking. He was throwing bottles. *Blam, blam.* I'm shot. "Help! Help! Help me!" Nobody was around. I was bleeding. I jumped into my car. I drove really fast. I could hear a truck horn blowing. "Don't, don't!" The truck was coming fast.

The mothafucka was standing on the truck shooting at me. I've got to duck. I could hear my car window breaking. "No, no, stop, stop!"

"Daddy, Daddy, wake up!" It was Goldie. "Daddy, you're having those nightmares again. Are you all right?" she asked. I was back in my room in my bed. I let one of my hoes sleep with me each night.

"Damn, light me a Newport. What time is it?"

"Daddy, it's 3:30 a.m.," she said.

"I'm sorry about that. I didn't mean to wake you up," I said.

"That's okay, Daddy. I'm glad I was in here with you. Daddy, you were yelling in your sleep. What happened?"

"It was the same dream again. I've been having bad dreams for a while. I don't know who is trying to kill me in my dreams, but they won't stop." I got up and walked into the living room. I pulled the curtains back to look at the ocean. That seemed to calm me down. I was being careful; that wasn't cool. I don't know why I was having these nightmares; it seemed like it was trying to tell me something. I just didn't know what.

*****

"Hi, Daddy, I've got $430. Do you want to come and break me for it?" Naomi said.

"I'll be down that way in about thirty minutes. Just keep it in your shoe."

"Okay, Daddy, I will." She hung up.

I was working Long Beach, Orange County, Hollywood, and Inglewood. I stayed on the move with my team. I couldn't get that dream out of my mind. I thought it meant to stay out of the way of Boline. He came on duty at 4:00 p.m. I never worked Long Beach at that time. That bitch-ass police wasn't going to get any more money from me. I was on top of my game. I had eight of the finest hoes on any ho stroll. Nigga was jealous and full of envy. Some of my own homeboys were envious of me. My pimping was on top of the world. I felt untouchable. I had over thirty tailor-made suits with my name in them. I had full-length mink coats, waistline minks, and custom-made jewelry on. Rolex watches and seven fly cars.

"What's up, Mac? I haven't seen you in a minute."

"Vinnie Mac, look at you. The streets are talking about you. You're on the top. How's your mom doing?" Mac and my mom were good friends. They used to work at big nightclubs.

"She's all right. I'll tell her you asked about her," I said. I hadn't been to Mac's shop since I started wearing my hair in a fade haircut. I talked to Mac for a while. I always respected Mac's opinion about things. He told me to watch my back, that niggas were jealous of me.

He said, "When you're on the top, everyone wants to be your friend, but when your down and out, where do all the people go?" That always stuck on my mind. I missed my friend and brother AD; he was in New York. I wanted to go there, but I couldn't right now. I had things to take care of. I liked going to see little Vinnie; he was three years old now. He was just starting to talk good. I loved my son. Ms. Price took good care of lil Vinnie; she treated him like he was her son. I always gave her anything she wanted; that was my second mother, even though Debbie and I weren't together anymore.

*****

"On the floor now!" the man with the mask ordered my sister, Ms. Hunter, and my mother. One was behind the counter, and another was behind the meat counter. "Where's the safe?" It was another person out in the front of the store. The one behind the counter, where the cash register was, walked over my sister and told her to get up. He walked her behind the meat counter. "Open the safe right now, bitch. Open it!" He slapped my sister hard in the face.

My mother yelled, "Don't hurt her. Don't hurt my daughter." The other man ran over and kicked my mother in the face and stomped her hand.

"Shut the fuck up, old lady!" he yelled. My sister opened the safe. They took all the money and dope then ran out of the store. The whole robbery only took a couple of minutes. It seemed like a lifetime to my family. One thing's for sure: it was somebody that knew us. They knew there were drugs in the safe.

*****

It's been a month since the robbery. My mother was mad as hell at all of us. She said it was our fault that my sister's store got hit by them stickup boys. My mother had to get five stiches in her lip, from them niggas kicking her in the face. Eddie and Kevin were out to kill, and so was I. My brothers lost $65,000 in cash and a kilo of cocaine. My sister wanted to call the police, but we told her not to. The store was in Boline's area. The last thing we needed was for that asshole to get wind of what happened at the store. I gave Eddie and Kevin enough money to buy a half kilo of cocaine and $5,000 in cash. We told my sister, Ms. Hunter, and my mother not to tell anyone what had happened. We didn't tell the homies what had happened, because it was probably one of them, or they had put somebody up on the lick. Eddie was from Twenty-First g's, and my lil brother Roach was from the rolling twenties; our younger brother split the neighborhood up. They didn't get along with each other. One thing's for sure, somebody had set up our family to get robbed.

*****

"Daddy, Don wants to see me. He's been begging to date me," Candy said. I had stopped my hoes from working in Long Beach on PCH, but I did let them date regulars they had from the LBC. It had been months since I let Candy see Don.

"Okay, Candy, you can date him, but if he trips on you, you let me know so I can knock his ass out."

"Daddy, I can take care of myself. You made sure of that sending all of us to judo class. Daddy, I know you got my back, and thank you," she said.

"Where's he going to meet you at?" I asked.

"He's going to pick me up on Tenth and Cherry, Daddy."

"At what time?"

"He said around 3:00 p.m., after he gets off work."

"Okay, and for how long?"

"Daddy, Don said he wants to see me for three hours," Candy said.

"Well, you'll have to stay home after that. Your wife-in-laws are going to work in Inglewood and Hollywood after that."

"Okay, Daddy, Don's got $900 off me."

"Cool, I'll drop you off. Make sure you take your keys with you. Don't let him drop you off by the penthouse, let him drop you off at Von's. I need some fresh fruits. I'll give you a list. After that, you catch a cab home."

"I will, Daddy," Candy said.

*****

"Don, the boss wants to see you. He told me to tell you to get to his office now," his coworker told him. Don jumped into his truck and headed to the main office. Don pulled up and parked in the company's parking lot. He walked in, and Don Wheeler, the real owner of the construction, was behind his desk. Everybody else had gone home.

"Don, pull up a chair."

"Yes, sir, Mr. Wheeler."

"Don, how long have we known each other?"

"Well, Mr. Wheeler, about fifteen years. Why do you ask?"

"Don, you've been stealing from the company's bank account."

"Mr. Wheeler, it wasn't me."

"Yes, Don, it was you. You're the only one it could have been. $70,000 is missing out of that account. I'm sorry, but you're fired."

"Please, Mr. Wheeler, I'll pay you back," Don said.

"No, Don, you're fired, get out now," Mr. Wheeler said.

Don got up and acted like he was going to leave then pulled out a gun and fired four rounds into Mr. Wheeler's chest. It killed him instantly. Don dragged his body out of the office then mixed up some cement. He stuffed his boss's body in a fifty-gallon drum and filled it with cement. He also cleaned up the blood. The boss always took business trips, plus he was single and didn't have a girlfriend. Don knew that his boss only dated hoes for sex and companionship. That made it perfect for Don. He had killed his boss, and nobody would find out. Don signed the paychecks of his coworkers. Don could also draw money out from the business account. Don also did the bids for jobs. It was a perfect crime. The truth was that he was a pathological liar. He lied because he can. He lied because he could get away with it. He lied for the pleasure of it. He lied because he enjoyed it. He lied because he's good at it. He was dedicated to lying. His words were his tools and instruments; now he's a murderer on top of that. Now he's meeting Candy for $900 and for three hours.

"Hi, Candy, get in. How have you been?"

"I'm fine, Don, and you?"

"I've been working hard and thinking about you. Here, I've got something for you." He pulled out a small box. It had a diamond bracelet in it.

"Don, it's beautiful, thank you," Candy said while kissing him on the side of the jaw. Don had over $20,000 on him.

He said, "Look, Candy, I can give you everything you need," showing her all the cash.

"Come on, Don, we've been through this before. I'm not leaving Vinnie," Candy said.

Don rented a room at the beach motel. "Candy, how much will it cost for you to spend the night with me?" Don asked.

"Don, give me $3,000, and I'll stay until tomorrow."

"You got it." Don pulled out $3,000 and handed it to Candy.

"Don, I'll be right back. I need to call Vinnie and tell him.

"Daddy, Don wants me to spend the night with him. He's going to give me $3,000. Daddy, he's got at least $15,000 or more on him," she stated.

"Okay, Candy, it's cool. Where are you at?"

"I'm at the beach motel, room 214."

"How do you feel, Candy?"

"Oh, Daddy, he gave me a diamond bracelet too. I'm okay."

"Okay then, I'll see you tomorrow."

"Okay, Daddy, I'll be ready at checkout time."

27

"Vincent, meet us at the Jack in the Box on PCH."

"I'll be there in twenty minutes. That was Kevin. He wants me to meet them at the Jack in the Box," I stated. My mother was at the bookie joint. She wanted me to drop her off at my aunt's house. I had taken her car to get the oil changed. I told them at the shop that I would be back before 5:00 p.m. to pick up my mother's car.

"Daddy, you want me to keep driving, or do you want to go home and get another car?" Red Bone asked.

"No. Mom is waiting in the front of Robert Charles's house. We will stop by, pick her up, and then you can drive me to meet my brothers."

"Okay, Daddy, I see your mother standing in the front."

"Hi, Momma, what's up with you?"

"Nothing much, Vincent. When will my car be ready?" she asked.

"Momma, it will be ready at 5:00 p.m. I'm going to have Red Bone take you to pick it up."

"Hi, Red, are you going to stay here with me until my car is ready?"

"I don't know, Momma, it's up to Vinnie," Red Bone said.

"Vincent, can she stay with me? I want her to help me pick out some horses."

"Yeah, Momma, she can stay with you, but she's going to drop me off and then come back." Red Bone pulled up at my aunt's.

My mother was getting out when she said, "Vincent, let me have some money. I'll pay you back when I get my check."

"Here, Mom, here's two hundred."

"Thank you, son," she said.

"Okay, Momma. Red will be back in a minute." She pulled up at Jack in the Box and let me out.

"Okay, Daddy, I'll see you later."

"I'll call you later," I said, and she pulled off.

"What's up, Roach, where's Eddie?"

"He's in the restroom." Just then he came walking out. I walked up to the counter and ordered. Both of them already had their food. "Vincent, we think we know who robbed Peaches's store."

"Who was it?" I asked.

"Do you know that nigga named Kenny?" Roach asked.

"Who in the fuck is Kenny?"

"That's that nigga Ray's cousin. The one that was robbing all those stores and shot you—that Ray," Eddie said.

"You mean that cherm-head nigga?"

"Yea, that's him. Check this shit out. Him, that nigga T. Powell, and that bitch Rohda—them mothafuckas robbed us. Kenny is the one that kicked Mom in the face. The bitch Rohda was driving," Eddie said.

Roach said, "Vinnie, we gonna kill them mothafuckas. After we break Kenny's neck. That bitch-ass nigga T. Powell's gonna get his throat cut. After we're done with them, we're going to make that bitch watch, and then we're gonna fuck that bitch in the ass then cut her from asshole to elbow. Then I'm going to cut T. Powell's dick off and stick it in Rohda's mouth."

"Eddie, we need to calm down and take our time. I'm not trying to go to jail for the rest of my life. We need to plan this shit out," I said.

Eddie said, "I'm madder than hell. We should have killed that nigga T. Powell the first time."

Roach said, "Vinnie, that bitch Pam told us that she was with them the day of the store robbery. She said that Rohda and T. Powell were talking about hitting a big lick and that Kenny was going to go with them, and they had to pick him up. Rohda was driving her mother's car. Pam also told us where Rohda's mother lives and that she keeps her car parked in the driveway."

"We had asked Peaches, Momma, and Ms. Hunter what kind of car it was on the day the store was hit. It was a brown station wagon."

I jumped in the car with my brothers, and we drove past Rohda's mother's house; the car was parked in the driveway, just like Pam said.

"Kevin, did she tell you where they are at now?"

"Pam said they came back to her house with a bag of money and a bunch of cocaine. They had divided the money and dope up. Pam said Rohda and T. Powell left together. Kenny stayed at her house for a couple of days. Pam also told us that Kenny had about $20,000 and some ounce of cocaine, and Kenny gave her $2,000 and an ounce of coke. Kenny bought a tan Camaro, with a bird sticker on the back window. She said she put him out because he got high and kept pulling his gun out and looking out the window. She said that Kenny wouldn't let her out of her own house for two days. She told him he had to leave. Kenny left early in the morning. Rohda and T. Powell left in a cab."

"Did she tell you where they went?"

"No," Eddie said. I asked, "Where is pam at now?"

"Pam showed us where Rohda's mom lived. Then we took her on a long drive and dropped her off at the end of Belmont Pier. She's sleeping with the fish," Kevin said.

*****

"Daddy, come and get me. I hit a lick for $3,000," Baby Face said.

"Where you at, Baby?"

"I'm on the Westside of Long Beach on Harbor and PCH."

"I'm on my way." I ended the call. I got in the Chevy, the one I got for Naomi. I backed out my mother's driveway and headed to pick up my ho.

I always went to my mother's house while my hoes worked in Long Beach; my mother stayed right off the ho stroll on Locust. On my way to pick up Baby, I saw a Camaro with a bird in the back, and it was tan. *Fuck, that's Kenny's car.* I couldn't turn around. I had to pick up Baby Face.

"Jump in, Baby."

"Thanks, Daddy. That trick dropped me off at Taco Bell. I didn't want to have to fight with that asshole if he found out his money was gone." I jumped on the 710 Long Beach freeway and headed downtown. I got off on Ocean then drove Baby Face to the penthouse.

"Okay, Baby, you go upstairs and kick back. You're done for the day. Your coke is under the couch in the living room. Go in my room and get the weed." I peeled off and headed for Kenny's mother's house. The windows were tinted on the Chevy Impala. I pulled over and parked. I waited for over an hour, but he didn't show up. I called my brothers and let them know that I had seen Kenny's car. I told them that I couldn't turn around and follow him because Baby Face had robbed a trick, and I had to rush and pick her up.

I drove by Kenny's mother's house every day looking for that car. It had been over two months since Pam told us who had robbed Peaches's store. T. Powell and Rohda were nowhere to be found. We took turns staking out Kenny's mother's house. If that mothafucka showed up, his ass was going to be leaking. I had noticed that Kenny was coming from the Westside. I drove all over Long Beach. I went to every motel in Long Beach. There was no sign of any of them. They had plenty of money; they could be hiding anywhere. I kept on looking; them niggas were dead once we got a hold of them.

*****

I had my hoes on automatic; they would set the alarm clock and get up and go to work. I had them working in Orange County on Harbor by Disneyland; the ho stroll was on full. I never told my hoes what had happened at the store. I didn't want to scare any of my hoes. Pimping is one thing, and killing was another thing. The less they knew, the better off I was. After Baby Face hit that lick for the nine grand, and I had seen Kenny, I stopped my hoes from working Long Beach. Candy was still seeing Don. They would get a room at the beach motel; it wasn't in the hood. It was right on the beach. The beach was 90 percent white folks.

I didn't have to worry about her. Don was spending $1,000 every other day. Eddie and Kevin continued to sell cocaine out of the store. They stopped my sister and Ms. Hunter from working, then Ms. Hunter still worked for my sister, but not in the store. She would help my sister with her two kids and cook and clean up my sister's house.

28

"Hi, Don, thanks for the flowers. How long would you like to see me today?" Candy said.

Don said, "I want to see you for the rest of my life."

Candy smiled and said, "Don, that's sweet. You're one of my friends. But it's business with us."

"I know, but I still care for you, and if you get tired of this business, you can come and live with me. Candy, I really care for you. I would love for you to be my wife."

"Okay, Don, I will keep that in mind."

Don pulled in to the motel and said, "I'll only spend two hours with you today. I've got a lot of things I've got to do." He handed her $400 in an envelope.

"Don, thank you." He and Candy headed to room 217 at the beach motel. Once they were in the room, Don got undressed then pulled out some coke. He made a couple of lines out of the cocaine.

"Candy, would you like a line of this?"

Candy was getting undressed and said, "No, Don, I don't mess with that shit. You know that."

Don got mad for the first time and said, "You date strange men all day, but you don't get high. Yeah, right."

"Don, don't ever talk to me like that again."

"I'm sorry about that, Candy, I've got a lot on my mind today," he said as he snorted the line of blow. They finished dating, and Don let Candy keep the room. He kissed her on the side of the jaw then went downstairs, got into his truck, and pulled out of the parking lot.

"Hi, Daddy, I'm done with my date. Can you come and pick me up? I need to talk to you."

"Yeah, Candy, I'll be there in fifteen minutes. I'm driving in your car. I'll blow when I'm out in front of the motel room." I got Candy a Cadillac Seville. It was baby blue and real clean.

Don had pulled down the street from the motel and parked. He was waiting to see who was picking Candy up. He had killed his boss so he could have the woman of his dreams. He had become obsessed with Candy and would kill anyone that came between them.

I pulled up in front of the room and blew the horn. Candy came out and was walking from the motel room. She was wearing a black minidress with a baby-blue thick belt and baby-blue thigh-high boots with a baby-blue purse. I had to admit she was looking good. I got on the passenger side so she could drive her car.

"Hi, Daddy, thanks for coming to pick me up."

"So tell me, what's on your mind?"

"Daddy, it's Don. He's starting to act…strange. Talking about marrying me. The mothafucka pulled out some coke and was snorting it. I'm starting to have bad vibes around him. He seems to be obsessed with me. Daddy, Don has given me over $80,000. He's starting to act like his little dick ass owns me. I don't want to see him for a while."

"Okay, Candy, if that's the way you feel, then you don't have to date him again." She started up her car, and we pulled out of the motel.

Don was pissed off. *That fucking pimp has to go. He's got my woman, and he needs to disappear. I'm going to make sure the black nigger pays for pimping on Candy. Then she will be mine.* Don pulled off after he finished daydreaming.

*****

I was on my way to pick up Cherri from the Greyhound. She finished doing her time after that fight she had. The prison added more time to her sentence. I took care of her while she did her time. Cherri was my first real ho. I had love for her. The bitch gave me the claps; my dick was sore, and it burned every time I had to pee. We had to go to the health department. Both of us got treated for STD. The doctor gave me a shot in the ass and stuck a long Q-tip in my dick. After that, we had to go pick up some pills. We had to take them for a week. The doctor told us not to drink alcohol. I pulled up in front of CIW (California Institution for Women). Cherri was standing waiting for me. I was driving my Rolls-Royce. The other prisoners could see Cherri getting into the car. Those bitches whistled and cheered as we pulled off.

"Hi, Daddy, I missed you. This is a very nice Rolls-Royce. I told them hoes you were coming in this car. That's why they were acting like that."

"I had to drive my best car for you, Cherri. You were the one that helped me start my stable of hoes. I owe it to you."

"Vinnie Mac, you were going to do that anyway, but thanks," she said. I took her to Sizzlers for lunch. We had a great time talking over lunch. I didn't tell her about the store robbery or that the bitch Rohda had anything to do with it. Cherri had gained some weight, her ass was thick, her skin had cleared up, and her breast was looking cool. She had her hair in braids. I had decided to take her shopping in downtown Los Angeles. I made it back to LA in an hour and a half. We parked down by the alley. I pulled into the parking lot and parked. Cherri kept rubbing on my dick. I knew she wanted to fuck. What the hell, I might as well put some dick on the ho. We walked, talked, and shopped. I got her a long black wig; panties and bras to match; seven minidresses; seven pairs of different kinds of shoes, boots, and sandals. I also got her a coat, blue jeans, and blouses. We were in the Alley for a couple of hours. It was noon once we got back into the Rolls. Next we headed to a McDonald's so she could change clothes. While she changed clothes, I was thinking about how we had to kill her friend Pam, and we were going to do the same thing to that bitch Rohda. Cherri came back to the car, and the next stop was the parole officer. Once we were done with that, I took her to get a room. I pulled into the beach motel. I got my favorite room. As we were walking to the suite, I noticed a truck that had Don's construction company logo on both sides of the doors. It was Candy's regular trick

Don. I wondered why he was there. It only took a minute. Don and another bitch came out of the room. I turned my head, and Cherri and I headed to the suite. I remembered that ho Don was with. It was one of Max-a-Million's bitches. I had been sweating that ho in Hollywood.

Me and Cherri made love and had a couple of drinks. After that, I took her to dinner. My other hoes were on automatic. I had them in Orange County. They would get a chance to meet Cherri tomorrow. Cherri seemed to be a little jealous of her wife-in-laws. My pimping had grown so much when she was gone that she needed to find a way to deal with it. My penthouse was full. I slept with a different girl every night. One thing's for sure: I would have to get another spot if I knocked any more hoes. Sexy, Red Bone, Velvet, and Goldie hooked Cherri up with some of their regulars. Baby Face didn't have any regulars. She dipped into all her tricks' pockets if she caught them slipping. She was a very good thief. She had also taught Sexy how to steal money from tricks. That bitch Cherri didn't want me to change her name. The bitch would tell my other hoes about the way me and her fucked and what we talked about. That shit I didn't allow. I had to check that bitch. I moved her into the suite at the beach motel. The bitch started fucking with different women in prison. All my other hoes weren't gay. They didn't like the way Cherri stared at them when they got out of the shower. Once they started to notice that, the bitch Cherri stared at them like she had a dick and wanted to fuck them. She also tried to tell them what to do. Cherri didn't take the time to find out my hoes all knew judo. Them bitches could whoop the hell out of her. The bitch ended up going back to prison on a violation of parole. The bitch was getting high off PCP cherm. That's why she acted strange. I wrote the bitch, firing her. I did give the ho $500 to help her out. I knew one thing: a scorned woman is a very vindictive bitch. I caught Cherri looking at the naked silhouette of Spicy in the shower. The bitch Cherri was high off that cherm shit. The bitch had on jeans and had her finger in her pussy, jacking off as she watched Spicy in the shower. That's why I moved the bitch out. The only mothafucka that was doing any fucking in my house was me.

29

"Hi, what's up?" Rohda asked.

"What the fuck are you talking about 'hi, what's up'? The rent is behind. You've been gone for months. You left me for dead. Bitch, you better have a damn good reason for leaving me like this. My family has called the jails, hospitals, and our friends are looking for you. Bitch, you know I can't hustle because of them punk-ass niggas robbing me and breaking my arms and legs. Your mothafucking ass runs off and don't call or nothing."

"My damn phone is fin to be turned off."

"Where are you at, bitch?"

"If you give me a chance to talk, I'll tell you.

"Daddy, I hit a huge lick."

"Keep talking."

"Remember when I left to go to my momma's house?"

"Bitch, how can I forget?"

"Well, I ran into somebody I grew up with. He told me about this plan he had. It was to rob this store."

"Bitch, who the fuck is he?"

"Daddy, please let me finish."

"Go ahead, I'm listening."

"It turned out to be Vinnie's sister's store, and his brothers were selling coke out of the store. He told me that Vinnie's sister, mother, and another lady worked in the morning. He said that Vinnie's brother sold dope in the evening starting at 4:00 p.m., so me, him, and his homebody Kenny hit the store around 11:30 a.m. before lunch. Daddy, guess how much money it was?"

"Bitch, just tell me."

"Okay, Daddy, listen. The nigga kicked Vinnie's mom in the face, and T. Powell slapped his sister up and made her open the safe. Daddy, all I did was drive the getaway car."

"Bitch, tell me about the money. How much did you get? And I want to know now!"

"Okay, I fin to tell you, but, Daddy, listen first. Kenny and T. Powell ran to the car, and I pulled out. We went to Pam's house and divided the money and cocaine up. Daddy, I got $20,000 and four ounces of coke."

"Bitch, where are you now?"

"Daddy, I'm trying to tell you. After that, me and T. Powell caught a cab to Los Angeles. We got a room at the Best Western on Sixth off Western. It's in the cut.

"Daddy, T. Powell is a trick. He has given me over $5,000 of his money, and he's paying for the room. Daddy, we can get this mothafucka for the rest of the cocaine and money."

"Okay, tell me how and when, and I'll send some niggas over there."

"Daddy, he has a gun on him. I'm going to take the ammo out. He's all fucked up on coke. It's a store across the street. I'm going to tell him that I need tampons and that I'll be right back. You have somebody come, and I'll give them the key, and they can walk right in on him. He has over $10,000 and three and a half ounces of cocaine."

"I'm going to have my cousins meet you at the store."

"Who, B. Boy and Lil Boy?"

"Yeah, bitch. I'm coming to pick you up, and you give them the key."

"Okay, Daddy, I'm going to park on the side of the store."

*****

"Hi, Daddy, I really missed you."

"Shut up, bitch. Hurry up and get in." Rohda got in, gave Mac Ton the money and coke she had. Then Rohda gave him the room key.

"What room is it, and which floor is the room on?" Mac Ton asked.

"Daddy, it's on the third floor to rooms past the elevator. It's room 317. I took all the ammo out of the magazine and the one that was in the gun."

"Give me a kiss. You done good." Mac Ton signaled to his cousins in the car behind them. His cousins came to Mac Ton's car. Rohda told B. Boy and Lil Boy how to get to the room by the stairs. After she was done telling them, Mac Ton told them to meet them at his house. Mac Ton and Rohda pulled off in his Cadillac.

*****

"You back already," T. Powell called out from the bathroom; he was taking a shit, with a mirror in his hand full of coke. He was snorting a line while he was using the bathroom. B. Boy and Lil Boy crept into the room. *Boom.* B. Boy kicked the bathroom door in.

"On the ground, mothafucka. Now." Lil Boy hit T. Powell in the head with a .45 pistol. Blood began to roll down T. Powell's face. B. Boy socked him in the jaw. T. Powell fell to the floor with his pants around his ankles. "Where's the money and coke at?"

"I don't have any money. Please, I don't." Lil Boy started pistol-whooping his ass.

"Where's it at? Tell me now, or I'm going to kill your ass."

"Okay, okay, I'll tell you. It's under the bed." B. Boy dragged T. Powell's ass into the living room with his underwear still down around his ankles.

"Where, mothafucka?" Lil Boy kicked him right in the nuts. T. Powell screamed. B. Boy grabbed him around his throat.

"Shut the fuck up, ho-ass nigga." He was choking T. Powell to death. T. Powell started pointing to the closet.

"It's, it's in there, it's in the closet." Lil Boy looked in the closet, and the money and dope were under some pants. After they got all the coke and money, Lil Boy knocked T. Powell out. They wiped all the fingerprints off everything.

"Let's kill his ass."

"No, Mac Ton told us not to kill him," B. Boy said.

Once B. Boy and Lil Boy got in the car and drove off, they called Mac Ton.

"Hey, it's B. We got the stash. We're on our way to meet you."

*****

"Did you do what I told you?"

"Yeah, Mac Ton, we cleaned up all the fingerprints, and we left his punk ass knocked out. The mothafucka was on the toilet when we entered the room. We dragged his ass out, pistol-whooped him until he told us where he had stashed the money and cocaine at." Mac Ton counted the money; it was a little over $10,000, and there were two and a half ounces of coke.

"Man, where's the rest of the cocaine at?"

"Man, that was all of it," B. Boy said.

"Rohda, get your ass in here."

"Yes, Daddy."

"You told me it was three and a half ounces of cocaine."

"It was, Daddy."

"Okay, then you can go back into the bedroom." Rohda went back in the room to finish getting dressed and snorting her coke.

"Mac Ton, we must have left an ounce there," Lil Boy said.

"Well, that's on y'all." Mac Ton divided up the money; he gave B. Boy $2,500 and an ounce of coke. Then he gave Lil Boy $2,500 and a half ounce of coke. Mac Ton kept one and a half ounces of cocaine and a little over $5,000.

"Thanks, cousin." They both were happy to get the money and dope from the robbery. B. Boy and Lil Boy stashed their dope and headed to the door. "All right, we're out of here, Mac Ton."

"Okay, I'll holler at y'all later." Mac Ton closed the door and made sure it was locked. Rohda made it back home with a great come up. Mac Ton was glad to see her.

"Baby, you know I wouldn't let you down."

"I know, bitch, but it sure took you long enough."

"Daddy, you're crazy."

"Yeah, I'm crazy about you. Now pass me the blow."

*****

T. Powell's phone was ringing when he came to. "Fuck, hello."

"Man, it's Kenny, I called you ten times. Is everything all right? You sound funny."

"Man, get over here, I've been robbed."

"What the fuck! I'm on my way." Kenny hung up the phone. He jumped into his Camaro and burned rubber trying to hurry up and get to T. Powell. Kenny ran up the back stairs and made it to the room. *Knock, knock, knock.*

"Who is it?"

"It's me, Kenny." T. Powell unlocked and let him in. "So tell me what the fuck happened." T. Powell had cleaned himself up by the time Kenny got there. T. Powell found the ounce the jackers left behind, and he had $437 in his pocket. T. Powell filled Kenny on what had happened. The bitch Rohda had set him up.

Kenny said, "Man, that's some fucked-up shit. That dirty-ass bitch. We put the ho up on the move, and the ungrateful bitch had you robbed. Man, if I see that bitch, we're going to kill her ass."

T. Powell said, "What's up with Pam? Have you seen her?"

"Man, that's why I was calling you. I haven't seen her in a while. I've been by her house, but nobody answers. I also went by her sister's and mother's, but they haven't seen or heard from her. Pam's mother said that she always does shit like that. Don't worry, Pam will pop up. I wonder if she was in on jacking you for your shit."

"I don't know, but what I do know is that the ho Rohda was in on it. Them niggas had her key."

"Well, man, so what's next?" Kenny asked.

T. Powell said, "I'm going to pack my shit up and get a room in Wilmington of PCH. It's cool over there. Is anybody talking about us? Eddie, Kevin, and Vincent's sister's store getting robbed?"

"Man, nobody's saying anything," Kenny replied.

"You know what that means?"

"No, what?" Kenny asked.

"That means they're looking to find out who did it. They don't want anybody to know. Did the police take reports?"

"I didn't hear anything about the police. Do you think they know it was us?" Kenny said.

T. Powell said, "Me too. I've got a lot of my money left. We can get a room together." T. Powell and Kenny walked across the street and got some liquor. T. Powell finished packing up, and they headed to Wilmington.

30

"Hi, Daddy, where are you at?"

"I'm at my mom's house."

"Me and Goldie had a double date for $150 each. Do you want to come and pick it up?"

"Velvet, how much do you have altogether?"

"I've had two dates. I got $70 from my other date."

"So you have $220?"

"Yeah, Daddy."

"Where's Goldie?"

"She's at the motel with another date. Daddy, let me call you back. A trick just pulled over for me."

"All right, call me back once you're done." I ended the call.

I had Red Bone and Spicy working on Temple and PCH. Sexy and Baby Face worked on Pine and PCH. Goldie and Velvet were working the Westside of Long Beach on Harbor and PCH. I moved Baby Face and Sexy off the Westside after Baby Face hit that last lick. Both of them knew how to peel tricks for their wallets. All my hoes had cars now except for Baby Face. She didn't know how to drive. And didn't want to learn. She told me she was in a wreck and that it scared her to drive. We—I and the rest of my team—now have eleven cars. It was a parking lot down the street from the street from the tower apartments. I had my hoes park their cars in the lot. I kept my Rolls in a storage unit. I parked my Cadillac, 450 SL Benz, and Lincoln Continental in the underground parking lot at the apartments. We had a private elevator, so my hoes would take the elevator down to the underground parking and get in the Lincoln and Benz, drive to the parking where the other cars were parked, leave the two cars, and then jump into the other cars and head off to work. That way nobody sees all those hoes leaving the apartment. It worked out great.

*****

"There you are, bitch. I want my fuckin' money back your nigger ass stole from me." It was a trick that Baby Face knocked off a couple of months back. He was a redneck on a Harley Davidson motorcycle.

"Man, I don't know what you're talking about. I didn't take your money."

"It's you. You're the cunt that robbed me." The trick parked and got off the Harley. The mothafucka was about 6'5" with a bald head. It turned out that the asshole was a white supremacist from the Aryan Brotherhood.

Sexy said, "Bitch, what the fuck are you going to do?"

"I don't know. We better think of something quick. That white boy is going to try and fuck us up."

"Give me my fucking money back, you black bitch." He started walking in their direction. Sexy and Baby were by the alley.

"Man, I don't have any money. Leave us alone."

"I'm going to kill you, nigger." He ran at them. The prick grabbed Baby Face. Sexy elbowed him in the face. He stopped, shocked. Then Baby Face took one of her high heels and hit him hard. It landed in his eye. Blood shot from his eye. That big mothafucka pulled out a knife; he swung it. Sexy sidestepped it then roundhouse kicked him in the chest. Baby Face took the bloody shoes and hit him in the neck. The asshole socked Sexy and knocked her down. He ran at Baby Face. He was bleeding like a hog. Sexy got up and jumped and kicked him. The man hit the ground hard; the back of his head hit the ground hard. *Boom.* It sounded like a boulder had hit the ground. The man was knocked out. Baby Face took off her other heel. She and Sexy ran out of the alley and jumped into Sexy's car, which was parked on the side street. As they pulled to the corner, they saw that trick coming out of the alley. He was screaming, "Help! Help! I've been robbed." He didn't see them as they drove by.

Sexy said, "Look, bitch."

Baby Face turned around and saw five police cars flying in that direction.

*****

I hated to lie to Velvet or any of my girls. I was parked down the street from Kenny's mother's house. My brother and I would take turns watching, waiting for Kenny to come home. I was eating a breakfast Jack and sipping on some orange juice. I was just about to pull when I saw the Camaro with that bird in the back window. *There, that mothafucka is right there.* A smile came over my face. We had been looking for that asshole for months. I got his ass now. I watched him as he parked. Kenny's mom had already left for work. He used his key and entered the house.

"Eddie. It's me. Kenny just came home. Where's Kevin at?"

"He's at Momma's house."

"Y'all get over here quick."

"Okay, I'm going to stop and pick Roach up. We'll be there in ten minutes." Eddie hung up.

My phone started ringing again.

"What's up, Eddie?"

"No, it's me, Kevin. Vinnie, if he leaves, follow him. Call us and let us know."

"Okay, my other line is ringing."

"Okay, Vinnie, see you in a minute."

"Hello."

"Daddy, Daddy."

"What's wrong, Sexy?"

"Me and Baby Face got into a fight with a trick. Baby Face got blood all over her."

"What the fuck. What happened, is she hurt?"

"No, Daddy."

"Bitch, put her on the phone."

194

"Daddy, it's me Baby. It was that trick I robbed a couple of months ago. He spotted me. I forgot and had the same wig on that I was wearing when I peeled him for his money. I hit him in the eye with one of my high heels. Blood got all over my clothes. Me and Sexy fucked him up. That mothafuckin' white boy was 6'5" or taller. Me and Sexy kicked his ass, and he fell hard and hit his head, in the alley. Nobody saw us. We ran and got in the car and smashed off. There are at least five police cars there now."

"Are you hurt?"

"No, we're both okay."

"Listen. Pull in an alley, change clothes, clean yourselves up. You did get both of your heels?"

"Yes, I did."

"Throw them clothes away in a trash can. Then go straight to the house. I'll be there in a little while. As a matter a fact, call the rest of your wife-in-laws and tell them I said to go home right now."

"All right, Daddy. Do you want to talk back to Sexy?"

"No, she's driving." I ended the call.

Kenny was still at his mother's when Eddie and Kevin showed up. I got in the car with them. "The nigga is still in there. We're going to follow him and see where he's been staying at. Eddie, you and Kevin should have got into Mom's car. Everybody knows you and Kevin's car."

"Vinnie we didn't have time to. We wanted to hurry up and get here," Kevin said.

I said, "Well, let's follow him in my car."

"Yeah, that's a good idea."

*****

"Hey, man. It's me, Kenny. Them niggas are at my mom's house. I saw them. When I walked out of the alley on my way to get the half stick of cherm, I noticed Eddie's car. Vincent, Kevin, and Eddie are in a gold 450 Benz. I don't know whose car they're in. I haven't seen it before. If I had to guess, I would say it's Vincent's car."

"Kenny, leave that car there. Don't let them see you. Can you get a ride from somebody back over here?"

"I don't know. I can try. My homie Steve might give me a ride."

"Okay, see if he will. Don't let him know where we're staying."

"Okay, I'm on my way over there."

*****

"Steve, what's up?"

"Nigga, where the hell you been? I hope you got my money. You owe me."

"I got it. That's why I'm calling you. Are you at your house?"

"No, I'm at my girl's house on Tenth and Orange Avenue."

"Well, if you want your hundred, you need to come pick me up."

"Man, I heard you bought a car. You come over here."

"My car is in the shop. If you give me a ride, I'll give you an extra hundred."

"Where are you at?"

"I'm on Fifteenth and Pacific Avenue at the burger joint."

"I'm going to bring my girl with me."

"That's cool. Hurry up. I ain't got all day," Kenny said, ending the call.

"Tee, I'm getting a ride. I should be back that way in about forty minutes. I'm going to have them drop me off at McDonald's and walk from there. I'm down on Pacific and Fifteenth. I'm leaving the car at my mom's."

"Okay, make sure nobody sees you waiting there."

"I know. I'll see you later." Kenny hung up the phone.

*****

"Damn, that nigga must be asleep in there. Vinnie, you sure that was him?"

"Man, I know what that cherm head looks like. Doesn't anybody have a car like that? That's him." We ended up taking a chance sending a bum to knock on the door. Kenny must have spotted us and slipped out the back door. Damn, that mothafucka was gone.

31

We missed catching Kenny at his mom's. He had spotted us parked down the street. We would have to find another way to find them. One thing's for sure: once we caught him, T. Powell, and Rohda, their asses were going to be in a world of trouble. We decided to stop staking out Kenny's house. We wanted him back in that car; it stuck out like a sore thumb. My brother and I stayed looking for them. Nobody knew what had happened that day at the store, and we planned to keep it like that.

*****

"Jerry, I'm going to be just fine. Nobody knows I'm still alive. Take me to Los Angeles, to my friend's house."

"I want to take care of you so nothing like that will ever happen again."

"Jerry, I'm coming back. I want my friend to know what's going on. If I don't, she might get murdered. I'm not calling the police. Please don't ask me again."

"All right, Pam, I trust your judgment," Jerry said.

Eddie and Kevin didn't kill Pam; they hit her over the head and knocked her out. After that, they drove her over five miles from her house to the fishing pier. They put her in the trunk. Pam played like she was still knocked out when they tossed her into the ocean. Pam swam under the pier. Once they were gone, she started swimming to shore. Jerry spotted her and helped her onto his boat. She's been with him all that time. Now she was on her way to Mac Ton's house. Rohda's mother told her that's where she was staying at.

"Jerry, park right here. Please don't leave. I'll be back." Pam jumped out of his truck and ran up the stairs and knocked on apartment 9. Jerry was in love with Pam. He watched to see which door she went in. He had a .38 pistol under the seat. If there was any sign of trouble, he was going to handle it. *Knock, knock, knock.*

"Rohda, it's me, Pam. Open the door," she yelled.

"Ton, it's Pam. Let me let her in."

"Wait, bitch, I'm fin' to cum." Mac Ton was fucking when Pam started banging on the door and screaming for Rohda to answer the door. Pam spotted Mac Ton's car downstairs in front of the apartment. Mac Ton's bedroom window was next to the front door.

Rohda slid the window open and said, "Bitch, let me get dressed, I will let you in." Rohda slid the window closed; she let Mac Ton get his nut. She rushed to the door and let her in. Rohda said, "Bitch, where have you been? I've been calling you for months."

"Ho, give me a drink and a snort of cocaine. You're not going to believe this shit." Rohda went back into the room and got a plate with coke on it.

"I'm going to give Pam a little."

"Fuck that ho. Make her buy some," Mac Ton said.

"Daddy, you know that's my best friend. Let her have a line. She's got something to tell me."

"Wait, bitch, I'm coming in there. I want to hear what that begging bitch has to say." Mac Ton and Rohda both walked into the living room. "Bitch, you're out of pocket knocking on a pimp's door like that. Then you want my coke on top of that. Ho, this better be worth my time."

"Fuck you, Mac Ton, I would never pay your ass."

"Pam, you better watch your mouth before you get slapped in it."

"Ton, stop that. Pam, what's going on, are you all right?" Rohda asked.

"That bitch is begging. She's not all right. The ho ain't got any money. She needs to hit the ho stroll and pay a pimp."

"Pam, have a seat," Rohda said.

Mac Ton said, "Don't give that bitch all my coke with her greedy ass," while walking back to his room.

"So, Pam, what's going on?"

"Rohda, I can't stand Mac Ton's black ass. Fuck him. He's always talkin' shit to me."

"Girl, don't pay him no mind. Where you been?" Rohda asked a second time.

"I've been dead. That's where I've been. Vincent's two brothers grabbed me and made me tell where your mother stayed. They made me take them there. After they beat the shit out of me. Those mothafuckas punched me and kicked me, questioned me over and over, then they made me show them where Kenny's mother stayed. After that, they drove me back to my house and questioned me over and over. They waited to see if Kenny was coming back. They made me call him again and again. Bitch, that mothafuckin Kenny started tripping after you and T. Powell left. He kept pulling out that gun and looking out the window. I put his ass out after he had me held hostage for two days. But anyway, wait, let me have another line and another shot." Pam started crying as she told the rest of the story. Rohda patted her on the back and hugged her friend. Pam got herself together and asked what happened to T. Powell. Rohda told her that Mac Ton had his cousins knock T. Powell out then rob him for the rest of the money and cocaine. Pam told Rohda about Jerry and how he saved her life, and that's where she has been, living on the boat with him. Pam told Rohda that she better watch her back and that if Kevin or Eddie caught her, they were going to kill her and Mac Ton once they found out that he has something to do with that robbery. Rohda gave Pam some coke, and Pam told her goodbye and good luck. She also told Jerry she was done working the streets.

*****

After all my hoes made it home, and Kenny slipped out of our hands, I headed over to my mother's house to talk with Eddie and

Kenny. My Benz was damn near new. It was gold with black interiors and a sunroof. I turned on the news.

"This is KNX, and I'm Ken Hunt reporting. The police have found another dead body on the side of Interstate 5 Freeway. The latest body found was of a black female in her late twenties or early thirties. She was found strangled and naked. This is the eighth female victim found. The other seven were identified as prostitutes. It's too early to tell right now. The police think that the victim may be a prostitute also. We'll let you know more as soon as we can. The police are calling the suspect the I-5 Killer. If anybody has information, call the LAPD Homicide Division. Also making the news is a story live from Long Beach. Here's Julie Walls."

"Hi, I'm Julie Walls. And as you can see, behind me is a crime scene where a victim suffered a brutal beating. The victim is a white male in his thirties. He was robbed by two black males after he parked his motorcycle and headed into the liquor store next to the alley. The victim said two black men approached him and demanded money. Then struck him with something that knocked out his left eye. Then the suspects kicked and beat him. If you have any information, contact LBPD Robbery Division. This is Julie Walls reporting for KNX. Now back to the studio."

I turned the radio off and called Baby Face and told her what I had heard on the news. I told her that nobody was going to be working Long Beach anymore. I talked to Sexy before hanging up. There was a psychopath out there killing hookers. I didn't want any of my girls getting hurt or killed, so I decided to only let them date regulars; they had about eighty tricks that paid a hundred or more in the black book. That was good enough for me. I had saved a lot of money. I had over $200,000 in my safe. After me and my brothers take care of our business with the bitch-ass niggas that robbed the store, slapped my sister, and kicked our mother, I was going to leave town for a while. Give it time to cool off. I pulled over in the front of my mother's, locked my Benz, and headed upstairs to her house.

32

"What's up, AD, where do you want to meet at?"

He said, "I'll be at the McDonald's on Sunset Boulevard and Western Avenue."

"Okay, I'll be there at 1:00 p.m."

"Vinnie, can you cop me some blow from Goldie's brother? My hoes like his shit the most. These niggas out here are cutting the cocaine too much and are charging more money." I told him that I would stop by Donald's on my way to meet him in Hollywood. The truth was I already had some coke. I had got an ounce from Donald last night. All my hoes were asleep. I had three phone lines put in my penthouse. I placed escort ads in the back-page of a magazine. They worked the new phone lines all night. Plus they had over a hundred regulars. The money was a little slower, but it was safer for them. I had them place ads saying Outcall or Incall. If my girls had to go on an outcall, I had another one of them ride with her. For the incall, I had my suite at the beach motel.

It's been a couple of months since the I-5 serial killer had found his last victim. The killer had picked up prostitutes from Orange County and Hollywood. That asshole had hookers scared to work the ho stroll. A lot of pimps were placing ads in the back page. A lot of pimps were leaving town. The track was on fire. If a pimp didn't get his ho off the ho stroll, he might get knocked for the ho. The killer picked up one of his victims in the daytime. The prostitute that was picked up and killed in the afternoon was from Orange County.

I pulled into the parking next to AD's Cadillac. I was bringing my Benz. I got out and started walking to the McDonald's front door when I spotted a fine-ass white ho. I was wearing a gold silk sweat suit and gold-rimmed shades. My jewelry was shining. I walked over to the ho; she was wearing blue jeans, a cut-off T-shirt, and sandals. She was about 5'8" with long blond hair.

"Excuse me."

She jumped.

"I'm not trying to scare you." She walked across the street once the light was green. I caught up with her. I started spitting game to her. She didn't talk at first. I said, "Everywhere I go, sunshine follows me."

She stopped and turned around once we were across the light and said, "Sunshine follows everyone," smiling at me.

"What's your name?" I asked.

She said, "My name is Dawn. What's yours?"

"Vinnie Mac. Can I buy you a sandwich lunch so we can get to know each other?"

"Sure," she said. We turned around and went into the McDonald's. We ordered. I got us a seat behind AD.

"Vinnie, I see ya, man."

"AD, this is my friend Dawn. Dawn, this is my brother AD."

Dawn said, "It's nice to meet you, AD."

AD said, "It's nice to meet you too." He picked up his tray of food and joined us. We chopped it up for a minute while we ate our food. After that, we walked out to the parking lot, and I opened my car door and let Dawn sit in it while I took care of my business with AD. "Vinnie, how's that escort thing working out for you?"

"AD, it's slow but steady. Business is picking up though. If I keep those ads going, in a few more months, I'll be making a lot more money. I'm thinking about keeping my hoes off the streets while I'm in LA County. That I-5 serial killer did me a favor. I would have never started my escort service without him."

AD said, "Vinnie, can we go into business together?"

"Let me think about it. I'll let you know. You don't want to start your own service?"

"Vinnie, you've already got it going. It would take me all those months it took you for my own service to start getting paper, ya dig?"

"I dig ya." I handed AD the coke he wanted; he gave me money, and I got in my ride and got on with my new girl.

Later on that month, AD and I started All Top Flight Escort Service. We rented a three-bedroom house and made an office out of one of the rooms. We had the house laid out. The house was on the top end of the ho stroll off Sunset Boulevard. We placed a full-page ad: the escort service was open from 11:00 p.m. till 9:00 a.m. AD moved into an apartment building off Hollywood Boulevard and Vine Avenue. He was staying in a three-bedroom penthouse. Dawn had been a phone operator in Connecticut. I had her working the phones and booking all of the dates for my girls and AD's team also. Dawn stayed at the new house; the rest of my team still stayed at the penthouse in Long Beach. All the calls in that area went to my hoes. All the calls in the Los Angeles area, AD's hoes went on. AD used tricks' motels for his incalls. The I-5 killer had three more victims since we started the escort service. The police were all over the ho strolls in Hollywood, Orange County, and the Valley. The killer's latest victim was picked up in the Valley on San Fernando Road. That was one of the ho strolls.

*****

It had been almost seven months since we had seen Kenny. He must have left town. His mother was driving his car. She left her car parked in the driveway. I would pass by there at different times; there was no sign of him ever being back at his mother's house. I would stop by my sister's store and hang out with my brothers; they were selling a lot of dope out of the store. A nigga named Harry that lived around the corner from the store was buying a lot of dope from my brothers.

"Eddie, where is Harry getting all that money from?"

"Vinnie, Harry's been hitting licks downtown and in Belmont Shores. He's been breaking into people's homes out that way. He's our best customer. He spends $1,500 a week with us."

"Damn, that nigga's getting it," I said.

Harry had just come and bought $200 worth of coke. I told Eddie I would be over that way Friday. It turned out that Harry was getting money from the narcotics officers. He had got busted breaking into a house in Belmont Shores. He ratted on my brothers; the police had followed Eddie and Kevin to Watts. Once they came out of the projects, the police jacked them and found a kilo of cocaine. They had search warrants for my sister's store. The police didn't find any drugs at the store. They had also searched Kevin's house and Eddie's place; the police found empty large bags and a scale at Eddie's. The police had a joint investigation with the feds. My brothers couldn't get bail. The mothafucka nigga Harry had set them up. I went to court to see what was up with the case. Eddie's lawyer told Eddie that the police officers on the case were dirty. It turned out that punk-ass Boline and five other officers had been breaking into suspects' homes and stealing dope and money and planting evidence. The feds dropped the case on Kevin and Eddie. The police used Harry to break in to dope boys' spots and take money and drugs. He also planted evidence. Boline and his boys were shaking niggas down and making them pay. Harry was a key witness in the Fed case. Eddie and Kevin had spent three months in jail and were released. All the police were indicted. It was all over the news. That fucking asshole Boline finally got what he deserved.

33

"Hi, Daddy, can we go shopping? I need some new clothes."

"Yea, Rohda, we can go to the swap meet. I got a run to make, and once I get back, we can go."

"Okay, Ton, I'm going to take a shower and get dressed."

Mac Ton backed up and then pulled off. He turned up the music and headed to Watts. His homeboy wanted a half ounce of coke. He stayed on 103rd Street. "Bone, I'm almost there, come outside."

"I'm on my way out now, Ton." Bone ended the call. He was standing out in the front waiting for his friend to pull up. "Park in the driveway, Mac Ton."

"Get in, Bone, what's up with you?"

"Man, I'm just trying to get this money. My people love that cocaine that you got."

"Here it is, all there." Mac Ton counted it again. Once he was done, he asked Bone if he could use the bathroom.

"Yeah, man, come on in. My mom is at work."

"Good, I'm going to bring us a line of blow in also."

"Cool," Bone said. Mac Ton and his friend talked and blew cocaine. Mac Ton lost track of time. Rohda called him and told him to come home.

"Man, I've got to go and take this bitch shopping."

"All right, Ton, I'll see you later," Bone said to Ton as he was getting into his car.

"Mac Ton, your clothes are ready. Come in and change."

"No, come on, let's go, Rohda." She jumped in the car. They took off and headed to the swap meet.

"Man, look, that's the bitch and her nigga right there." Butch called Shawn. "Say, homie, that bitch is at the swap meet on Slavson. What do you want me to do?"

"Follow them and see where they live."

"Okay, Butch, I'll be waiting for your call." Shawn hung up the phone. He called Eddie. "What's up, cousin? It's Shawn. My homeboy is following Rohda and the nigga that we jumped on."

"You found the bitch. I'm on my way over to your house."

"Eddie, wait till we find out where they live, and I'll call you back," Shawn said, ending the call. Eddie called me and Kevin. We met up at Kevin's house. Shannon called a couple of hours later. He told us where Mac Ton and the bitch Rohda stayed. I, Eddie, and Kevin headed to Watts. Our cousins were outside smoking some weed when we pulled up.

"What's up, cuz?"

Shawn said, "Let's go inside and have a drink and come up with a plan."

We decided to take care of it ourselves. I paid Shannon's homeboy for the information. We stayed in Watts till after midnight. Then we left to take care of our business. Me, Eddie, and Kevin pulled down the street from Mac Ton's spot. We watched as customers came and left from the apartment. We spotted a bitch heading to Mac Ton's to get some coke.

"Say, can you come here for a minute? I just want to ask you something." The lady came to the car.

"Yeah, can I help you?" she said.

I said, "Do you know where I can get some coke? I've got three hundred to spend." Her face lit up.

"Yeah, come with me, I'll show you. Are you going to hook me up with some blow?"

"I've got you covered, don't worry."

"Okay then, come on." I got out of the car, and we walked and talked. Eddie and Kevin were in another car; they watched as we were going into the apartment building. Sharon was the girl's name.

"Give me the money, and I'll be right back."

"No way, I'm coming too."

"Okay then, come on."

I could hear the music coming out of the apartment. The apartment was dark. I guess somebody unscrewed the light bulbs. It was perfect. Sharon knocked on the door. *Knock, knock, knock.*

"Who the fuck is it?"

"It's me, Sharon."

"Bitch, you better have more than $20 at this time of the night." I was standing behind Sharon when Mac Ton opened the door. "Who the fuck is that with you, Sharon?"

"It's my friend. He's spending $300."

"Well then, y'all come on in." As we were walking in the door, I pulled my .38 pistol out and pushed Sharon into Mac Ton. Eddie and Kevin rushed to the apartment once they saw the door open. "What the fuck is this! Nigga, do you know who I am?" Mac Ton said. Rohda heard the commotion and came running into the living room.

"Daddy, what's—aw! Fuck, I'm sorry. Please, please." By that time, Eddie and Kevin were behind me. "Please, mister, I don't have nothing to do with this!" Sharon shouted.

"Shut the fuck up and sit down." Eddie had a shotgun, and Kevin had a knife. I hit Mac Ton in the head, and blood flew everywhere; he hit the floor. I kicked his front teeth out. I tried to kick them down his throat.

"Where's my mothafuckin' money, bitch!" Kevin shouted. Eddie turned the music down a little bit then hit Sharon in the head with the shotgun. She fell and was out cold. Kevin grabbed Rohda by the hair and put the blade to her throat. "I'm going to ask you one more time. Where's my dope and my money at?" Kevin stabbed her in her leg. "Bitch, give me those rings you got on and those gold chains." She pulled them off and handed them to Kevin.

Eddie said, "Nigga, where's T. Powell at?" I kicked him again.

"He's not here. We took his—"

"Shut up, Rohda, don't tell them niggas shit," Mac Ton said. I pulled a pillow off the bed as I searched for the money. I heard what Mac Ton said, and I came running back in the living room with a pillow. I put it on Mac Ton's face and fired the pistol three times.

Kevin said, "Now, bitch, where's the money and dope at?" He reached over and slit Sharon's throat.

"Please don't kill me. It's in the room under the rug. Pull it up in the corner. The money's under the rug. Please don't kill me. Please, please." Kevin stabbed her again, this time in her stomach. "The coke is in the kitchen cabinet." Eddie took the drugs and money out to the car and came back with some gas. We set the apartment on fire and burned all of them mothafuckas up. It was too bad that Sharon was the one that came to the car that night. She was at the wrong place at the right time.

*****

We made it back to Long Beach and counted the money that Eddie got from under the rug. It was only $18,000. Rohda and Ton had spent a lot of the money. There were only two ounces of cocaine left. Rohda had set up T. Powell and robbed him for his part of the money and cocaine. I knew she was a dirty bitch; now she was a dead dirty bitch. We took that shit personal. They kicked my mom in the face and slapped my sister in the face.

The *Los Angeles Times* newspaper read: 3 DEAD IN APARTMENT FIRE. "The bodies are not yet identified." Once Kenny and T. Powell find out that Rohda and Mac Ton were killed, they were going to wonder if it was us that had killed them.

34

Me and my brothers decided to lay low for a while, unless we spotted T. Powell or Kenny. Boline and his rogue cops were out of jail on bail. The FBI had Harry in witness protection.

"Eddie, what's up, are you going to the store today?"

"No, Ms. Hunter, and Peaches will be there."

"Okay, then I'll holler at you later." I ended the call. Kevin and Eddie stopped selling cocaine after they got their case thrown out of court. All the arrests and convictions were overturned after Harry told the FBI what was going on with him, Boline, and the other police.

*****

"This is Chuck Henry reporting for KNX Radio. Here are the stories coming up at the top of the hour. The manhunt for the I-5 Killer has spread out north to Bakersfield and south to San Diego. The reward is now $100,000 for info leading to the arrest and conviction of the murder suspect. Also news at the top of the hour: The three bodies that were found buried in the apartment building in Los Angeles have been identified. The names of the victims will be released after their families are notified. It is now 8:45 a.m. This is Chuck Henry reporting for KNX. Sports is next."

I turned the radio off and parked at the penthouse. I sat there for a minute and then got out and headed up to the house. I had all my hoes working outcall, incall. The I-5 Killer had killed four more girls, and the streets were on fire; the police were warning all the hoes to be careful and report anything that looked strange or any trick that tried to strangle or hurt them. I stuck my key in the door and was about to turn it when Baby Face opened the door.

"Hi, Daddy, can I talk to you for a minute?"

"Sure, Face, let me use the restroom, and I'll meet you in my room." I kept my room locked. I gave her the keys, and she went to open the bedroom door. Most of my hoes were asleep. They had worked all night. Red Bone and Candy were on a call for $300 apiece. The call was an outcall in Lakewood. I had been noticing that Baby Face was acting funny; she had been getting real high off the coke and was drinking heavily. She didn't like working the escort service. She wanted to work the ho stroll so she could steal money from the tricks. "Hey, Baby Face, what's going on?" I could smell the liquor on her breath.

"Daddy, can I close the door?"

"Yea, go ahead." She closed the door and started to cry. I pulled her close to me and hugged her. "Baby, what's wrong with you? I've noticed that you've been real high all the time. Is it me? Tell me what's going on. Please stop crying and talk to me." She couldn't stop crying. This has been going on for months. I had to find out today what was really bothering her. I loved Baby Face, and I could tell something was very wrong in her life right now. She told me it was about her mother. I had called and talked to her mom; that wasn't it. Then she told me she was missing being in Texas. I asked if she needed to go home for a while. She told me that this is her home and that I was trying to get rid of her. "Baby Face, look at me. I want to know now. Stop lying to me. Tell me, Baby." She pulled some coke out of her pocket and tried to make a line. I stopped her. "No, you can't have any more of that shit till I find out what's wrong with you."

She looked at me with her eyes full of tears and said, "Daddy, you're going to hate me."

"No, I'm not. I love you."

"Daddy, Daddy, I'm not some punk-ass ho. I killed him. I killed that bitch-ass nigga." She started crying and fell on the floor. I pulled her up by the arms.

"Who did you kill, Baby Face! Tell me now. Who the fuck was it? You killed who? Some trick? Who?"

"Daddy, I'm sorry, I'm sorry. I killed him. He won't leave me alone."

"Bitch, who did you kill?"

"It was Stone. I killed Stone."

"What the fuck! I told you to leave that nigga alone, didn't I?"

She stopped crying and got mad and said, "Daddy, he said he was going to kill you unless I got back with him."

"Baby Face, listen. Tell me exactly what happened." I pulled her very close to me. I gave her a kiss on the lips. "Baby, please sit down. I'll be back." I went to the bar and made myself a drink. I couldn't believe what I had just heard. My phone started ringing.

"Hello. Who is it?"

"Daddy, it's me Candy. Are you all right? Your voice sounds different."

"Yeah, Candy, I'm fine. I'm just a little tired. What's going on with you?"

"I called to let you know that the trick wants us to stay for another hour."

"Okay, beautiful, y'all be careful. Call me when you're on the way home."

"Okay, Daddy, I'll see you in a little bit." I was glad to get some more time to talk to Baby Face and see what the fuck happened. I finished making my drink, and I also made Baby a drink to calm her down so she would tell me everything that happened, and I wanted to know where she killed him at and how she killed him. I entered back into the room, and Baby Face was putting on makeup.

"Daddy, I'm going to tell you everything."

"Here, I made us a drink. Take your time. You can have a blow now. After you're down, I want to know what happened." She made a line and snorted it and downed her drink.

"Okay, Daddy, this is what happened. After Stone left the motel, he called me before you had gotten to the room. He said he would kill you if I didn't get back with him. I told him to fuck off, and if you found out, you would take care of him. He told me that he would kill my mother if he had to. He also said that I would have never made it to California without him. Then he said that he went to jail trying to make the money back he had lost in Las Vegas. He also said that you had taken me from him and that he was in love with me. I told him to meet me by the racetrack in Inglewood. Remember when you had us work out there and I was gone for over two hours? I lied and told you I was with a trick all that time. I had made up my mind that the only way to get him off my back was to kill his ass. Anyways, I met him at the gas station, and we pulled into Hollywood Park Racetrack. We parked and got into the back seat. I had an ice pick. I brought it with me from Texas. Before you sent me to self-defense classes, I kept it for a trick if he found out that I had stolen his money. Daddy, you know I have a lot of heart. I couldn't steal money if I didn't. I used it on two tricks in Texas. That's why I wanted to come to Hollywood. I wanted a fresh start once Stone went to jail. Then I met you, Daddy. I was in love with Stone. Once I got with you, your game was so strong, and you take real good care of your girls. I fell in love with you. I never wanted this shit to happen. Stone had slapped me and tried to bully me into going with him. Daddy, don't get mad. I started sucking his dick. Once we got into it, he closed his eyes, and I pulled out the ice pick and stabbed him in the heart. He died right away. I got out, looked in the trunk of his car, and got some towels and blanket out. I wiped all my fingerprints out of the car. I put the blanket on him. I then drove to the store and bought all the cat litter they had. Then I drove to another store and got some more. Once I got enough cat litter, I drove him back to the horse racing parking lot. I parked in the space I told him to get. He had a room right down the street. Daddy, I'm not going to lie to you. I was giving him money after I told you where his family lived. I told him what I had done. I had him get the room by Hollywood Park. Daddy, the bitch he had was a cokehead. I gave him money to eat, and I was giving him some of the cocaine you had given me. Anyway, I poured the cat litter all over him. Then I cleaned up all the empty bags then covered him up with the blanket. Then I went back to work like nothing had happened. Daddy, I'm not mad I killed him. I was upset because I was lying to you all this time."

I couldn't believe what she told me. I loved her, and her telling me that made my dick hard. I grabbed her, kissed her with passion, and led her to the bed and fucked the shit out of her, then I slapped the shit out of her. It seemed to turn her on and me too. After we were done, I drove out to Inglewood so we could move the car.

I knew they were going to tow his car. He only paid for a couple of months. He had no idea that my bitch was going to kill his ass. Once we got to the parking lot, the car had tape all around it, and the police and news crews were all over the place.

"Baby, are you sure you wiped off all of your fingerprints?"

"Daddy, I made sure the car was clean and nobody saw me leaving."

On our way home, I drove in silence. I turned on the news.

"This is Bob Hunter in for Chuck Henry. We're reporting live from a gruesome scene. A man was found dead in his car covered with cat litter. The police are investigating. It seems as though the man was murdered and left in his car for an unknown amount of time. Once we learn more, we'll let you know the details. This is Bob Hunter reporting live from Hollywood Park."

I pulled into my parking space, and we talked. I told Baby Face not to ever tell anybody what had happened. I kissed her and told her that I love her. Baby Face was cool and calm. She was back to herself. It seemed like once she told me the truth, she was relieved of all those lies and deceptions, and she could now relax, knowing I had her back. If she only knew I had killed someone also.

I know one thing's for sure: if you fucked with me or my team, payback was a mothafucka. I was on top of the top, and I planned to stay there. I was one of the biggest pimps on the West Coast. Niggas were hating on my game. This game ain't for the weak. You've got to be real Mac to stay on the track. When niggas hear the name *Vinnie Mac*, they better watch their hoes on the track.

I sent Baby Face up to the penthouse. My phone started ringing.

"Hello, this is Vinnie Mac, one of the deepest on the track. Can I help you?"

"Daddy, this is Red Bone. We made it back, Where are you at?"

"I'm downstairs. I'll be up there in a minute, Red."

"Daddy, you're sounding happy, you must be feeling better?"

"Red Bone, just talking to you makes a pimp feel better."

"Daddy, you're crazy. I'll see you in a minute."

"Yea, you're right. I'm crazy about you." I hung up my phone. I locked my car and headed up to the penthouse.

35

The police were getting all kinds of tips and leads, but they still hadn't made an arrest. The I-5 Killer was still at large. He hadn't killed in over a month. The prostitutes were carrying all kinds of weapons for protection. The news stations reported daily updates on the murder investigation; the vice cops had undercovers on every ho stroll. A lot of pimps had left the area; the killer had the tracks hot as ever.

*****

"Well, Don, let me count that money and make sure it's all there." Boline counted the cash. It was $50,000. Boline spotted Don dragging his boss's body out of the office on the Westside. The construction company had won the bid to build a Job Corps on Santa Fe Boulevard. Boline was meeting a drug dealer at the site when he heard a shot coming from the office. He kept quiet about the murder.

"It's all there, Boline. It's always all there."

"Shut the fuck up, Don. If I didn't need this money, I would blow your ass away. You fucking prick." Boline put the bag of cash in his car and said, "I want $100,000 next month." As he was pulling off, Don had made up his mind that he had to kill that no-good ass cop. He wasn't going to pay that police another dime. Boline was bleeding Don dry, and Don was trying to figure out how he was going to get rid of him. The only problem was Boline had taken pictures of Don dragging his boss's body out of the office and hid it while Don was mixing up the cement. Boline told Don to freeze and don't move. Don left the gun he used on his boss sitting on the desk while he was moving the body. Boline had called the drug dealer he was supposed to meet and changed the time and the location of the money drop that he extorted from the drug dealer Cruz, a Westside Longo gangbanger. Boline had walked Don back into the office and recovered the murder weapon. He had watched Don bury his boss in the fifty-gallon drum; after that, Boline kept the pictures and the gun to extort money from Don. The only problem Don faced was finding the pictures and the murder weapon.

*****

The police had gotten a break. The I-5 Killer had finally made a mistake. He had killed a college girl and left some evidence at the scene where he had dumped the body. The police called a news conference.

"This is Chuck Henry live at the police headquarters in downtown Los Angeles. The chief of police reported that the latest victim of the I-5 Killer was identified as the missing college student. The murder suspect has now started killing other women. The chief stated that the reward is now one million dollars for information leading to the arrest and conviction of the I-5 Killer. The chief also asked that no student walk along or take a ride from a stranger, and he also suggested that the prostitutes not work alone. The police chief also said the killer had left some evidence behind. There was some concrete mix and blue rope fibers. This is Chuck Henry reporting from downtown Los Angeles."

"I hope they bust that mothafucka soon. The city is in an uproar over the latest victim," Don said as he and Candy drove to his house.

"Don, this is a very nice place you have."

"Thanks, Candy. This can be yours. All you got to do is say yes."

"Say yes to what, Don?"

"I want you to be my wife." Don pulled out a ring.

"Don, we've been over this before. I like you a lot, but I can't be your wife." Don poured drinks for him and Candy.

"Here you go, Candy," he said as he handed Candy her drink.

Candy had lied to me and told me she was going to meet someone else. She decided to date Don. After he told her he would give her $5,000.

"Don, let me use your restroom." He showed her where it was at. Candy called me and told me what she had done.

"Say, bitch, you hurry up and get back to the house. What, you like that fucking trick or something?"

"No, Daddy, I like giving you his money. I'm only going to be here for two hours."

"Candy, I don't trust him. Where does he live?" She gave me the address to his house. "Okay, Candy, if you're not home in a couple of hours, I'm coming over there and fuck that trick up."

"Daddy, if he doesn't do what he says, I'm going to fuck him up. Don't worry."

"Candy, just watch him and don't drink or eat anything there."

"Okay, Daddy, I won't." Candy ended the call. I told Candy not to date Don again. I loved Candy and all my other hoes. I worried about them even more because of the I-5 Killer. I knew my girls could protect themselves, but I was still concerned.

"Here, Candy." Don handed her the drink he had made.

"Don, I don't want a drink. We need to go ahead and date. I've got another date waiting on me." Don had put something in Candy's drink, and now she wouldn't drink it. Don had decided to kill Candy; if he couldn't have her, nobody else could either. He insisted on her taking a drink. "Okay, Don, can I have some more ice?"

"Sure, Candy, I'll be right back." Once Don went to get the ice, Candy switched the drinks. "Here, Candy, here's your ice."

"Thanks, Don. I need to use the restroom, then I'll be ready to date."

Candy called me from inside the bathroom. "Daddy, come and meet me. Don is acting strange. I don't trust him."

"Bitch, I told you. It's going to take thirty minutes to get to his house."

"Okay, Daddy, I'll be ready once you get here."

"I'm on the way." I hung up. That little short mothafucka is going to get his ass kicked today. I never liked that trick anyway; he was always trying to con my bitch into leaving me. I jumped into Sexy's car and headed to San Pedro.

"Oh, there you are, Candy. I was fin' to come and check on you."

"I was fixing my makeup for you. I always try to look my best for you." Candy was stalling for time; she already had the $5,000 in her purse.

"Well, Candy, let's drink up."

"Okay, Don, here's to us."

"Yeah, to us." Candy downed her drink. Don felt bad about the drugs he put in her drink. He knew he was going to kill Candy. He downed his drink. Candy lit a Newport.

"Don, I'll be ready in a minute. Don, so tell me, did you build this beautiful house?"

"Yeah, Candy, I built my dream home." Don was lying his ass off. Candy kept talking to him. She noticed that he was starting to look sleepy.

"Don, let me give you a rubdown. It will relax you."

"Good, I need one bad." Don pulled off his shirt, and Candy started to massage him.

*****

Boline had followed Don and Candy back to Don's boss's house that the fake Don had moved into. Boline had set up Don. He put the blue-fibered rope in the back of the construction truck that Don was driving along with evidence from the other murdered women. It turned out that Boline was the one that was killing the prostitutes. He was waiting to sneak into the house and kill Candy and make it look like a suicide. Then he was going to call his ex-boss, the chief of the Long Beach PD, and tell him that he followed up on a lead, that he spotted the I-5 Killer picking up a hooker in Long Beach, and that he had followed them to the suspect's house. Boline was trying to set up Don so he could get the charges dropped on him and become a hero.

"Daddy, Don had tried to drug me. He put something into my drink, and I switched our drinks. Don's passed out. How close are you?"

"I'll be there in ten minutes. Candy, clean up all of your fingerprints."

"Okay, Daddy, but why?"

"Candy, I heard on the police scanner that Boline said he had followed y'all to Don's house and that Don is the I-5 Killer." Boline told the homicide investigators that he wants to make a deal, and he wanted to talk only to the chief. I eased up and parked. I saw Boline in a car parked across the street from Don's house. Boline was so busy trying to make a deal that he didn't see or hear me creeping up to him. Boline was outside of his car talking to the chief when I cracked him on top of his head, knocking him out cold. I wanted to kill his ass bad. I called Candy and told her to get the fuck out of that house now. She had a towel in her hand, wiping herself as she came out. "Candy, hurry up. The police will figure out where Boline was calling from." Candy ran, and we jumped into Sexy's car, and I pulled off. Don lived up in the hills in San Pedro. Once we were about ten blocks from the house, we saw all kinds of undercover police cars. The police chief was in one of them.

"Candy, are you all right?"

"Yeah, Daddy, I'm sorry I fucked up bad. I could have lost my life if it wasn't for you."

"Candy, don't tell any of the other girls."

"Okay, Daddy, I promise I won't." I pulled over to a liquor store and got a drink. I needed one bad. I paid for the drink, and Candy and I drove off. I jumped on the freeway and just drove, not heading anywhere in particular. I just wanted time to clear my head.

"Daddy, here." Candy handed me a bag she had stashed in her gym bag that she used to carry different costumes that she used for her dates. The bag had about $80,000, ten gold watches, diamond rings, and gold chains. I pulled off the freeway and got a hotel room at the Sheraton. We checked in. Candy and I took a long hot shower. I called home, and Naomi told me to turn on the news. That Don and the cop Boline were on there. I told my other hoes to just relax and take the day off and that me and Candy would be home later. The police arrested Don for the murder of his boss, the prostitutes, and the college girl. Don was the I-5 Killer, the news said, and that the bust came after a tip led them to the scene, and the caller said the dirty cop Boline was Don's accomplice. Both men were taken into police custody. Me and Candy made love and went to sleep after counting the money; it was over $100,000 and about $70,000 worth of jewelry.

*****

We woke up and had the hotel deliver us room service. I ordered steak and eggs for both of us. I turned on the news. It turned out that Boline told the police that Don had a partner and that he was knocked out by the other person. Boline told the police that he followed Don and an unknown hooker that was picked up on PCH; he also said in his statement that he had suspected Don of killing his boss. While investigating Don, Boline noticed Don moving a fifty-gallon drum. Boline said Don had taken the drum back to his house. The police found the boss's body in the cement and other evidence pointing to the murders of the other women. Boline was called the hero of the investigation. The feds dropped the charges on Boline and the other cops after the witness Harry changed his statement. It was a bizarre twist in the case. The feds didn't know why Harry changed his mind. Don said he had paid Boline over a million in cash. The feds suspected that Boline paid off Harry but had no evidence to support the fact. Boline and the other officers were reinstated.

Epilogue

The news media was parked all up and down Temple where the courthouse was located. This had to be one of the biggest murder cases of the century. Don's arraignment was at 1:00 p.m. I and all my hoes and the rest of the world watched TV to see how things were going to unfold in court. The news reporters were standing out in the front of the court building.

"This is Mark Burns live in downtown Los Angeles. The man known as the I-5 Killer is being arraigned today with over fifteen counts of first-degree murder. A Long Beach police officer was the one that led other police officers to the house where the I-5 Killer had committed the gruesome acts. His boss was found stuffed in a fifty-gallon drum. The suspect had shot his boss and then placed the body in a fifty-gallon drum that was then filled with cement. The crime scene unit also found a blue-fibered rope in the back of the truck the suspected killer was driving. They also found cement bags in the truck. Blue fibers and cement were found on all of the murdered women. The prosecutors are seeking the death penalty for these heinous acts. This is Mark Burns reporting live in downtown Los Angeles. Now back to the studio."

My other girls were stunned by the murders they were hearing about. I was planning to leave town after I had found T. Powell and that asshole Kenny. The ho strolls were filling up again. After the news spread about the arrest of the I-5 Killer, I had my hoes working Long Beach from 4:30 a.m. till 7:15 a.m., then I would work in Orange County from 11:30 a.m. till 1:00 p.m., then they took the rest of the day off; at 11:00 p.m. till early morning, they would work the escort service. Baby Face was glad to be back on the track. She hit some cool licks; one was for $3,500 and another for $7,000. She didn't rob every trick, just the ones she caught slipping. Sexy dipped on a trick for $1,300. I never took Baby Face back to Inglewood. Naomi and Spicy got an outcall for $500 apiece.

It had been months since I've heard anything about T. Powell or Kenny. One morning I had Sexy, Baby Face, Candy, and Goldie work early morning in Long Beach. A blue truck pulled over and picked up Sexy; she hit a lick for $2,000. Once she got out of the truck, the trick pulled into the store parking lot. The trick went into the store and noticed his money was gone. He ran out looking for Sexy, but she was gone. Candy, Baby Face, and Goldie stayed down. The trick drove around all morning looking for Sexy. Baby Face, Candy, and Goldie gave me about $900 altogether. Baby Face and Sexy were always trying to top each other to see who could steal more money. A lot of the times, I had them working different tracks.

*****

"What's up with you, AD?"

"Man, I just knocked a bad new bitch."

"Where did you knock her from?"

"She called the escort service looking for work. I'm meeting her at Denny's."

"All right, pimpin', I'm on my way out there to pick up the credit card slips and take them to the bank. I'll see you in about an hour."

"Okay, Vinnie, I'm going to get fresh for the new ho." I ended the call. AD never showed up again. The new girl was an undercover vice cop. They busted AD for pimping and pandering. The Hollywood vice cops raided the house where the escort service was. They didn't find anything. The escort service was a legitimate business. The police couldn't close it down. I bailed AD out; he sold me his part of the escort service for $50,000. AD packed up and headed back to the East Coast; he was going on the run. The most he would get was two years. He had some down hoes, but he wasn't going to keep them if he was sentenced to a prison term. Them hoes would choose up with another pimp. I never hired any new girls to work my escort service. I had to be careful. The vice was trying everything to bust the owners or owner of the business. I had a sign posted in the office that no prostitution was allowed, and anyone that violates will be fired and/or prosecuted. So the escort business couldn't be held responsible.

The news reporters were following up on a tip that Don had an accomplice. Don's lawyer made a statement to the media. He stated that his client was innocent and that he was set up by the police. He said that there were no fingerprints from another person found at the house where the arrest was made. His client was drugged and framed. The media went crazy with the story. They asked on the radio and TV for the woman that was allegedly with him to come to the police department and make a statement.

I decided that before they found out what had really happened, I was leaving town. I knew Boline would put it together that it was me that hit him over the head. I told my brothers to meet me at the store so I could talk to them.

"Vinnie, what's up? You sounded like it was very important."

"I'm going to leave town for a couple of months."

"Why?" Eddie asked. I told them everything that had happened on the day leading up to the arrest of the I-5 Killer. It was hard for them to believe what had happened; they told me that it would be best that I did leave for a while.

I had all my hoes working the escort service. We only took calls from Orange County and Seal Beach and other coastal cities. We didn't take any calls from the Hollywood area. Things were going smooth until Candy went on an outcall in Seal Beach. I had Red Bone drive Candy to the date's house. The trick was giving Candy $500 for two hours. Red Bone dropped Candy off and drove to a local Jack in the Box. I always had the girl that drove her wife-in-law on the call to wait at a different location in case the vice had set up the date. Red Bone called Candy after she didn't check in once she was in the trick's house. Red Bone kept on calling. After she didn't get an answer, she called me. I called her also. She didn't answer. I told Red Bone to come home. I had Red Bone drive me back to the location. I got out and banged on the door; nobody answered the door. I walked around the house and looked into the window. I couldn't see anything. A lady came over to where I was standing in front of the house.

"Are you looking for someone?" she asked.

"Yeah, I'm looking for the person that lives here."

"The man that owns this house died, and his family is selling the house."

"What's his name?"

"His name was William Baker. His daughter Pat is married to a police officer."

"If you can remember, can you tell me what city he worked for?"

"Sure, it is the Long Beach Police Department. He's the one that helped catch that killer. His name is Markus Boline. He's a hero." I couldn't believe what I just heard. "Mister, are you okay? This is a nice house. Are you trying to buy it?"

"Yeah, yeah…I mean, I'm all right, thank you." I had to shake it off.

I knew that no-good ass cop was going to do something to Candy. I had a bad feeling about it. I was walking to the car and got in and closed and the door. I watched as the lady went back into her house.

"Daddy, what did she say?"

"She said that she just woke up."

"Daddy, I hope Candy is all right."

"Me too, Red." She and I stayed there another hour then headed back to Long Beach.

*****

I sent my other hoes on the road. A week after, Candy's body was found. The girls all cried all throughout the night. Their first stop was at Bakersfield. Then we were going to Fresno and then San-Jose. I was going to meet them in San Francisco and then head on to Portland. I was sick after I found out that Candy was found dead early in the morning on the beach. She had been decapitated with a needle in her arm. She had been beaten with a blunt object. I broke down and cried. I was mad as hell. I was going to kill that fucking cop if it was the last thing I did. I wanted to beat that son of a bitch to death just like he did to Candy. I had to figure out a way to catch Boline slipping and then make him pay for what he did. I didn't know if he had help from the other rogue cops. I had to be careful because Boline knew I had to be the one that hit him over the head. He didn't know if I knew he had set up Don to take the murder rap for the female victims. My brothers and I were trying to come up with a plan.

Boline worked patrol by himself on Thursdays; he was still extorting drug dealers for large amounts of money. Including Babs and our other homies. We decided to have a meeting to handle the problem. I found he was fucking this bitch on the Westside. He would meet her at lunchtime. He would drive down by the bridge and park; they would have sex in the patrol car. He would drop her back off in the alley by her house. I, Eddie, and Kevin came up with a plan. Boline didn't know that Eddie and Kevin were brothers. We rented two cars. Eddie had hoes back to the alley next to Kevin's car. I was hiding in the next yard. I called Eddie and told him that the cop was out of the alley.

Boline spotted my brother making a fake dope deal. He pulled up and told them, "Freeze! Don't fucking move." His greedy ass didn't call for backup. He made them lie facedown on the ground. He picked up the money off the trunk of the car and started counting it. I crept up from behind and shot that mothafucka right in the back of the head. Me and Kevin moved quickly. We grabbed all the money and cocaine, and I jumped out of the car with Kevin. Eddie was driving the other car. We pulled over and got out fast and headed to the penthouse. I had the scanner that I had bought to keep my girls safe from the I-5 Killer and from the murder investigation. Boline was on his lunch break when I caught him in the head.

Once we entered the penthouse, I heard the police put out an all-points bulletin alert. The helicopter spotted his patrol car and his body lying in the streets. The damn police department responded to the "officer down" alert. It was a one-way alley that ran into the side of the bridge and led up to a light on PCH. Nobody heard or saw us.

I poured myself a drink; my brothers did the same. I took a shower and changed clothes. Eddie and Kevin changed also. We watched on TV as the murdered officer made headline news. We got away clean. No evidence was left at the scene. I loved my brothers; they put their lives on the line for me. Kevin and Eddie didn't want the $40,000, but I made them take the money. I followed them back to a rent-a-car place. They turned the car back in and jumped in my car, and I drove them home. Then I drove to the Belmont Pier and threw the gun into the ocean. This shit consumed me. I killed people; this is not the life I expected. Pimping is a noncontact sport unless a person fucked over your ho, then their ass would be out. Surprisingly, it didn't bother me that I had killed someone.

*****

My team was in Fresno. They sent their traps to me by Western Union. I had them send it to me in different names.

"Hi, Daddy, what's going on?"

"I'm great, is everything all right?"

"Yeah, Daddy, things are good. Dawn is doing okay. She's getting used to working like Sexy. Okay, Daddy, here's Red." I talked to my whole crew. I was going to leave the next day. I gave my mother the keys to the other cars, and she moved in to the penthouse. I kicked it with my homies and family at King Park. I gave a barbecue. I wrapped things up at 8:00 p.m. so I could get some rest before I started my journey.

*****

My phone was ringing. I had Goldie call to wake me up. I took a shower, got dressed, kissed my mom, and got in the elevator then headed to my Cadillac. I felt great going on the road and putting things behind me. I gassed up and started toward the freeway. I had three blocks to the freeway. I lit my blunt while waiting for the light to change. I turned up the music. Johnny "Guitar" Watson came on. I stepped on the gas, then a car came flying through the light. *Scrrrrrrr! Bam!* I banged my head; it hit the window. I didn't have my seat belt on. The last thing I remember was going through the windshield.

The End

About the Author

Born under the sign of Aries, Vincent E. Jordan went to the Job Corp and got a Culinary Arts degree. He also attended Long Beach City College and studied creative writing, sales and promotions, and was the senate president for two terms. He had a 4.0 grade point average, and sat on the bord of directors of the Associate Student Body (A.S.B.).

He was inspired by Ice Berg Slim and Donald Goines to create these new urban novels about the inner-city ghettos.

He says to readers, "I want to thank you for taking the time to read my work and supporting me as an author. It means the world to me and my family, my sister Lenora Shell, and my two brothers Eddie Jordan and Kevin 'Roach' Kendricks."

Milton Keynes UK
Ingram Content Group UK Ltd.
UKHW011352260624
444777UK00033B/365

best journalist of the century as far as writing, style and content are concerned. Gentle. Sweet. Courageous. And a great man at the bar.'

I do know enough about the British press not to lecture you on how you should ply our chosen trade of journalism – what Walter Lippmann called 'a refuge for the vaguely talented' and what H. L. Mencken described as 'the life of kings'. The strengths of British journalism and American journalism lie in their differences, not their similarities. So I would like to speak from my own experience, with my own government and with my own newspaper, with the caveat that I have worked for only one daily newspaper in my lifetime. I would like to talk about government lying. Calculated lies. The wilful deception of the public for political ends, especially under the disguise of national security, and what an awful price we pay for such lies under any name: misinformation, disinformation, deceit, deception, or even economical with the truth.

In America, the press is curiously shy, even embarrassed, when faced with the need to use some form of the verb 'to lie', even now when public tolerance for the unexplained and for the unbelievable explanation is wearing thin. We seem to drop quickly into a defensive crouch, even when we are accused of abusing our power by not accepting explanations which often defy acceptance. We are, too often, close enough to the establishment ourselves to be comfortable in calling a lie a lie.

I am not talking about little lies, as in Vice-Admiral Poindexter